S*The*eer

a historical novel

The Seer

a historical novel

EVA SHAW

Light Messages
Torchflame Books
Durham, NC

Published 2021, by Torchflame Books
an Imprint of Light Messages Publishing
www.lightmessages.com
Durham, NC 27713 USA
SAN: 920-9298

Paperback ISBN: 978-1-61153-419-1
E-book ISBN: 978-1-61153-420-7
Library of Congress Control Number: 2021910411

For Jennie Ernestine Miller Klein.

Mama, you were my model of kindness and creativity.
I think you'd have enjoyed this book.

ABOUT THE BOOK

THE SEER WAS SPARKED BY CURIOSITY, a host of historical details that would not leave my mind, a love affair with New Orleans, and plenty of what-ifs. I have been assisting, writing for, and working with an incredible gentleman, Frank B. Stewart Jr. for two decades since the publication of my award-winning book, *What to Do When a Loved One Dies*. Frank and his gracious-as-all-get-out wife Paulette have shown me the faces and places in NOLA that few tourists ever get to see.

Working with and ghostwriting for Frank for many years, I've especially enjoyed hearing his oral history of the Crescent City, Louisiana, and the glorious South. These marvelous accounts brought the energy, flavor, and thrill of the city to life for me.

I've often compared New Orleans to an older aunt who wears far too much perfume and packs on foundation, blusher, and fire-engine-red lipstick. Hanging out with her means you and I will definitely step out of our sedate routines and go wild, and what fun that will be. I love the city like she's my favorite aunt, so how could I not set my next novel in my second, unofficial hometown?

If you haven't been to NOLA, you are missing one of the great cities of the world for music, the people, the architecture, and the food. I've often wondered if it's illegal to serve a bad meal in the city. I've certainly only had the best food ever.

At the end of Poydras Street, where it meets the Mississippi, the Algiers Point–Canal Street ferry goes from New Orleans to the town of Algiers. Algiers, today, is a charming community, yet I wondered what it had been during World War II when New Orleans was a military hub and powerhouse transportation port. Apparently, it had been a gritty second cousin, ignored by the elite of the city, and much to my surprise, there in Algiers was a prisoner of war camp.

That led to diving into the history of Algiers, New Orleans, visiting the World War II Museum, and digging out documentation of a possible Nazi invasion, and terrorist activities, up the Mississippi. While not formed into anything resembling a book, the thoughts, shadows of characters, and the what-ifs and fragments of the plot began to blossom.

Historically correct, the novel you're holding is the result of extensive research about NOLA during World War II, including Camp Algiers, a mystery even to some who have lived in the Crescent City their whole lives. If you go there or search on the Internet, you can still see crumbling buildings of the camp established in conjunction with the unlawful Enemy Alien Control Program, established and run by the State Department. This ugly part of our history, under the guise of keeping Americans safe from the Nazis, apprehended over five thousand German Jews who had fled Hitler's genocide for the safety of Central and South America. These religious refugees were targeted and kidnapped as our government transported men, women, and children to war camps on US soil. What shocked me was that the program housed the innocents, along with known Nazi sympathizers and Nazi prisoners of war, as pro-Nazis were allowed to fly the swastika flag and sing Nazi songs. The Jews had no rights. There were no laws to protect or defend them. The State Department may have meant well, but the truth remains that Jews were abused, harassed, and even tortured by the Nazi inmates.

About this time, too, I started wondering more about my protagonist and her backstory—what made her tick and how was she going to fit into the novel. I started asking myself questions. One that stuck in my mind was, What if the protagonist has come to the city to find her birth mother, and using her skill with reading people, and a sympathetic ear, pretends to be a psychic to gain access to the movers and shakers of the city, as well as the local gossip? What if she has hyperthymesia, a condition that allows people to retain details with great precision. Great memory would certainly help a fake psychic, so l wondered, What if our government hired psychics during the war? It's documented that the British, Russian, and Nazi governments used them, so why not the US? Yes, back to what if ... and the book and characters just took over from there.

Since I'm a ghostwriter and online writing professor, my spare time to write fiction (which l love to do) is limited, as l have a wonderful extended family, including our feisty little dog, Coco Rose, and hobbies galore. That said, even when l wasn't writing about Beatrix Patterson, my protagonist and self-proclaimed Robin Hood of psychics—as she likes to believe—the intriguing scientist Dr. Thomas Ling and the characters who inhabit the novel, l was thinking of them. Yes, okay, l was talking with them.

If this is the first time you've heard a novelist say they talk to their characters, it does sound wacky, and we writers try not to spread that around. Yet, if most novelists were to be honest, they do. l certainly had long chats with the people who have peopled the mystery.

Any mistakes with the historical details in the book are all my fault, and as this is a novel, l fictionalized connections with my characters to real people such as the Higgins boat inventor, Andrew Higgins, and then First Lady Eleanor Roosevelt. My hope is this novel will encourage you to wonder "what if" and write the book you want to read. That's what I've done here.

Remember, the person who waits and waits for the right time to write is called a waiter. The person who writes, published or not, is a writer.

Thanks for reading this and my book. I'd love to hear from you.

—Eva

ACKNOWLEDGMENTS

LOTS OF WRITERS SAY IT. And you know what? It is true. It takes more than a good story or a writer sitting at her computer to bring a novel to fruition. It takes people helping people and lots of them. This novel started in my mind, and countless others added their thoughts, comments, and ideas into the workings of my brain before the story came together.

The book took about three years to complete and wouldn't be what it is today without a battalion of help from friends, readers, my online students, my extended family, and the gracious and super-smart staff at Torchflame Books.

Ellen Hobart (the best BFF ever) read the book a few times, knowing I'd grill her, and she was more than prepared to step up to that, tell me the truth, and laugh my angst. Ellen's friendship is something I do not deserve. And gosh, we really do have fun together, as Ellen's mother always said.

Thanks go out to Lisa Patterson Walton and Danielle Light Corwin, who joined the first reading group with Ellen when I nearly had a book I wouldn't be mortified to pitch to a publisher. Your feedback, comments, and catches for some writing faux pas were invaluable, and like Ellen, you were ready and eager to field my questions. Thanks, too, to Susan and Andy Meilbaum for reading yet another rough copy and their enthusiasm.

Backing this truck up a bit ... Paulette Stewart, who lives and breathes the love of New Orleans and of reading, said yes when I asked if she'd read a version so rough, I'm embarrassed to say I put her through that. Even though the book has morphed three different directions since that time, she's still my friend.

It's been humbling and overwhelming to have received such an outpour of joy on the publication of the book from my extended family, my church family, and friends, including those in New Orleans, like the incredible Tommie Fagan. I love you all and hope I've told you that enough.

While my husband Joe has been, in years back, among the first readers, Alzheimer's disease has long since robbed him of the ability to communicate. Nevertheless, I know if he could, he'd be cheering with those I admire and love.

This book would not have been possible if Frank B. Stewart Jr., my friend, mentor, and favorite ghostwriting client, hadn't introduced me to his beloved hometown, New Orleans. I've been to debutant balls, sipped cocktails on Bourbon Street during the height of Mardi Gras, tasted the best gumbo possible, along with countless delicious meals, in diners and dives, all the way to the high-end culinary legends, and mingled with fascinating and delightful friends and colleagues of Frank's. Frank knows everyone in the city, and everyone knows Frank, and they all consider him to be a friend. They accepted me without hesitation as their friend, too. Southern hospitality is alive and well, and I can't get enough of it.

Big thanks to my online students and the writers in my Facebook group, Eva's Writeriffic Garden, headed up by Tad Clark. Thank you, Tad, my TSAB. Teaching writing for the last two decades has made me a better writer while mentoring you, answering your questions, and juggling my workload. What a blessing to continue to teach; thanks go to Vicki Diaz and the staff at Education To Go.

Beatrix Patterson, the main character in this mystery, is a powerful, independent woman. Like her, I believe all girls and women should have the opportunity to achieve their potential and know Beatrix would agree. Hence, fifty percent of the profits of "The Seer" will be given to Days for Girls International, a global nonprofit that advances menstrual equity, health, dignity, and opportunity for all. They transform periods into pathways. Please join me and support this organization where they are working girl-by-girl and woman-by-woman to shatter the stigma of menstruation. Visit daysforgirls.org for more information.

Special thanks to my editors, staffers, artists at Torchflame Books: Elizabeth, Meghan, Ashley, Betty, and Wally.

Now, thanks back to you for reading this book. Pass it on if you like, just as I do when I've enjoyed a novel.

CHAPTER 1

Royal Street, New Orleans, Louisiana—
February 16, 1942

BEATRIX PATTERSON WAS A LIAR. And a good one.

"It's for everyone's best interest. I take from the rich and give to the poor."

At least the second part of the statement was true. She gave herself credit for that.

Tucking her film-star-inspired page boy into a navy-blue snood, the fish-net hair covering supposedly trendy at the time, the slight woman with dark circles beneath her eyes and a sweetly innocent appearance that made men and women instantly feel they must nurture the dear little waif, avoided looking at her reflection by the storefront window.

She grabbed the grapefruit-sized crystal ball from the middle of her desk in the shabby chic and cluttered room that looked more like your elderly aunt's parlor than an office, took aim at the front door, lifted her arm like a baseball pitcher, and stopped. She inhaled, and with the might of a hundred exclamation marks, flung it as a means to punctuate her shame. Rather than shattering as it collided with the doorframe, which was the longed-for result, there was an unsatisfying thud before it dropped to the worn Persian carpet.

The shadowy figure who had been lurking on the doorstep jumped, and the door handle rattled, but that didn't surprise

Beatrix. Someone was always watching, she believed. She didn't care anymore because she knew if that door opened, her lips would tell more lies—only if the visitor was willing to part with the money in his pocket and needed to know the future.

Far earlier that same day, and long before Thomas Ling reached Beatrix's storefront, he'd scouted the surroundings, created a plan, checked the routes, and determined the viability of his escape with the meticulousness of a scientist—which he was. His mind reeled, his palms were damp, and as if repetition could bring reassurance—which it had not so far—he recited the instructions he'd been given: "Be the illusion. People see no more than what they expect. Have them ignore you."

Hence, he had swaggered, like a sailor on shore leave—which he most certainly was not—attempting to blend into the late afternoon shadows of gritty Magazine Street, keeping his eyes down, lest they give him away.

To the casual observer, he was nothing more than a slender man in a crisp white uniform, in a sea of sailors, marines, and soldiers ready for a Sazerac, distractions of either gender, and to unwisely use limited hours before being hustled into a troop carrier shipped to war-torn Europe, and if the war gods were smiling, perhaps even return to the girl or guy next door. That assessment would have been wrong.

With deliberate determination, Thomas glanced behind him before disappearing into an alley's inky darkness, then huddled against a packing crate to confirm he hadn't been followed. People dashed by the alley, seemingly never noticing that a pedestrian had vanished, and that's what Thomas hoped for.

If Beatrix had been gifted with second sight, it would have been clear that Thomas flinched as he huddled in a backstreet when a taxi backfired as it maneuvered through crowded lanes lacing the French Quarter. She would have seen him skirt inches from the bricked wall, trembling at each sound. He had moved as if a million eyes were on him, and without warning, memories of his superstitious grandmother flashed in his mind. Because of his logical nature, the crazy thoughts were temporarily suppressed yet would return, lapping without end, much like the murky tides do in the Mississippi River Delta.

In the growing dusk of early February, a cat screamed, and another replied even louder as a well-fed rat streaked over Thomas's expensive shoes. Somewhere high above the street, hoarse woozy laughter intensified, only to be replaced by squealing breaks and bellows of a bar fight. The lithe sailor flinched with each sound yet stealthily continued from one grimy doorway to the next, crouching behind overflowing trash cans, beer crates, and the debris generated by the city. Once more, he stopped as if to catch his breath, but in fact, he was too frightened to breathe, still unable to shake the notion that he was being watched.

If Beatrix could have psychically followed as he turned abruptly and entered another backstreet—an even tighter one— she would have seen him turn left and move to where a door had once been but was now rudely bricked over. Thomas' loose-fitting uniform concealed his strength as he easily lifted a stinky metal garbage can and silently placed it out of his way. Then he smoothed a hand above the pock-marked wall, and with razor-edge swiftness, stopped and pulled out a brick. *It is all as I was instructed.*

Like powdered sugar sprinkled on a beignet, flecks of the loosened mortar silently tumbled into the polluted puddles that had lingered from the afternoon's storm. And while everything was still, it took seconds before Thomas could breathe again.

Reaching inside the enclosure, he felt the paper, and it was exactly as he'd been told. "Remove an envelope and take it to the courier and leave the message you have been given," were his orders.

The envelope, perhaps ten-inches square, was crisp and formal. Flickers of light had crept in the alley, so he could barely make out the blob of red wax seal with its distinctive symbol. He slipped the envelope into the waist of the uniform, replacing the brick, and left as purposefully as he'd come.

Finally, nearing the street, he dared to straighten his posture and will his heart to stop pounding with the intensity of a kettle drum.

Thomas peered three times in both directions as he reached the appointed location and slipped into a tiny chaotic laundry at the end of yet another alley. Like a ghost, he disappeared through the door marked SAM'S CLEAN SHIRTS and into steamy vapor that clung to the window, making rivulets down the panes of speckled glass. More steam billowed out of the door of the establishment, mingling with the fog swirling through the checkered neighborhood. A sad-eyed woman leaned heavily on the counter and did not blink as a stranger seemingly dissolved into the recesses of the building. She had merely lifted one finger to point to a side office and then gave her undivided attention to flipping a page of *Photoplay* magazine, and with the other hand, stubbed out a cigarette in the overflowing ashtray.

The evening quickly closed in, as happens in February in the South, and fingers of mist circled up from the river, resembling the Hollywood set of cheaply made horror flick. No one seemed to notice that zombies or vampires would be lurking if this was a movie, and instead, workers bustled home to be with their families, stores' clerks pulled down blackout shades, and secretaries covered their typewriters, giggling and whispering plans to stop for a whiskey or mint julep before hopping on the streetcar and heading home. Throughout the city, office lights turned off, and flickering bar lights came on. In the distance, the once-joyful bell chiming at St. Charles Cathedral seemed to moan with each clang, echoing the fears of the citizens of New Orleans as the war escalated and the daily statistics in the newspaper grew more unspeakable.

With the declaration of war on December 8, 1941, the *joie de vivre* felt as if it had been sucked right out from a city whose slogan was *laissez les bons temps rouler*. The good times were not rolling anymore, except for those taverns and restaurants that catered to the masses of sailors and soldiers who knew but would not admit that it could be their last chance to have a wild time. Forever.

For residents of the Crescent City? Most were holding their breath, personally kicked in the gut from the tragedies at Pearl Harbor and Hitler's aggression through Europe. For Beatrix, these tragedies were good for business. Extremely good.

Fear gripped the city from Rampart Street to Canal Street and all the way to Esplanade Avenue, including the parlors of the leading citizens who lived in the always-upscale Garden District. The often-heard question was, "Can it get worse?" Of course, it could and would, especially since the Navy had begun to build heavily armed ships right in their harbor. With a shudder, one of Beatrix's customers would say, "What will happen here, now that everyone says the Port of New Orleans is next on Hirohito's hit list? We'll be just like Hawaii, bombed to smithereens. You know what happened there."

Beatrix would nod, look into the crystal ball, and twist it just so in order for the overhead light to make it sparkle as if it were alive. Then she'd blink as if tears were about to be shed while selecting an all-knowing, yet vague, response: "Humans have freewill. What 1 see in the future could change." But she'd let them stew because that meant more time with her. More time equated to more money she could send to the cause.

Even out that storefront psychic office on Royal Street, everyone seemed to agree that Orleans Parish was the next target for Axis to attack. Some even repeated hearsay, as if it were gospel and they were the preacher: "The Nazis are right at the mouth of the Mississippi. They're cruising the waters of the Caribbean, just waiting to invade. We all know them Germans have been up and down the river, spying on the docks, setting fires at the railyards to keep us terrified. They're too close, and you know what'll happen to our women and children when they come. ..."

The gruesome details ran wild, and like a break in the levee, the sinister theories exploded as the war intensified.

When it seemed as if a black curtain of apprehension had fallen over the city with all the discomfort of a wet, woolen overcoat when rationing gasoline to shoes to coffee wasn't enough, and when enough fathers, sons, brothers, and sisters had volunteered or were drafted, until one lost count, the city founders decided that the spectacle of lights and laughter and parades, and lavish parties, had to be canceled. There could be no Mardi Gras.

Oh, the wailing of mamas whose daughters were this close to being presented to society and the sobriety of many well-heeled fathers in the community was shattered, as drinking was easier than trying to console their grieving womenfolk. Between whining and crying, most ladies in that circle went straight to bed with the vapors and swore they'd stay there until Hitler was wiped off the earth if they couldn't have the debutant balls.

"Whatever shall we do," was the wail of the collective lament. "Our daughters will never find suitable husbands because of this stupid war going on."

Once the shock settled, and like decades of Southern belles did in the past, they became fearless. They knitted scarves for soldiers, wrote letters to the men overseas, collected newspapers, rolled bandages, and everything else to be recycled for the war effort. Gathering in circles, they sipped peppermint tea or something stronger and exchanged local gossip. But first and foremost, they were Southern women. They might pretend to be frail and needy, but only a fool would believe that they would do anything but soldier on. But not without letting their husbands, their parish presidents, and even congressmen know that they would need to make things right in their well-heeled world, promptly ... or else. Period.

Beatrix, while not born with the backbone of a steel magnolia, knew at her core that even though the values of the city were as bogged down as thick as Mississippi mud, her business would get better. As one socialite client had put it earlier that day: "Why it is all the fault of those egomaniacs

Hitler and Hirohito and their minions." It was a simple explanation, but didn't make the loss of Mardi Gras any more acceptable, and at least a half-dozen wealthy women had paid Beatrix to find out when they should schedule the fittings for their daughters' ball dresses ... "Once that war madness is over, of course."

With so much gloom on the minds of citizens, no one had taken unnecessary notice of Thomas as he disappeared into the laundry. Moments later, he reappeared. Gone was the snappy white uniform, replaced by gray, threadbare work clothes that were better to blend in with the shadows. He had picked up a sack near the door, slipped the envelope inside of it, and then flung it over a shoulder. Keeping away from the partially covered streetlights—part of war safety and dimmed as a precaution against enemy aircraft zooming in on the city—he trudged along Royal Street, stopping from time to time as if the bag was heavy.

If I keep walking, I will deliver this message and be on my way, he thought for the millionth time, doubting the sanity of accepting the task. *To what?* Demanded a seemingly terrified voice that tortured his brain.

It had been arranged that in seven days after picking up and then delivering the envelope if all worked out, he would board a steamer to the Caribbean Island of San Lucia. If that happened, he was to find a certain fishing boat in the harbor to eventually sail into Nassau and then onto a trawler heading to Cartagena, Columbia, by the middle of March. He'd memorized the instructions, daring not to keep written evidence on his person, of how he should seek out his contact at the Windsor Court Hotel before maneuvering his passage to London if all went as planned. "So many *ifs* ..." he repeated once more.

Yet the immediate concern was worse than the what-ifs, as armed police suddenly swarmed the streets, checking the identification of the sailors and civilians, which made just getting to the docks treacherous.

I can do this. I can deliver the envelope and find somewhere to hide until early morning. The plan after that? With the message delivered, he would disappear amongst the throngs of the uncultured side of the Algiers River—an ugly second cousin to New Orleans—and book a room in a boarding house, as requested. Supposedly, the owners expected him and were sympathetic to his cause. He'd wait out the days until the boat got him free of America ... unless the police stopped him first.

In less than twenty minutes after he'd snatched the precious envelop from a brick hiding place, Thomas stood in a doorway of some type of enterprise, unsure exactly what it sold. In Britain, where he'd spent his life, he'd never heard of a finder of lost things. Trying to blend into the doorway's shadow, he thought briefly of well-ordered days and the science that he'd chosen for his life's work. Perhaps, once the war was over, if England survived, he might tell his father, confidently, about his foray as a secret document courier. *I must not think of that now.*

He suddenly crouched down as if sorting dirty laundry in his sack but was stealthily observing two burly Marines being questioned by the police.

Before Beatrix heaved the crystal ball at the door, causing the unexpected visitor on the other side to jump, she had spent that afternoon pacing like a caged tiger, heels of her shoes silent on the Persian carpet, with eyes ringed with disappointment.

"Why can't I do this?" Her voice echoed throughout the room as she twisted the two-carat ruby ring on her right index finger. "Other psychics, not three blocks from here, create visions from animal entrails, or even read tea leaves," she muttered. "I can't even figure out how to pay for next month's rent. I can't see my way out of this."

It was then that she flopped into the desk chair, grabbed the orb, and propelled it at the door, barely missing the window and the black, bold-lettered business sign: FINDER OF LOST THINGS.

It had been the word *see* that triggered a memory she grabbed like a starving street urchin diving in a dumpster for a meal, and she remembered how she and Addie, her childhood nanny, had played endless games to memorize rooms and to make note of small details. "Always see, and always believe in what you see," Addie had said in her gentle French accent.

She hadn't thought of Addie in years but now wondered what had happen to the little woman after some type of argument had erupted between her mother and the nursemaid.

Beatrix frowned. "Oh, Addie, if I were to see anything right now, it would be a crazy woman pacing in an office—a woman who thought she could come to New Orleans and be a spiritualist and find her truth. You said, *Always see and remember*, Addie. What I see is a dead end for this illustrious career as a charlatan amongst established and frightening French Quarter voodoo priests, and flamboyant palm readers who have been doing this since the place was a swamp. A dead end to me being here, searching for my real self. This was crazy, and I was insane to even think of it."

Beatrix's back was to the door, or she would have seen Thomas staring at her as if weighing whether he should enter the business or not.

She turned, staring down at her desk, and whispered, "What did I just see? A small man or a boy. Running and then crouching in the shadow. He's avoiding someone."

She focused again and remembered seeing him throw what looked like a bag of laundry onto the horse-drawn truck from Happy Day Laundry service.

Beatrix clicked on another table lamp that made the furnishings of her compact office glow in gold tones. Two overstuffed chairs faced her desk, and a painting of a woman holding a parasol in the technique known to Monet hung behind her. In the corner was a small settee covered in heavy brocade, and a curtained doorway was directly to the left of where she sat.

She waited. "What if he comes in, turns the handle ..."

She'd seen enough in that glance to know he was in trouble. Appearances, she knew, were deceiving. Maybe he needed help, and she'd give it—if he had money. If not? She'd deal with that, but not without disappointment.

Out on the street, thickset police officers were knocking door-to-door and peering through windows. Thomas had overheard that they were looking for a man dressed as a sailor. Two men in uniforms joked as they continued the search, but only a fool would assume they were negligent in their duty to apprehend a suspected felon, a murderer, a traitor, or all three in one man.

Thomas put his head down, as if investigating the laundry sack, and the police looked right through him as if he were not there. Moments before, he felt like a noose was tightening around his neck—police were everywhere. Then a horse-drawn wagon with a wooden sign saying, HAPPY DAY LAUNDRY, lumbered down the street. In one swift movement, Thomas yelled something, waved to the driver—who looked confused but acknowledged the worker—and tossed the white sack into the bed of the wagon.

Thomas twisted the doorknob. The front door creaked as he inhaled and moved over the threshold, and Beatrix straightened. She spun around before tucking her wavy hair back into the snood.

"Don't just stand in the doorway. Someone might see you," she snapped at the stranger. "What can I assist you in finding, sir?"

She sized him up, as one might do with a job candidate,

noting peculiar details, and then adjusted the scarf around her neck, making certain that it concealed the scar, white and deep, that always produced far too many questions.

"I know you understand English, so make a decision. If you stand there, someone will see you." She smiled in the practiced way to invite confidence and used her most compelling psychic lines as she whispered, "Come in, sir. I have been waiting for you."

Looking at the man in the doorway, she continued to play the guessing game the French nursemaid had taught her to improve her sense of observation, and it was called *What if*.

Thomas stood halfway into the office, flinched, and quickly decided he could overtake the diminutive woman, but not half the New Orleans Police Department, who seemed to be on Royal Street, stopping every man in sight.

With the decision made, Thomas bowed to the occupant. Finally, he reached behind the red velvet curtains and grabbed the HELP WANTED, INQUIRE WITHIN sign from the window. He nodded three times, keeping his eyes lowered.

"You need laundryman, missy?"

"No, I do not." She stood, walked around the desk to be closer to her visitor, and twisted the knob to lock the door.

He inched into the office. "Missy, need houseman? I no get knackered. I good worker."

Thomas's eyes widened at how quickly she moved, which bothered him more than being locked inside with her. Yet the locked door meant that if he were followed, as he had to admit seemed true, he would be safe. For a time. However, his precious communication was in a laundry sack, atop a wagon headed God only knew where.

"Your name, sir? Do you use an English one? Or do you prefer to be recognized in Chinese?"

"Yes, missy. Ling. That my name. I good worker. You give me job?" He stared at her with intensity, then demurely at his feet. "You wait for me? You know me, lady?"

"I have been waiting for you. And now, please sit down.

Dispense with your terrible broken English. We both know you are British, with impeccable language skills. And you slipped up in the faulty dialect by using the word *knackered*, you know."

She based everything on the smoothness of his hands, his use of the British slang word. The giveaway? Pricy tan Northampton wingtips.

"No, missy. I work in laundry." He still diverted his gaze but noticed the quiet of the office.

The woman was alone. That was odd as he'd certainly heard an angry voice. She must have been yelling at herself.

Beatrix returned to her desk. "I know why you chose to come into this office rather than meet up with the police that are, at this moment, closing in on the front door. You see, I can read minds, and I know things normal people cannot."

It was a lie—one she'd used so often, it rolled out of her mouth. He was running from the law, so she could work with that until he revealed more.

Out on the street, deep voices barked a conversation, and although Thomas could only guess what they were saying, he knew they were looking for him.

If he's hiding from the police, either he's committed a crime or has no passport or documentation. And while he seemed harmless enough, Beatrix would rely on the tricks of the night trade and have him believe she knew more about him than she could, of course. Yet, there was an alternative. She could simply let him know he was safe and that all the hubbub on the street had nothing to do with him. In fact, it was a case of mistaken identity since the real felon was Japanese.

Yet she said, "The police are looking for someone who has assumed the disguise of a sailor, not a laundryman."

She had overheard about the criminal that afternoon. But she wouldn't tell him the truth. Not yet.

Before the war, Thomas often spent evenings in a darkened cinema, never revealing to his mates or family that he wanted an adventurous life like Humphrey Bogart or Ronald Coleman. In fact, his life in England was so far from anything cloak and dagger that when a colleague at Cambridge asked him to retrieve an envelope to take to an address in New Orleans, he replied, "Most certainly I will do it," even before all the details were explained. It seemed so much like a game, like a stage play he and his peers had put on during boarding school.

How could this woman know so much, especially since he'd had no plans at all to enter her office disguised as a laundryman or as the sailor he'd been impersonating just minutes before? Who had told her? Who could have?

"I am afraid you are mistaken, madam," Thomas said, returning to the cultured British accent.

He straightened the bent posture of a laundryman and again resembled the compact scholar he was while calculating that there must be a back door on the other side of the curtained wall.

Beatrix saw his gaze dart to the curtain.

"I do not make mistakes, sir. Kindly sit down. The back door is locked from the inside, and the key is here in the desk. If you want to leave after we have finished our conversation, I will hand it to you. But I do not think you will need it. Or want it."

Thomas Ling had a classical education but was also trained in the martial arts. It was true he had never set foot on Chinese soil. Nonetheless, he still considered Shanghai his home.

He took the guest chair and put his shoulders against the soft green leather, his feet squarely before him, and his hands clasped on his lap, yet every muscle remained alert. The questions engulfing his mind were not obvious, except to the observant woman sitting across the desk from him. His gaze darted around the room, and she knew he was in danger.

Thomas finally realized the woman was waiting for him to speak.

"Madam, what is that you want from me?"

"My name is Beatrix Patterson. I am a seer, a knower of things. You are hiding, running from someone. It's true because I have seen it. You've lost something that is most precious to you."

She hesitated, as she always did with a new client, reading his face, looking for micro-facial changes. And honestly, she did see him lose the laundry bag. Or at least toss it in the back of the laundry truck.

His eyes widened for the briefest second, and she knew there was more.

"No, the prized possession that you lost is not yours, but it's for China."

This time, his pupils dilated even more.

"I know of nothing about which you are speaking," he replied because that was what he was told to do should he be questioned after pretending he didn't speak English.

Beatrix Patterson did not look strong enough to even withstand one blow that he could administer, thanks to his training, so he tilted his head and said, "You have mistaken me for someone else, and now I must—"

"Sir, cut your chatter. We have little time to talk."

Beatrix knew she'd guessed correctly. If he was pretending, he wouldn't have chosen an upper-class accent.

"You are a courier," she said. "Is that not true?"

Certainly, a courier wouldn't have money or want a reading. But with a bit of trickery, perhaps he could be useful. The HELP WANTED sign had been for a weekly office cleaner. But right then, a plan—fragmented, at best—came together.

She jutted her chin out, and in the dim light, he could now see that she was not a crone but a woman with chiseled features, smooth hair tucked into some type of covering, creamy skin, and who looked much younger than he'd originally thought, fooled by the tone of her commanding voice. In this light, she looked no more than thirty.

Then the most unusual thing happened. Beatrix smiled and looked into his eyes. Suddenly, Thomas felt relaxed, and that went against everything he'd been instructed to do.

He leaned into the leather chair, and for the first time in a week, he seemed to be able to breathe.

Beatrix saw the muscles in his neck loosen and thought it was time to reel him in.

"I can help you, doctor. ..."

"Thomas Ling," he said and then realized he'd given away the one thing his handlers told him not to: his full name.

Beatrix now had all the information she needed.

"Dr. Ling. As a man of logic and the sciences ..."

He nodded, confirming her guess.

"I will protect you from the police for now. They are looking for a felon, and not a scientist. In return, you will become my secretary and bodyguard."

"I have another matter that must be completed. I cannot accept employment, nor do I want to, because ... you know, I am a scientist?"

She smiled. "In about five minutes, two or more police officers will bang on that door, Dr. Ling. They are looking for a small Japanese man who has impersonated a sailor. That man set fire to the munition's depot near the warehouse district. I know you are not him, and only an uneducated dolt would think you were anything but Chinese. However, these men always think the worst, and will not stop because you insist that you're not Japanese. They are determined to apprehend someone, and even your change of clothing won't alter that they'll arrest you. Trust me on these facts. They will drag you to the patrol car, where the worst may happen since the entire country is horrified by the destruction in Hawaii."

"I will explain. They will see the truth here." He stood, ready to bolt.

"Be real, Dr. Ling. The country is at war with an Asian empire. You are Asian, even if you are Chinese and have a cultured British accent. They won't take time to discuss your heritage, and I'm sorry for that. However, it's the truth. Stop talking, will you please."

Beatrix shoved her palm at him, and he jumped as if he'd been cursed.

"Unless you immediately head to the rear of the shop, change into one of the suits and a tie you'll find in a small room near the back door, they will arrest you, and your mission will come to nothing. Those who have depended on you will fail, and perhaps die. The object that you have lost will be gone forever if you do not take my advice. Now."

Thomas looked into her eyes. They were the color of the pale jade statues his parents displayed in their parlor. Then his gaze was drawn to her hands. The ruby glistened in the lamplight, making it look huge.

With more of a physical outpour of fear than common sense, he dashed through the curtained opening, down a hall to the open door. It was a large supply room, and just like the woman said, there were at least a dozen suits lined up on racks like bodyless soldiers and stacks of old-fashioned white dress shirts. Black ties hung neatly on a rack near the door. Thomas quickly surmised that the storefront had once been a haberdashery. Yet, the men's fashions had not been in style for two decades but seemed ready if need be.

He yanked off the gritty, soiled denim trousers and the rumpled cotton shirt, tossing them to the floor to madly put on a roomy woolen suit—he grabbed the first suit he saw, not taking time to see if it was the right size.

Thomas slapped a tie underneath the collar of the unstylish shirt to create a Windsor knot, and then his fingers froze as he heard pounding and shouting behind the door.

CHAPTER 2

BEATRIX GLANCED AT HER APPOINTMENT DIARY. It had been filled with consultations throughout the day, and there was one entry for later that evening, but she knew that. She ran a finger down the list of names—names she constantly read in the newspaper's society pages.

Since the outbreak of war in Europe, even more of the lonely, fearful, and brokenhearted came to Beatrix for advice, comfort, and a form of therapy to unburden themselves to a sympathetic ear. She accepted whatever money they offered, and for those who had little, she took even less. Some believed Beatrix could connect with the departed, and it gave them hope that their deceased loved ones were happy or perhaps had left a fortune stuffed beneath the floorboards of an old plantation.

She had told a client that morning, "If you can return for another session, perhaps your loved one will trust you enough to share where it can be found, or—wait … he's telling me right now that you must search the house again. You've forgotten to look in that special place."

Now, the client would pull everything apart, and if she didn't find the hidden cash, she would assume it was in a nook that only her deceased husband knew. Either way, she'd return for more information from Beatrix, either about the hiding place or for more predictions of the future.

While some believed, others called Beatrix a trickster, saying so with a practiced sneer for all things spiritual. Yet, they surreptitiously booked appointments to have their future revealed or an event explained, such as why a certain husband suddenly had to travel on business every second Tuesday of the month. The haughty Protestant minority, and the few others who didn't drink, smoke, swear, or gamble—hence, not part of true New Orleans' society—asserted that she bilked the grieving and unfortunates who believed in otherworldly things, doing so to the last penny of their life's savings. That wasn't true, but it made for excellent gossip.

It was established by rumormongers who fed on any tantalizing details that she lived alone in the mansion once built by her grandfather William Randolph Patterson Sr., who had created a goodly measure of tittle-tattle. After a miscalculation with a friend, and two pistols, which was a duel over a gambling debt, the spacious home went temporarily into the hands of her great aunt and uncle, whom Beatrix loved to visit during school holidays, and especially after the car crash that took her parents' lives. Her father, William Randolph Patterson Jr., was as much of a ladies man and scoundrel as his father. That is, until being swept off his feet by a Spanish heiress and moving to California. Some said the law was after him. But then again, the genteel mamas who had urged their debutante daughters to make Mr. Patterson's acquaintance were miffed when he up and married a *foreigner*, even if the heiress's extended family had been in California since the missions were established.

After that, the house was taken over by an aunt, the recently deceased Miss Cornelia Beatrix Patterson—Beatrix's namesake and total opposite of her scandalous brother, who bequeathed the ten-bedroom Victorian to Cornelia, and it was eventually passed to the psychic.

The Garden District's grapevine thrived on the scandalmonger that would never let a good story go, true or not, especially about the misdeeds of the nouveau rich, as all sides of the Patterson family certainly were deemed to be.

A few of the most senior gossipers might relish in whispering how champagne flowed like water or how the *first*

Mrs. Patterson never shopped anywhere except Paris. As for the wartime resident of the stately home? Even if the family had been there since the French Quarter was the hub of the city, Beatrix would most always be an outsider because, to fit into the tight-knit social rung, one must be born in the city, go to school in the city, and make one's debut with other upper-class young women at their first fashionable appearance in society.

The gossiped questions were endless: Could Beatrix Patterson talk with the dead? Was she able to predict the future?

It would seem that was all true, according to a segment of New Orleans society who wanted it to be so. Everyone knew about one particular woman or knew someone who did and her sessions with Beatrix Patterson. Supposedly, one well-connected matron blotted the corner of her eye with the edge of a silk hanky and whispered, "She put me in touch with Arnold, and told me straight away that he still loved me. Oh, how I miss him." She wiped another tear. "Miss Patterson assured me that he's waiting for me on the other side, and we'll be together again."

Heads turned, but not one of the supposedly close friends— diamonds glittering in the evening candlelight as they sipped fine sherry and played bridge—dared to ask the obvious: How does Miss Patterson communicate with a cat?

They looked hopeful, and if truth be told, a few considered booking an appointment with the psychic.

Even stranger things were said that made the most ardent adversary have doubts about Beatrix's *game*, as they kindly put it. Rumor had it that, "Miss Patterson doesn't charge for her service like a common fortune-teller, or those types in the Quarter."

This was not exactly true because Beatrix's patrons wanted all their friends to believe that the woman with the special gift for finding things and telling the future was doing it out of the joy of helping this or that moneyed person. Instead, they slipped a hundred dollars in a pocket of their outfit, which could discretely be placed in their palm, and more discretely passed to Beatrix.

"Pay her? Oh my dear, she never charges me," was a typical comment. It was a matter of perception. Offering money was quite another issue, and one never discussed that because ... well, it was about money.

The gossip that February was particularly vivid with comments: "You know she's not from around here. I remember what my grandmother told me about the Patterson family and how they'd always been high society here in New Orleans, until there was a little matter that sent young William Randolph Patterson away, although the details were covered up. As usual."

"Miss Patterson? Why, she is a lady. From Hollywood, I believe. Have you been to the West Coast? Everyone knows movie stars, and the parties last for days," they'd whisper and repeat the latest celebrity gossip from the movie magazines they'd have their maids acquire at the local drug store.

They wouldn't have been seen dead buying such filth. But behind the closed door of their bedrooms, they poured over every sorted detail.

The mere mention of inhibition-free California—teaming with glamorous movie stars, with its perpetual sunshine, and streets with lined riotous bougainvillea bushes—added to the psychic's cache, and it was socially agreed that Miss Patterson's *gift* was never to be spoken of in the same sentence with voodoo priests and those unspeakable dark practices that had previously crawled from the streets and opium dens into New Orleans' upper echelon. Certainly, no one would publicly announce that they believed in the paranormal world, except they never denied its presence either. That could be just as dangerous. After all, this was New Orleans. Anything could and did happen here.

The doubtful chose to look the other way, and the believers were relieved and felt safer now that they could take their questions to the lovely, gifted Miss Beatrix Patterson.

Beatrix thought of this as she waited and pondered it as if one might from reading a good novel. Beatrix understood the role of gossip and having a great memory for intimate details that were shared in off-hand ways, cared little of what others thought, and was happy that people talked because that brought in more clients. She was in the city for one reason, and certain events had to transpire before that could take place.

"Open up in there. Fists shook the door, then voices thundered, "We can see you. Police. Open up. We are here to search for a dangerous criminal. A criminal against our country, madam. You are safe. Just kindly let us enter your, um ... office. Someone saw a man come in here just moments ago."

With the country on edge, this had not been the first time the police had barged into her office and other businesses on Royal Street.

Beatrix unlocked the door and faced the puffy officers.

"You have a search warrant?" She stood out of their way and casually moved in front of the curtained doorway, hearing Thomas's light footsteps stop on the other side of the fabric.

"It is wartime, in case nobody told you, lady," said an officer, his twang abrasive compared to the New Orleanian accent.

His brown eyes got harder, and anyone who messed with him faced trouble. He poked a finger at her as if he wanted to use a gun instead.

"Yes. I am well-aware of this, sir. Hence, it is imperative that I am careful with whomever enters my office. Countless people are not what they would like others to believe, don't you agree?"

She reached out and took the Southerner's hand, and his erect finger softened, and he gently shook her hand.

Beatrix now spoke slowly, and with the practiced calm voice she used when clients became agitated.

"Gentlemen, would you care for some refreshment? Tea, or perhaps something stronger? The bourbon is smooth and will warm you on this blustery night."

She gestured to the discrete table across the room that held crystal bottles of rich, golden liquor, as well as a tea service that seemed to be at the ready.

The officer who held her hand dropped it and mumbled,

"Yes, ma'am. Thank you, ma'am. Ah, I mean, no thank you, ma'am." He blinked. "We are looking for a dangerous felon. Now if you'll step to the side, we want to look around. That spy might somehow have gotten in here without, well ..." he looked down, apologizing, "without you knowing it."

"You will only find me here." Beatrix turned slightly. "Oh, how awkward. You will also want to meet my secretary, Dr. Ling."

Beatrix pulled back the curtain, and Thomas shoved his shoulders back and stood as tall as his five-foot-six-inches allowed.

"May I help you, gentlemen?" he said in his upper-class British accent.

Beatrix caught Thomas's eye, pulled back the cuff of her velvet jacket, and looked at her watch. Then she looked at her new secretary once more.

He said, "This won't do. We have absolutely no time for an interruption, as Miss Patterson is going to be late for an appointment."

Beatrix smiled. He was quick.

She withdrew a small black diary from her jacket pocket and handed it to Thomas. He opened it to February 16, and there was a note that read, *Meeting Major Davies at his office, 6:30 p.m.*

The taller of the two officers snatched the diary from Thomas's hand, clearly disbelieving that there was any notation.

"This is your secretary?" He looked Thomas up and down as he spoke. "He's a doctor? He's—"

He saw Beatrix tighten her face.

"Yes, Dr. Ling is correct," she said. "We must leave at once. I assume you have met Major Davies? He doesn't appreciate being kept waiting, I've heard, and we're meeting because I've been hired to find something that concerns national security."

The officers' eyes widened.

"Ah, Major Davies," said the taller one. "Solely in charge of military police matters in all of the South, and particularly Orleans Parish?"

Before she could assure him that her meeting was with the commander, the man blurted out, "Ma'am, you find stuff? Like dogs and gold coins?"

Beatrix smiled. "I reveal the truth, and that has always helped my clients find things that have been lost. I bring to light things not known, and know of things that cannot be heard," she replied in the practiced intimate tone, lowering her voice to a whisper, which always made the questioner lean in. "You've lost something."

It was a statement that inferred she knew his mind, but he wouldn't have asked if that hadn't been the case.

"Yes, ma'am." He gulped and would have said more, but the other fellow glared, and the Southerner stopped.

Beatrix smiled and nodded. "Dr. Ling and I would appreciate your protection to the trolley since there's a dangerous criminal on the loose. Be assured that no criminal or evidence is concealed in any corner or closet of this office. Is there, Dr. Ling?" She waited and then gestured toward the curtained hall. "Better yet, Dr. Ling will show you the rest of the office." She smiled.

Thomas couldn't move. *What is her game? She's going to have me take them to the back, where I've just tossed the laundry worker's clothing to the floor?*

He fought hard not to accept the answer that filled his mind: Beatrix Patterson was a *wu*, a Chinese shaman. A witch, and straight from the frightening stories his grandmother had told him from the moment he was big enough to crawl onto her lap. Beatrix had lured him into her den, just like in the childhood folk stories, and now she'd probably smile, or maybe laugh, as he was carried off by the police.

The *wu* were evil spirits and ungodly creatures of the underworld who traveled the ether, concealed as the most beautiful women and handsome men, greedily grabbing humans and destroying them while they laughed at the pain and suffering.

Now, for her perverse pleasure, Beatrix would expose him

to the police by forcing him to walk them down the dark hall, where they'd find the pile of clothing. He could deny all he wanted that he was Chinese, but from the hostile and arrogant look on their faces, they wouldn't care. The *wu* would watch him being beat and then smile. He would surely die by their hand, on the way to jail or in a cell, before trial.

His devotion to science made the thoughts of evil spirits absolutely ridiculous. He'd always dismissed the supernatural possibilities as ways to frighten children. Yet right in front of him was a *wu*. As if in slow motion, Thomas watched her green eyes take in every movement and follow the expressions of the policemen as she calmly buttoned the tailored maroon suit jacket and then took a black alligator clutch purse from a cabinet.

Then those eyes, as if penetrating his flesh, turned on Thomas. With what? Trickery? Revenge? Was he the mouse in a game where the cat only won? What if he reached out and grabbed her by the throat, twisted that scarf, waited for her to scream? Would she react and fight, or would she disappear into a mystical vapor?

Squaring his shoulders, Thomas futilely attempted to recall any literature supporting that one could go mad by simply thinking they were, as he feared he was doing then.

Beatrix watched Thomas's eyes and hoped that the know-all, see-all look she'd practiced for her paying clients would stop him from doing something stupid, like confessing to the police. She knew they'd beat him to death before they would drag his body back to the police station because his eyes were shaped like almonds. Apparently, her stunt worked, as Thomas flinched but didn't object as she tucked her hand around his elbow and then looked deep into the eyes of each officer.

"I think we're finished here," she said.

Thomas watched as the officers looked like they wanted to go past the curtain that concealed his clothing and who knows what else, but their feet would not budge.

Thomas balled his fist behind his back and whispered to himself, "The *wu* has the power to mesmerize even the police."

Beatrix laughed when she heard him call her a witch. Then, as if breaking a spell, she turned to the officers.

"You will not find anything here of interest."

The officers stepped back with a jerking movement as if shocked by electricity.

"We will not find anything of interest."

At the door, the taller officer said, "Thank you for your time, ma'am. Sorry to bother you. Just doing our job."

"We'll be on our way, ma'am." The Southerner leaned toward Beatrix. "Do you find people?"

Beatrix withdrew a gold-trimmed business card from her jacket pocket.

"If they are truly lost, then they can be found. But if it is of the person's choosing to be lost, then it is impossible. Good night, gentlemen." She turned to Thomas. "Oh, one moment please. I've left the address for our meeting in the pocket of my other jacket. I won't be long. Please wait by the door."

The police left, but Thomas's breath was ragged, as he was acutely aware that he may have walked into the clutches of a *wu*.

CHAPTER 3

THE STICKY FOG HAD RETREATED and was replaced by a stiff wind flinging itself through the French Quarter like a charging rhino. *The devil's wind*, some locals called it, and each told stories of tragedy when that wind barreled through the city.

Less than five minutes later, Beatrix shut the door, locked it, and handed Thomas the key.

"You may want to be in the office when I am not here. Take it. Just beyond where you left the worker's clothing, there is a staircase to the second level. You will find a comfortable, small apartment there. It is yours."

"How did you know I needed lodging, Miss Patterson? Oh yes, you are the great knower of things." He tried to bluster a casual laugh with a hint of sarcasm but only ended up hearing a quiver in his voice.

Witch or not, he'd be crazy to take her up on the offer. Nobody—at least, not in his circle of scholastically egotistical colleagues—would ever do something generous as this without an ulterior motive. If she were a witch, this generous offer would only be so that she could destroy him. If she were not a witch—and Thomas tried to hold onto that particle of reasoning—her game was a mystery.

He'd never liked Sherlock Holmes or Miss Marple. He liked facts and formulae. At the moment, he didn't much care for the game Miss Beatrix Patterson was playing. Whatever it was.

He weighed the truth against bravado and blurted out, "If

you do know things—and my dear lady, I find that impossible to believe—then help me find the bag that I tossed into the bed of a laundry wagon."

He knew this was not logical or possible. How could it be? It was a lie. Part of him did not believe, but it gave Thomas a thread to hang onto so he'd stop imagining her as a *wu*.

She walked on, not turning when he spoke.

Suddenly, Thomas was spinning a ridiculous plan, foolish even, in his currently trembling mind. *I must find the wagon and the sack, but the streets are filled with police hunting for that Asian criminal dressed like sailor. My only chance is to stay close to the witch, at least for the next few hours. Then after she meets with this military officer, I will force her to tell me where the sack is because I know she knows. This is part of the witch's evil plan. After that, I will escape into the night.*

Thomas stopped walking as he thought the strategy through and then had to run to catch up with Beatrix, who put out her gloved hand and turned to him. Was that a smile on her face? Was it confidence? Ridicule? He wanted to turn and walk away. Or better yet, run. But to escape from this crazed woman, if, in fact, she knew where the laundry sack was, would mean failure to his mission. And if that happened, thousands of his country's people could die. The truce with the enemy might not be approved by the United States, but even if that caused national discord, it would buy time—time for many of the stranded in the war zone to escape.

The brisk February wind pulled at the collar of Beatrix's jacket, but she barely noticed it as she walked toward the streetcar at the end of Canal Street. She knew Thomas would follow, even though his thoughts about her were inaccurate. At least, about being a witch.

Had it been a shock when he had seen that she could convince people to do her bidding? That was a part of her polished act that she rarely exercised, and it was simply the power of suggestion and a good strong stare. There was a trick to it, but only if the unsuspecting wanted to be fooled, as many did.

Beatrix walked up the steps of the streetcar, then turned to Thomas.

"I've called Happy Day Laundry. They have your sack."

"You called the laundry, madam?" Thomas followed her to the middle of the car. "When? We were there with the police. You and I were standing right with them. This is preposterous."

"Things are not always what they seem, Dr. Ling. As someone who has studied sciences such as the work on relativity by Dr. Albert Einstein, you must believe in the unbelievable. Do I have a special gift? Perhaps. But I am not a witch. If anything, some prefer to think of me as a clairvoyant. I hear the truth, even when I am being told lies. It is no good to be anything but honest with me. The laundry sack with your precious cargo would have been dumped, scrubbed, bleached, and destroyed by the time the sun had come up tomorrow had I not acted quickly. Instead, it will be waiting for us when we arrive there."

It was all a big pack of lies, and yet she saw Thomas nod. Beatrix knew a tiny part of Thomas wanted to believe it, so she preyed on that superstitious element and succeeded. In fact, she had seen Thomas toss the bag into the laundry truck and knew Happy Day Laundry was the only service in that part of the French Quarter. She'd have to sell a few more antiques from her home to pay the laundry's manager for his time, but that was the cost of business. She might need this contact again. One never knew. The irony of the situation wasn't missed. She was paying to have someone believe in her, rather the other way around.

Thomas tried to remember the details of Dr. Einstein's theory. *Can this woman bend time? What she does is not logical, not possible.* In his well-organized life, situations like this did not happen. In analytical thinking, there were formulas and expected outcomes. *She's able to break the laws of science.*

He punched the trolley seat in front of his.

"What is stopping me from going now?" he said.

"I have helped you, Thomas. Why, you could even say I

saved your life. And if need be, I'll do so again. It's your turn to help me. At least for the next two hours. Then you can leave and be rid of me. I will not hinder you."

He looked about at the neighborhood as yet another idea took hold. *Since this wu, or shaman, or sorceress can stop people from doing what they want, like the officers, and can read minds, perhaps disappear or make people forget—as she must have done when making the telephone call to the laundry—she will be of use to the cause unless it is all foolishness.*

The plan was incomplete, at best, and as a scientist, that made Thomas anxious. But if Beatrix Patterson needed a secretary and a bodyguard, then he would agree to get what he wanted.

He bit his tongue as he hatched the ideas, remembering from tales his grandmother had told him that a witch cannot attack you if you are in pain. He kept waiting to taste blood, but he couldn't push himself to that extreme as he wrestled with the shocking possibility: *Can I conceal my thoughts from her?*

On the trolley, shoulders bumped, and knees collided as passengers, like sardines in a can, pretended it was otherwise. Each strained to look through the drippy foggy windows, wishing their stop would be next.

Beatrix enjoyed feeling invisible as she stood near the rear of the trolley, where everyone avoided eye contact, and she could make educated guesses about their work, marital status, and even what they did for fun. It was psychological gymnastics for her as clues would appear about the people crowded together for ten to fifteen minutes of their lives each day.

In front of her, close enough to feel the heat from her body, was a buxom woman in her forties—one of those ladies with a perpetual look of exhaustion etched on her face. She grunted and pulled a shabby woolen coat tighter to her throat, although the trolley felt like a Florida afternoon. She smelled of strong disinfection soap, like from a hospital, and her hands were red and raw around the cuticles—*a laundress at Touro Infirmary.* Beatrix wondered why she was on the Canal Street trolley.

Directly to Beatrix's right was a child, no more than ten years old, clutching a worn copy of *Anne of Green Gables*. *Alone?* Beatrix wondered until the washerwoman snapped, "Glory bee, Amelia. Can't you stop reading for one full minute? What is it about you and books? When we get to your granny's for supper, you'd better not be reading."

Beatrix bent low so the washerwoman couldn't hear her, but the mother was now complaining to another passenger who had accidentally pounced on her foot.

"That was my favorite book when I was your age," Beatrix said. "Please keep reading and learning. Knowledge is power, and you're going to grow up to be a marvelous, educated, and strong woman."

"I want to be a writer," the girl replied, soulful eyes pleaded that the stranger would keep her secret.

"Then you must."

"Amelia, what have I told you about talking to strangers. Sorry, ma'am. Honey, this is our stop, silly girl. Or have you decided to ride the trolley all the way out to the cemetery?" the woman snapped but then gently patted the child's shoulder. "Momma's just tired tonight, baby girl. Wonder what Granny's going to fix tonight. Think maybe she's still got enough rationed sugar for pie?"

It was a harmless game of trying to tell everything about someone from a snatch of conversation, and Beatrix was thoroughly glad she was wrong about the impatient and tired parent. The girl would be fine, and she was loved in a way that Beatrix had never been.

She turned to Thomas, who seemed well-practiced at holding a swinging strap from the ceiling of the trolley and not touching others.

"You are inquisitive, Dr. Ling, and I think you've figured out my game of profiling. I've been curious all my life, and I study people and their actions, much like you know the sciences. However, there's an American saying, *Curiosity killed the cat*. Be careful what you think and do from now on. If you do not want me to read your thoughts, please tell me. Everyone should have privacy."

Beatrix pulled at the scarf around her neck and longed to get off the trolley and into the fresh, night air. She had studied the sciences of the mind and discovered that psychology allowed her to know a great deal about people, including things they wouldn't tell a new acquaintance, but Thomas didn't need to know that.

She moved toward the front of the trolley and their destination.

Now's she's toying with me. Tell her not to read my mind? That will only make her more inclined to do so. Thomas shuttered, unable to not believe she was as powerful as she said.

An icy wind ruffled the hair on the back of his neck as he stepped down from the trolley, and he obediently followed Beatrix across the street to a building that seemed grungy for that of a military meeting. Whoever the man Davies was, Thomas wondered if this was the meeting where she'd need a bodyguard.

After reaching the landing on the second floor, Beatrix stopped before knocking, listening to the voices inside arguing, and in the distance, the wail of a saxophone crying out the blues. The tavern below was alive, and even in wartime, those who needed it could find comfort, drink, and a party. With luck, they might catch a smile or join a second-line parade and temporarily forget the world's troubles with the help of alcohol, dance, laughter, and music.

Beatrix rapped, and the door swung open.

"Miss Patterson," came the drawl from a puffy-faced man with pink cheeks and a dusting of gray hair.

The US Army officer's uniform fit snugly around his middle as if he'd partaken in too much of New Orleans' excellent cuisine.

"Thank you for coming on this short notice." He looked past the small, competent woman. "Wait, I said to come alone." He threw a meaty arm across the doorway, stopping her from gaining entrance, and making Thomas bump into her.

Beatrix stepped back, even closer to Thomas, and looked up at the officer, chin high in the air.

"Major Davies, this is my secretary. He accompanies me everywhere I go. I keep no secrets from Dr. Ling, nor he from me. If you have changed your mind about needing my help, then we will be on our way. Good night."

Beatrix turned, but not before she saw the major about to touch her maroon jacket. She didn't smile—that would have been a giveaway—but she knew right then that he had heard the rumor about this California voodoo mystic who could cause bodily harm should she be touched.

She stopped and said, over her shoulder, "Did you want to say something, sir?"

"Miss Patterson, yes. Why, of course. I just didn't imagine you'd have a person of this persuasion in your employ. I mean, this is wartime. But we have requested this meeting, and if you can vouch for a J-person such as this, considering our war efforts in the Japanese war theater, and the carnage that just happened to our boys in Hawaii ... well then, I suppose—I mean, apparently all the cards are on your table," Major Davies growled, spitting out the final words.

"Major, gentlemen." She made a point to look into the eyes of those who clustered around the table, holding each stare so that the man believed she was reading his thoughts. "Dr. Ling is Chinese. I grant you; he is not American. He is a British citizen, and as you know, England and China are currently allies. Consequently, if you trust me—and apparently you must already, or we would not be having this conversation—you will do the same for my secretary."

The sideways glares continued from Davies and the four other men circling a table in the small, sparsely furnished room. Yet the whispering stopped.

The major stepped aside. Thomas followed Beatrix into the room.

Sure, she trusts me. She can read my mind. He caught Beatrix staring back at him as if he'd just said as much out loud.

The officers stepped back from the table, and two tried to smile, but their faces showed they trusted no one, perhaps not even their colleagues. In these times of war, anyone who looked different, spoke with an accent, or was out of the ordinary in any way—including a finder of lost things—was suspected of being a spy.

They were right about Dr. Ling. At least, in one way. He was more important than merely a secretary.

Thomas kept his eyes lowered yet was keenly observed the military men. *There is no reason for the United States government to be concerned with me, as the battles I fight involve forces within my ancestral country, and even if that was known right now, it would mean little. So much bloodshed and, oh, the children. I cannot let my mission fail. I will get the envelope somehow to the operative tomorrow. God willing, it will not be too late.*

Major Davies dragged a chair up to the table and motioned for Beatrix to take it.

"Tea, madam. Or perhaps a bourbon? It's a chilly night."

"Perhaps when we have more time," she replied. "How is it that I can help you?"

Thomas withdrew to a corner of the room, where he watched the *wu* listening to the military men. Within moments, they seemed to have forgotten he was there. Or perhaps the witch had magically persuaded them to tell the truth.

Major Davies said, "We have known since Hitler's forces began trampling every blasted corner of Europe that the Third Reich would do anything to celebrate a victory by exterminating everyone in the land of the free and the home of the brave. Army intelligence and the local law enforcement talk on and on about having a strong hold on things here in the city, trying to bamboozle us into thinking it's Japan we must fear more. That said, madam, there are reports of German U-boats throughout the Caribbean Sea, and of course, waltzing straight into places like Caracas. That's in Venezuela."

Beatrix studied Davies as he jammed an finger on the map,

right onto the word Caracas, as if he was killing the Nazis with the action.

"You disagree with the intelligence reports, is that right," she said. "There is no use hiding your thoughts from me, Major Davies, as you know by my reputation that I can hear what you're thinking and know what you're feeling. You believe that the entire city of New Orleans is not safe from saboteurs. Am I right, Major?"

The major pulled a skinny black cigar from his breast pocket, lit it, and puffed deeply as ecstasy betrayed his addiction to nicotine, and Beatrix wondered what other vices he might have.

He refocused, walked to the window, and blew the smoke into the air, again relishing the pungent smell as if he were Adam sampling forbidden fruit.

"Damn right," he replied. "Hirohito and his gang of crazies have plenty to keep them occupied, conquering all of the Asian Pacific. Which, by God, we won't let happen. Sure, my bet is that he's got eyes on America, and our troops are falling right and left. On the other side of this confounded pond, those damn Nazis are war machines. They're steel and spitting out tacks. They're mad as hell at us because we're a free country. We'd never hurt those people like that."

"Are you referring to *those people* being exterminated because they're Jews, Mennonites, disabled, scholars, artists, herbalists, and even midwives," she retorted. "They're murdering anyone who does not bow to Hitler."

"Yeah, well, all those people are still people." The major grunted, unaccustomed to being corrected by anyone, especially a woman.

He ground the cigar into an ashtray with a vengeance.

"If I could get my hands on that crazy-eyed Führer, or just his stinky little moustache, why, I'd tear him to shreds."

"That's valiant of you, sir," Beatrix said. "Nonetheless, what does this have to do with me?"

She learned early on to wait for the client—and in this

case, the United States Army—to give out the information she needed to evaluate the situation. Otherwise, the truth would not be spoken. It was after those awkward quiet moments that the client, Beatrix knew, always told her exactly what they wanted from her.

"Quite rightly, madam. Now, to the point. Miss Patterson, we are certain that Nazis are shipping armies and munitions to South America, and it's all clustered in Venezuela and Brazil. There have been reports of German ships unloading cloaked cargo in the port of Punta Piedras, and training missions into the jungle to give them practice when they get to our shores, because as sure as shootin', they'll move up and into our Louisiana and Florida swamps. That has to stop. If the Nazi's establish themselves with strongholds there in South America, with the approval and greed of the current Venezuelan government, they'll take over all of South America from top to bottom. Hell, that's just a start."

"I do not see the Nazis here, Major," said Beatrix. "But instead, they plan to control the Panama Canal, not cripple it. In doing so, they can conquer Central and North America."

"Damn straight. How could you know that? Nothing of the sort has been in the newspapers about spies being caught in Panama." He gulped

"I'm getting a psychic message." She touched her forehead.

It was better acting than she'd done before, and when the major's face paled, she realized he was putty in her hands.

She opened her eyes. "I have just been told that there are German operatives working with the local criminal faction here in the city. These enemy cells, with guerrilla training, are here to disrupt the city, transportation, government, and of course, travel and transport on the river."

"Well, hell, if you know that, then you're not going to be surprised to learn that before, we spotted German operatives on the Yucatán. That's in Mexico. That means we've got Nazis on our doorstep and spies in our backyard." The major slammed a palm to the table to punctuate his outburst, looked surprised when no one jumped, and then patted all the pockets in his uniform jacket and came up empty.

One of his minions handed him a cigarette, which he dismissed with a grunt and a wave.

"You believe that an invasion is eminent, Major? I do not. But of course, free will is the right of all humans. Are you sure of this?"

Beatrix watched his face and hedged her bet because, honestly, she did not have a clue, except for what he had unintentionally told her.

"I'm here to ask the questions," he growled. "You supply the information, missy."

"Major Davies, if you are uncomfortable with my tactics, I will leave. If not, please be respectful. Because you, sir, invited me here, and the visit was requested by Washington, DC."

The major's jaw worked as if he were chewing gum, and he dug through his uniform pockets once more. This time he grabbed the cigarette pack from the table, pulled one out, and looked at it but didn't light up.

"I am in charge here, Miss Patterson, in case you've forgotten."

"I thought we had established it does no good to lie to me, sir." Beatrix tilted her head and stared at him.

"Hell, yes. Okay, these are stressful times, and lots of lives hang in balance. My temper runs hot. Just ask these goons I work with."

He looked at his subordinates, but none met his gaze, and both Thomas and Beatrix took note of that.

"The psychic messages I am receiving are that there a few now, and shortly, many more, Nazi sympathizers planning to cause chaos, enlisting unsuspecting Americans, perhaps to side with the Germans to supposedly end the war."

"When? How? What will they do?" Major Davies withdrew a handkerchief from his trouser pocket and patted sweat beads from his bald head.

"This city is a target," she said, "and to prevent a full-out attack by homegrown terrorists, you must act quickly."

Major Davies sank to a chair. "Homegrown for sure, and now terrorists. These are American traitors, plain and simple, and a rotten bunch would probably sell out their country for a dime and a promise." He poured a measure of golden liquid, kicked it back, and sat next to Beatrix. "We got off on the wrong foot, madam. Let me apologize. We need your help. The US government doesn't believe in psychics or clairvoyants, or whatever you call yourself. But I've been told from the best folks right here in the city, and some in Washington, right at the top, how you know stuff that you couldn't possibly know. And you find the truth. I want the facts. I'm bone tired of cloak-and-dagger negotiations. Just look what happened with the Brits when they tried to negotiate with Hitler. Trampled. We need information, and the government will forever be in your debt if you truly can get it using your supernatural abilities. Are you willing to be a true American and help us?"

"Are you asking me to identify the Nazis in the city right now, Major? Grab some psychic message from the ether and tell you names and addresses? Or are you asking me to reveal the future when I know it?"

"We have ways to deal with spies, conspirators— filth of the earth who take money to destroy all that's good and wholesome about our great country, Miss Patterson, and what I want is information now. But no, I cannot imagine that you could give us names and addresses. Can you?"

"Major," she looked into his eyes as Thomas watched in horror and fascination, again seeing the witch at work, "If I am able to help and alert you to those who are enemies of America, what can I expect in return?"

It was obvious to Thomas that the commanding officer hadn't expected this. He rolled up a map of the parishes, with locations of armories and munition depots circled in red.

"In return? Madam, the threat will be resolved. Citizens will not fear for their lives. Isn't that plenty?"

"You see, Major Davies, I am a businesswoman. While I

do not expect the government to pay me, as would a patriotic citizen, I require something more. May I have your word that if I help, you will grant me one favor?"

The officer gulped. "I will grant you one favor," he growled.

Beatrix headed to the door. "I will need full access to some government facilities under your command. Of course, accompanied by my secretary."

The major reached out as if to grab Beatrix's arm and then thought better of that.

"I don't know about that, Miss Patterson. You see any person who looks Japanese. I apologize, Ling, but it's true. Any person who looks Japanese is in danger at our operations."

"That, sir, is your problem. Dr. Ling accompanies me, or we do not have a deal." She shrugged and twisted the doorknob.

"Wait, perhaps we can say he is an interpreter." For the first time, the major looked at Beatrix's associate. "I assume you speak Japanese, Dr. Ling, even if you are Chinese?"

Thomas smiled without meaning to, and the stress of the last days turned into a chuckle and then into laughter far louder than he anticipated.

"Not all of us of speak Japanese, nor do we want to." He let out a caustic snicker.

"Don't be a wise-ass with me, mister. I don't need your kind here."

His minions came to attention as though Hirohito himself had barged into the room.

"Have your men stand down, Major, as you must see the humor," Beatrix said, watching red anger sink from the major's cheeks to his chin and neck. "You'll find that my associate is extremely well-educated, and if you could put yourself in his shoes for a moment, you'll see the irony in this line of questioning."

Thomas continued, ignoring the rage on the military man's face.

"I speak Cantonese and Mandarin, along with a few other dialects from my ancestral homeland, including one called

Pinghau. Furthermore, I speak French, Italian, German, some Polish and Russian. I am also fluent in English," he replied in the clipped upper-class accent reminiscent of the British Broadcasting Company.

The major huffed at Thomas's sarcasm, and in that second, Beatrix liked her new colleague even more.

"Then it is agreed," she said. "Dr. Ling will more than satisfy my need for an interpreter, should I require German or French translated during this investigation."

Beatrix stood, gathered her leather clutch bag, and left the office.

Thomas turned back and whispered, "The major is watching us, you know. Did you not want to rebuke his final comment when he said, 'Damn psychic and the fools that run this country have no idea what it's like being the boots on the ground and dealing with self-important idiots all day'?"

Instead, Beatrix continue to walk. She'd heard the comments and instinctively knew they were being watched. "That went better than I expected," she told her associate.

He caught up and walked next to her. "No need to apologize, if you were going to, Miss Patterson."

"For their crude assumptions? Please. Dr. Ling, it might surprise you that conjectures have been made frequently about me, even uglier than what they threw at you. For your information, I am not a witch or a *wu*."

"You know the Chinese word? But you have the power. I've seen it."

They reached the trolley stop.

For a microsecond, she wanted to tell him the truth, but being such a good liar was easier. The more he believed in her supernatural powers, the more pliant he'd be.

"Yes, that is true," she replied. "Now, are you ready to find that precious envelope before it disappears into a tub of hot water, courtesy of Happy Day Laundry?"

"Yes, yes, the letter. The envelope. May I ask a question?"

"It depends." She stepped back from the curb as taxis

splashed through murky puddles that edged the street.

"I know you insist that you have a psychic gift. But how do you plan to expose Nazi sympathizers from right here in New Orleans?"

"More important than finding them—which will only require asking questions of the right people at the right time— will be to find out what they plan to do in the city and when."

"But the major, Miss Patterson ... he didn't ask you to do that, did he?"

Beatrix smiled. "No. But that is what he wants to know. Additionally, Dr. Ling, once I am in possession of those specifics, I will have more leverage. Trust me. The details will be most helpful in the near future. You see, not everyone is what they seem, and most prefer to lie over telling the truth. I hear the truth, even when the liar is saying something quite the opposite."

But of course, that last sentence itself was a lie.

They boarded the trolley, empty now. Thomas knew there was nothing to gain by attempting to conceal anything from this woman, whether he liked it or not—which he did not.

"Then you know that inside the envelope I need to retrieve is a diplomatic pact between China and India," he said, "along with a letter written by Japan's foreign minister, promising never to invade Hong Kong. I am not privy to the details, as I am merely a courier."

No, she did not. But that bit of information could be important.

"Dr. Ling, if you chose to know those details, I will tell you. But from the intelligence I have gathered, regardless of what treaties are signed and what pacts are made, the Japanese Army has the power to crush the American soldiers in India and your people in Burma. Japan will invade Hong Kong. The battles will be fierce, and losses will be horrific."

Her prediction gleaned not from the ethers but from listening closely to those in Washington and New Orleans who gathered intelligence and shared that with their wives.

"Then it is hopeless," Thomas replied. "Wait. How do you know this? How?"

He was shocked by his inability to do something to save these people.

"How stupid I've been," he said.

His brain wanted him to run, but his body seemed powerless with fatigue.

He said, "That's it. You are a Japanese sympathizer."

Indignation pulsed in his veins, and he feared he might do something regrettable to this woman.

"You are a traitor to your country, Miss Patterson." He attempted to quiet his voice.

"Do you remember how I said that not everything is as it seems? I was speaking of myself, actually. You can start breathing again, Dr. Ling. I am not pro-Japan or pro-Germany in this horrible war. I'm attempting to fight the evil in this world."

Could he believe her? He had to stay with her at least until he got the envelope, or he would never see it, never give it to another courier, and it would never reach the government headquarters in Shanghai. But he would desert her the second the envelope was in his hands.

Beatrix squared her shoulders and lifted her chin, now with her eyes level to Thomas's.

"What of you?" she said. "What do you call yourself, if you're willing to admit that you're assisting, even as a courier, to develop a possible peace treaty between China and the enemy forces who are controlling Japan? Where do you stand on the war? You can accuse me of whatever you want. Most of it would be true, as I take money and give information."

She tried to grab his arm, but he pulled away, fearful of the witch if he were honest with himself.

Beatrix duplicated the piercing stare she used when convincing anyone she could read their mind. This time, it felt beyond theatrical, yet she voiced her spiel.

"I am a messenger of the truth, and through visions of knowingness and messages from the unknown, I relay the truth.

Frankly, I'm much like you are, as the courier for the treaty found in that envelope and the secret message that you left in its place ... and your homeland is trying to work with America's enemy. What does that make you?"

Thomas pulled away, wishing he could stop the sting of the truth as Beatrix's words tumbled out.

"Look here," she said. "Do you really think it requires psychic abilities to listen to conversations and understand the dynamics of war, once one knows how, and to pass that information along to unseen forces who can save lives?"

What she didn't add was that the First Lady of the United States, and a handful of high-ranking diplomats and generals and their spouses, were among her confidential clients who discussed war effort. She admitted to asking them leading questions, and they willingly confided small bits, which she used to link facts together.

All the weeks leading up to his arrival in New Orleans, Thomas felt that his mission was altruistic, that a treaty between Japan and China and India would stop the massacre. Now, for the first time, he wrestled with the theory. Was he a pawn being controlled to place his homeland in further jeopardy, to create further death tolls that had already reached the millions throughout the Pacific? Did he truly know if the aging Chinese colleague was pro-China? What did he even know about the next courier he was to meet?

As the Canal Street trolley rocked on the tracks, Beatrix continued.

"Leave whenever you want. If China, India, and Japan forge a truce, it could avert two of your Chinese armies under US General Joseph Stilwell's command, crossing into the Burmese frontier. If the truce is just useless writing on a fancy piece of parchment, which I believe it is, before the end of that month, the Chinese forces defending Toungoo in central Burma, between Rangoon and Mandalay, may be annihilated by the seasoned fighters that the Japanese have become. British and Indian units in Burma will not do any better and will retreat seeing the enemy's numerical superiority both in the air and on the ground."

Beatrix got off the trolley at Royal and could feel Thomas close to her. Instead of returning to the office, she walked east.

Thomas scrambled after her, stunned by her predictions.

"I must get this information to my government," he muttered. This is more important than the worthless offer for a peace treaty."

"Do you believe anyone in government will listen?" She turned slightly before crossing the street.

"I'll make them," he growled, shocked that this witch could make him shout. *No thought is safe when she's nearby.*

"You see, Dr. Ling," she said in a lyrical tone, "I can assist you, and you can provide a useful service for me. I need a bodyguard, and you need information to pass along to your government. I know what you're thinking. Unfortunately, until the potential slaughter of soldiers at the Burmese front happens next month, your government will not accept the intelligence gathering that you want to give them."

"If I tell them, and then they change their plans, countless lives may be saved. But if they do not believe me, then what?" He rubbed his hands over his face.

"Accept my employment. Then I'll go to your consulate, speak with the diplomat in charge and attempt to convince this person of my ability to know the future. I do know some powerful decision-makers in Washington who have influence over the individuals in charge. Now, please stay here while I go inside." She motioned to the entrance to a warehouse and the sign that read HAPPY DAY LAUNDRY. "I'll return in a moment with the envelope."

Thomas's head felt like it was on fire. Two hours before, he was a frightened, adrenaline-filled courier who should have stayed in Britain and continued his study of the power and intricacies of the atom.

He paced. On a lark, he got caught up in what he thought would be a grand adventure. He'd carry a message from one party to another. It was playacting, a way to shake off the cobwebs of studious life and help out an elderly Chinese professor he knew at Cambridge. Now, unless he agreed to be the accomplice of a possible traitor to the United States, his hands would forever have blood on them.

Don't be stupid, Ling. He jolted. *I am arguing with myself. She's telling the future, the truth.*

Beatrix handed Thomas the envelope with its red seal of wax intact.

"Goodnight, now," she said. "If you choose to accept my proposal, I will see you at nine o'clock tomorrow morning. Stay at the apartment above the office if you want. Take the information about the potential slaughter in Burma to your contact or the consulate or do whatever you want with it. If you're not in the office, I'll assume you've changed your mind to help me so I can help you and those in China."

Thomas wanted to snarl or lash out, which was the polar opposite of his personality. *How dare she tell me that I would not at least attempt to stop bloodshed in my homeland?* He turned his back, avoiding any possibility that she would hypnotize or bind him in a spell, as she had done to the police and the army officers.

Thinking she'd gone, Thomas flipped around to find that she was staring at him, and he felt heat radiate from the envelope in his breast pocket. Whatever spell she had concocted to hex the police either wasn't working now on him, or for some reason, she had chosen not to mesmerize him. And even though he had not turned into a zombie, Thomas was certain that she could still read his thoughts.

He bowed slightly. "I will see you in the morning, madam. Have a good night."

CHAPTER 4

February 17, 1942

ALTHOUGH THE MANSION on Audubon Place was comfortable, Beatrix's night was anything but.

"I've got a gift, all right." She often swore between those words. "A gift to for excessive remembrance. I can recall every detail of every sentence, every place I've been, every person I've ever met or thought about meeting. Some stinking gift."

Yet, her ability as a skilled liar allowed her to connect possibilities and put together conversations and facts that quite often turned out to reveal the truth.

Until all the facts, images, and conversations that bombarded Beatrix's brain had been sorted, categorized, and prioritized; she knew it was hopeless to try sleeping. Instead, she walked through the house, switching on and off lights and pulling down and then throwing up blackout curtains, which were required by the government to avoid possible air attacks, as were happening in London. Those activities only confirmed to neighbors that the house was possessed.

At daybreak, the telephone rang. She heard the static of a long-distance call and then a shrill voice.

"May I speak with Miss Patterson, please?"

"This is she. Please let Mrs. Roosevelt know that I would be happy to chat with her."

The president's wife routinely called at that hour, so it took no psychic ability to know it was one of her most influential clients, even if few government officials knew about their association. Still, the loud gulp at the other end of the call made Beatrix smile.

"Beatrix, my friend. I apologize for calling this early," said Eleanor Roosevelt. "You see, I have a long day ahead and need a quiet word, in private."

In January, Beatrix had met with the president's wife to discuss helping families affected by the deaths in battle. But later that day, Mrs. Roosevelt said, "I know you have the gift. The Secret Service has warned me, Beatrix. But I know from mutual friends that you can be trusted."

Beatrix nodded, and Mrs. Roosevelt confided in the younger woman. Since then, they'd spoken every few days. Yet, that morning, the First Lady was hesitant.

"Mrs. Roosevelt, is this about your husband?"

"Franklin is suffering with the after-effects of polio. Do you see an end to this terrible disease that has disfigured my husband and turned him into, at times, a tyrant?"

"Be assured that in the next decade, a researcher and Dr. Jonas Salk, and others, will stop it," Beatrix replied, half-heartedly confident. "Right now, they're working to find a cure. One day, polio will be obliterated from the earth.

She attempted to keep abreast on medical news and knew a few scientists were searching for a cure, but her guarantee was a lie.

"What a relief, dear Beatrix. Another reason for my call ..."

Beatrix gave the First Lady time to phrase her question as awkward as it might be, and when she hesitated, Beatrix replied, "Your husband's romantic affairs will not hurt the country or his presidency. Never admit that you know. You see, a woman is like a tea bag. You cannot tell how strong she is until she gets in hot water."

Mrs. Roosevelt's breathing steadied, and there was a long pause. Then she laughed—a glorious sound that could light a room.

"Oh, I must write that down."

"We all gain strength, courage, and confidence by each experience in which we really stop to look fear in the face. We must do that which we think we cannot."

"I will take your advice, Beatrix. And with your permission, I'm going to use those sayings in my next weekly column for 'My Day,' the newspaper articles that are published to help Americans cope."

"Be well, my friend." Beatrix replaced the receiver.

Yet, as she dressed, twisted her chaotic hair into a loose bun at the back of her neck, and slipped into the black gabardine wide-legged pants and tan-trimmed suit jacket with black velvet piping, Beatrix continued to think about the First Lady.

What weight she carries on her shoulders. In private life, a woman with an unfaithful husband might quietly divorce him. The president of the United States and the First Lady live by other standards, and with the world watching their every step. We so often are afraid to care too much, for fear the other person does not care at all. I must tell Mrs. Roosevelt that during our next telephone conversation.

As she caught the trolley into the city, Beatrix focused on the previous evening's meeting with Major Davies, confident that if there was a Nazi cell in New Orleans, her trusted contacts would reveal them. No psychic gift required.

Beatrix walked slower than usual toward her office and saw the antiquarian bookseller, John Brockman, her neighbor on the block, as he peered out his front door. He'd approached her twice before and then demurred with fabricated excuses. Even in the early morning, now that America was at war, the city was electric with factory workers flocking to manufacturing plants, and every other person on the street was dressed in military garb, their hopes, and fears as clear as the insignias on their sleeves.

Mr. Brockman left his shop and stood out from the crowd in a shabby suit, waiting for his neighbor.

"Miss Patterson?"

"Mr. Brockman. Good morning."

Beatrix's hand connected with his cold, trembling fingers. His teeth were crooked and stained from cigarettes, his hair thinning, yet Beatrix guessed him to be about fifty. She'd seen him limp by the front of her office and knew there was a story behind that disability, one she'd never hear. He wanted to talk with her, and it had nothing to do with his condition.

She quickly critiqued his appearance, as one could tell a lot from the clothes and shoes of choice, but those decisions had to be based on fact. She had asked around and knew he was a man of significant power who had moved from New York City to New Orleans right before the Great Depression. It was then that he'd changed Brockhaus to Brockman, although one Saturday, as she was strolling through the city, she'd seen him head into the Touro Synagogue on St. Charles. Once established in this city, he was quickly launched as the decision-maker for gambling and speakeasys, along with the X-rated district, Storyville. Anything could be gotten anytime if John Brockman was involved. Beatrix knew all this because of the contacts she'd made around the city and by asking the right people in the right way. That said, she liked the man. He was an entrepreneur and an opportunist, much like her.

"Please call me John, ma'am." He tipped the gray flannel hat that had not been fashionable for years. "May I buy you coffee? My business is private. I wish to hire you."

"Hire me? Have you lost a book?"

She knew the answer, but it was a game she enjoyed playing. How much truth a person would reveal without her having to pretend to read their thoughts?

"Not at all," he replied.

John Brockman's tentative smile assured Beatrix that he also felt comfortable with her. In the past, she'd visited his shop, and they discussed literature and their mutual admiration of countless, primarily obscure authors.

"It's the future I need to know," he said.

"I can help you. Madam Flambeau's bakery and café next to your office now has a few sidewalk tables. Shall we stop there?"

"No, not her. The woman has the ears of an elephant, and is the most gossipy, unpleasant, bitter piece of—"

The Parisian baker was reported to spread gossip that melted out in all directions like butter on a hot croissant while adding juicy details of her own making.

"May I suggest Café du Monde," Brockman said.

Beatrix agreed, and they walked to the French Quarter. For an onlooker, they seemed an odd couple—perhaps an out-of-work relative hoping to borrow money from his smartly attired niece. Yet Beatrix, ever-sensing and seeing things, realized that Mr. Brockman's gaze swept the street ahead as if he were protecting her. Or was he protecting himself?

Café du Monde had not changed since its inception in the mid-1860s, and the citizens of New Orleans liked it just that way. Even in war, service was quick and polite, as if everyone who entered was a valued client or a persnickety Southern debutant. The café au lait was rich, dark, and creamy, and beignets were fluffy enough to nearly float off a plate.

Beatrix declined the sweet beignets but held the coffee mug between her hands and waited.

"I know you only as a true bibliophile, but I've learned about your business concern, ma'am, from others." John Brockman swallowed half-cup of hot and intensely fragrant liquid in one scorching gulp. "I've been residing in New Orleans long enough to have my own sources to weigh what's bunk and what's the gospel truth. You are astute and intelligent. Many swear you are a seer. I do not care to weigh in on that. You see, I've been approached by an unusual business opportunity, quite out of the norm for me, Miss Patterson, and I find working with the sorts who are involved much against my better judgment."

Beatrix looked into his eyes and knew it was true. Then she touched the ruby ring on her index finger. She smiled at him, and for effect, placed that same finger on the sleeve of his tweed jacket. The gesture worked, and she could see the older man relax.

"Please call me Beatrix, John. Yes, it does little good to

misrepresent anything to me. I appreciate how quickly you have arrived at the point of our meeting."

She'd said this hundreds of times, but now the lie felt painful in her throat. She wanted to help him. But could she?

He finished a second beignet and had the server refill his coffee.

"This is a matter of delicacy," he said, "dealing with government officials, and the odd part is that I'm often on the other side of the law."

"As a bookmaker, money lender, and money launderer, among other trades, you have a brisk business," she replied, reflecting on the flow of visitors that would go in and out of the back of his office building. "Nonetheless, with such a number of our city's electorate in your pocket, I doubt this matter has anything to do with your regular business transactions. Rather, you have been asked to finance something? Is it part of the war effort?"

She could tell by the tiny lines around his mouth that she was right. She'd struck gold.

He nodded and seemed to be relieved that she understood so much already.

"Last week," he replied, "one Major Davies came to me in the bookstore and asked about you. I thought perhaps the war department was going to hire you. He inquired about your patriotism, and since I could not, nor would not, answer that, he left in a huff."

"He returned?" Beatrix said.

"Yes, and this time he came with Admiral Peterson. Jack Peterson. Guess they brought in the Navy's big cheese to convince me."

"Major Davies. My." Beatrix sighed. "Interesting. They came to your back door the second time. An attempt to intimidate you?"

"Quite right. It didn't work. If I didn't know secrets about most of the politicians in Louisiana, I would have been in prison long before you were born. The admiral seemed to be a likeable sort. Southern man. Now, that major? He was twitchy, looking at his watch like he had someplace better to go."

Beatrix closed her eyes for a moment, as that always made the client feel she was connecting to the spirit world. She grimaced as if in pain. This cinched the deal about spirits and psychic messages.

"Are you aware that the admiral is in charge of evaluating production of a lightweight boat, something amphibious?"

She kept involved in the commerce of the city.

Brockman blinked. "Exactly, ma'am. As you may have ascertained, I am prosperous and well—"

"They want you to bankroll the entire operation for the government. Is that correct?"

Brockman blinked again. "I heard you were good, but I couldn't imagine it to be true. Yes, Beatrix, Davies has a good argument. I hate Hitler, and my reasons are thoroughly personal, as well as political. Yet something is suspicious. I need to know their real reason for asking me to pay to take an amphibious craft out of small-scale production and build factories to launch the crafts into battle. You know, America is not prepared to fight a long war. The admiral said, 'America just doesn't have the resources without the financial help of citizens who are true patriots.' Or so he told me."

Brockman continued about how the admiral pulled out the roll of plans and talked about the bookie's American duty at length.

"I ask you, Beatrix, what were those politicians thinking if they declared war and didn't have the money to finance it?" He rubbed his forehead.

"Are they lying to you, John? Could it be that the government wants you and other businessmen to fund projects because they're too risky? That doesn't sound too objectionable. What do you see as my role in this, John?"

"I want you to meet with Admiral Peterson and young Andrew Higgins. He's the man building the boats. I've known Higgins for years. He built that lumber business up well. Now he thinks he can produce boats. I don't know a thing about boats. I want you to tell me if these men are as good as their word or their contracts. I'm a businessman, and while I care for America, and maybe more than the next guy, I'm mighty skeptical. The bottom line is, why come to me, a crook, a bookie?"

"When will you meet with these men?" She slid her chair back from the café table.

"Later this afternoon. I know the time is short, but Beatrix, there is no one in the city I can trust."

"You trust me?"

"You have nothing to gain by not telling me the truth." He withdrew a fat envelope from the inside pocket of his jacket. "There is one thousand dollars in here. If you will attend the meeting with me at the boat factory on Lake Pontchartrain at three today, there will be another thousand for you. Give me your views on their reasons. That's all."

Beatrix accepted the envelope, keenly aware that the bookmaker didn't ask her to read their minds. Perhaps he knew, sensing finally that she was as much of a trickster in her business dealings as he was in his?

"Agreed," she said.

"May I have my driver pick you up?"

If others in the restaurant knew their business or the amount of money that had just been accepted, they would have been flabbergasted, as it was enough to buy a car and almost a house. It was more than bankers and lawyers made in a month. She knew it would help fund a clandestine war effort, one close to her heart, and support the disenfranchised of the city, too.

Beatrix went straight to the office. The door was unlocked, and the smell of a jasmine tea wafted around her. The mail was neatly stacked on her desk, and the appointment book was open. There was a notation for 11:00, in a neat script: *Flynn Howard requested an appointment.*

As was her routine, she walked through the office and up the stairs, checking corners and even inside floor lamps to make sure there were no listening devices planted anywhere. Her clients' secrets needed to remain so, and this daily task made her feel comfortable with whatever confidences she learned.

That morning, she was curious about items her new employee had moved in.

She was seated back at her desk when Thomas moved silently from behind the curtain, dressed in the same ill-fitting suit but now sporting a tie of shocking orange, with a purple, green, and gold fleur-de-lis, as if it was ordered for a Bourbon Street Mardi Gras party. He'd found it in the recesses of a closet in the storeroom, among the more conservative men's wear items leftover from the previous business.

"Good morning, Miss Patterson."

"Dr. Ling. Glad you accepted my offer of employment, and that you have settled into the office and apartment. Are you aware that tie will not let you blend? Besides, the colors are so loud they're shouting at me." She grimaced.

"I'm quite aware." He flapped it up and down, then waved it like a flag. "My plan is that people will need to cover their ears, and hence forget my ethnicity."

For the first time, Beatrix caught a smile in his eyes, one that made him boyish. She saw him relax, but the moment passed, and his face changed back to stony concentration.

"Oh yes, the unremarkable police officer who would have gladly beaten me to death, one Flynn Howard, charged in at nine and brutishly demanded to speak to you right then. Whilst I attempted to explain that you were otherwise engaged, he was unpleasant in the way a pit bull might be if one snatched his last meal."

"Yet he agreed to return?" Beatrix said.

Thomas nodded.

"Good. Did he mention the purpose of the appointment?" She removed the trim suit jacket that hit just at her hips, then poured tea and settled behind her desk.

"He preferred to bark orders and told me to *chop-chop* about adding his appointment to your calendar." Thomas let out a cynical laugh. "I will be in the storage room organizing boxes of leftover handkerchiefs, straightening clusters of cufflinks, and straightening the lapels of a hundred out-of-style suits, rather than sit here twiddling my thumbs. It will be ready, should you decide to end finding lost things and open a men's haberdashery."

"I hope you did not count on twiddling, Dr. Ling. There are a few errands that require your attention."

She withdrew the fat envelope from her purse, counted out five-hundred-dollar bills, wrote a note, and slipped everything into a crisp new envelope. On the outside, in cursive, she penned *Poydras House*. In another envelope, she added two bills and wrote a name. Finally, she handed the envelopes to Thomas.

"The first goes to an orphanage on Saint Charles and Julia Street. You can't miss it. The second should be given only to Miss Gillette Pierre. You will find her on Bourbon Street, at the Old Absinthe House. This time of the morning, the bar will be closed, so use one of the back entrances." Three hundred-dollar bills remained on her desk. "Take this one, Dr. Ling, and outfit yourself with whatever clothing you will need—coat, suit, shirts—so you look like you're living in 1941, rather than 1920. And buy some nicer tries. We have an appointment with the Department of the Navy this afternoon, and those trousers are far from flattering unless you are trying to show off your socks and those fancy English leather shoes."

Thomas was stunned. She'd known him for less than twenty-four hours, yet in his hands was $800. In China, this would be considered a fortune.

"Dr. Ling." Beatrix interrupted his thoughts. "What you and I are doing here will have a huge effect on the world and alter the outcome of this horrible war, along with the aggression in China toward the people you care about."

Thomas hated that she could read his mind and thought it was ludicrous that the money in an envelope could crush Hitler or Hirohito. He was going to say that, but she spoke first.

"Be careful. It's dangerous to be Asian in this city. I haven't been to Britain in a few years, but as you have noticed, American men seem to be nothing without a hat, and if you don't wear one, you'll stand out even more. Take a look in the cupboard near the storeroom. There are Fedoras that might conceivably still be in style."

He'd learned everything he currently knew about Americans by watching Hollywood's gangster movies. Everyone carried guns, and he thought of the one he'd secreted away and patted his suit jacket pocket.

"Thanks for reminding me," she continued. "That pistol you have hidden under the mattress in the bedroom upstairs? It is a good idea to take with you."

Thomas's face paled at her ability to read his thoughts. She placed the last two bills back into her purse before slipping it into the middle drawer of the desk.

"I hope you have the bullets for the pistol," she said, "and that you are willing to protect me with it when we are out and about."

"We seem to have a language barrier, as you speak an American version of English, and 1 speak true British English. You asked for a bodyguard, Miss Patterson. 1 am more than adequate to do that because of my intensive martial arts training. Nonetheless, if you are looking for a hot-headed cowboy or some New York gang leader with a loaded pistol and a speedy trigger finger, our association is over."

He realized it was a line from a gangster movie he'd recently seen, but he had never even touched a gun before leaving London, and the idea of concealing one on his person terrified him. He didn't know how to load one, nor could he ever shoot anyone. But when he'd boarded the fishing transport in Liverpool, he had been forced to accept the weapon.

"Having a gun and using it are two different things, Dr. Ling. But if you are incapable of handling a firearm, then please bring it here. That'll save me time trying to purchase one on the black market. If you choose to stay in my employ, to get information to help the Chinese war effort against the Japanese taking over the entire country, I must warn you. Not everyone in the city agrees with my political objectives. Besides, while attempting to shoot me, who knows? Someone might want to shoot an Asian, too."

Thomas grudgingly retrieved the gun, stood in front of the witch, and slipped it into the waistband of his trousers, just as he had seen in Hollywood gangster movies. He held the bullets he'd retrieved from a nook in the bedroom and showed them to Beatrix before taking the envelopes.

"These will never go inside a gun when that weapon is in my possession." He shut the office door with a bang, not caring about her opinion of him. He was a lifelong pacifist caught up, because of his own naïve doing, in a plot that could now get him killed, Beatrix Patterson killed, and end the lives of countless Chinese innocents.

He turned the corner, heading west away from the river. *She looks so docile, yet I have no doubt she would have me shoot anyone who might stop her. But from what? How can a woman that size think she can change the course of the war? I should have kept my first opinion of her. Beatrix Patterson is bizarre, calculating, and dangerous. She is a wu. Grandmother was right. They do exist. I am a fool.*

CHAPTER 5

THOMAS GRUMBLED at his own stupidity and all but walked into a handful of pedestrians, and they looked at his face and scurried away as if he had leprosy.

Anger made him walk straighter and faster. *How dare that woman have the cheek to doubt my reasons for this trip, and how could she have the audacity to demand I shoot someone on her behalf?*

The internal tirades continued, block after block. The angry explosion he aimed at Beatrix should have been targeted at himself.

I am a man of discipline. My work is with physics, formulae, and atoms. I have no business pretending this is some great lark to save the world, as I did in London when asked to be a message courier. Now I am involved in playacting in a dangerous drama of gangsters and hooligans. I am employed by, and taking orders from, a crazy woman who may or may not be a psychic, and I am carrying a lethal weapon. What has happened to me?

He cringed when he recognized that he was shouting and realized he was as crazy as Beatrix Patterson because he had taken a job that wasn't a job and involved because he'd failed to deliver a potentially destructive piece of information. Yet when he could have walked away from the witch and returned to Britain by a circuitous and cautious route, he did not. He chose to stay.

He looked up and doubled-checked the sign: POYDRAS HOME, FOUNDED IN 1817. Then he took the marble steps two at a time, toward the orphans and women's asylum, never thinking until he reached the top that whoever Miss Patterson was warning him against might be following him.

He swung around. There was a man leaning on a lamppost, sucking a cigarette as a child might with a lollypop. Everyone else seemed in too much of a hurry for wherever they had to go. Unable to do otherwise, Thomas stared until the man checked his watch at the same time a truck pulled to the curb. The driver and the pedestrian talked, the man hopped in, and only then did Thomas exhale.

"The sooner this charade is over, the better." He grunted and opened the heavy wood and glass doors leading to the asylum, patting the money in his breast pocket and feeling the heftiness of the pistol in his waistband.

The huge foyer smelled of orange oil and reminded him of the grand entrance to a theater rather than a shelter for children and older destitute women. Standing in the middle of the hall, he was lost as to which direction to go. Once again, unlike his former orderly self, he cursed because he'd neglected to find out who the money was intended for.

There was a reception desk to the left but no clerk. There were three long, wide hallways, and any of them could lead to a place where the mentally unstable, the sick, or just someone who was eccentric or peculiar would be kept behind locked doors. Thomas was aware of how cruel the world could be for those who were unique. In dozens of countries, including his ancestral homeland, those who did not fit into whatever society considered to be right, which most of the time was wrong, would be stuffed away like criminals. He knew the Nazis were rounding up and killing not only Jews and scholars but midwives, homosexuals, herbalists, the Roma groups, Africans, Asians, Mennonites, the infirm, and those needing special care.

Is this place any better? But of course, it was. Nazism contaminated the mind and exterminated those who were even

Eva Shaw

slightly unusual. And *unusual* was a term defined by Hitler's zealous henchmen.

A side door opened, and children of all shapes, sizes, and colors poured out, giggling and scurrying around Thomas. One of the smallest grabbed his hand, and he allowed himself to be pulled down.

"I love you," she said in his ear, then dashed off with the others, like bees escaping a hive, and headed out to the playground adjacent to the building.

When had been the last time he'd heard those words? He tried to remember some Bible quote his mother had read about—*from the lips of children*—wondering if he'd ever know the joy of fatherhood and have the same glow often seen on his father's face.

He headed down the corridor and heard the voices of women singing and glorious music echoing through the building. He was familiar with some of the hymns and songs from the Church of England, which were somber and pious. These were jubilant melodies, and there was clapping, too. *Definitely not the Church of England.* Thomas remembered services he'd attended with his parents and colleagues and realized they'd be horrified by the celebration of the voices rather than the dour dirge that was supposed to be reverent singing. He smiled as the heavenly music floated through the marbled hallway.

Then a touch, as soft as a whisper, came to his shoulder, and Thomas's reaction was that of a ninja, although one in an ill-fitting suit. He grabbed the hand and stiffened. Instead of facing a calculated murderer ready to end Thomas's life, the hand was lined with sapphire veins, connected to a tiny arm and eventually the body of a nun.

"My goodness," said a woman even smaller than her voice, but she did not try to fight his grasp, which loosened instantly.

She was draped in a long white habit, and there were no crosses or emblems on her clothing. *A supervisor, a nurse, or a teacher.*

"I did not mean to frighten you, young man." She took three

steps back as if to give him the opportunity to run away if that's what he needed.

It had been what he'd originally thought he could do because she seemed to come from the ether and get soundlessly close enough that he could smell a fragrance he'd known long ago but could no longer figure out from where.

"I am Mother Adelina. You are safe here, young man. No matter what you've done or what has been done to you, fear not. How can I help you? Are you here to visit or retrieve a child, or perhaps your mother, wife, or sister? I do not remember any Japanese children here with us, but often the young ones who have just arrived are kept in the hospital wing until they're well-fed and strong," she whispered, and the words dissolved into the quiet that once again shrouded the shelter, a harbor for the lost, disenfranchised, and traumatized.

"I am Chinese, madam."

Not to clarify his ethnicity could jeopardize his safety and his mission, even if this was a fragile elderly lady.

As Thomas knew, appearances were deceiving.

"These eyes are too old. My apologizes." She squinted at his features as if taking mental note but then looked at her feet.

He did, too. The footwear was in contrast to her saintly garb. Impossible. He must be hallucinating. The witch must have drugged his tea. But for what reason?

This entire city is inexplicable. I am speaking with a nun who just happens to be wearing combat boots while standing in a hallway filled with the singing voices of angels.

Thomas blinked, cleared his throat, and realized the sooner he got out of the asylum, the better, or these people would probably take him in for mental evaluation. He reached into the breast pocket of his suit jacket.

"Yes, madam, I am here to deliver this." He held out the fat white envelope.

She cocked her head, hands at her sides. "What is it?"

Should he tell this woman that there was a large sum of money inside? Thomas had assumed the staff members at the home would be expecting the funds, perhaps as regular payment for some debt or food for the children. But Mother Adelina looked just as confused as he felt.

"My employer asked me to deliver it to Poydras House. This is Poydras House, correct?"

The tiny woman put one finger on the envelope. A moment passed, and then she said, "Oh yes, of course. I understand now. I've been expecting it."

There they stood. Thomas held the envelope because to do otherwise would have let it drop to the floor and focused on the woman's index finger suspended in midair.

Blinking as if coming out of a trance, Thomas said, "To whom should I give this?"

She snapped the envelope and stuck it inside the voluminous covering.

"I bid you a good day, then," she replied, and it was only then that Thomas heard a faint Parisian accent. "May God bless you, my friend. Be safe. You are in danger that lurks beyond these walls. Please give my best to your employer."

Thomas returned to the blustery day, and while the woman seemed as befuddled as he was, something in their meeting felt calming. He wanted to return to her.

"The craziness of New Orleans has rubbed off on me."

He scanned for the man leaning on the lamppost. The avenue was crowded with men and women in military uniform, intent on whatever mission had brought them to the city.

Next time, if there is a next time, I must find out if it is permissible to reveal Miss Patterson's identity. If she is a psychic, she should have told me exactly what to do.

He huffed and headed back toward Bourbon Street and to the bar called the Old Absinthe House. What oddness would happen when he found Miss Gillette Pierre, whose name was scribbled on the second envelope? It was now close to eleven. The errands had eaten up too much time. He still had to deliver the second envelope and stop for whatever clothing he could find for whatever deadly assignation was ahead of them at three.

And he still had to get the sealed treaty offer to his contact that day.

Thomas stopped, and the pedestrians flowed around him like a rock in a river. He'd been determined to tell Miss Patterson that he was not cut out to be her bodyguard. Yet now, after meeting the funny little nun at the safe house and heading to Bourbon Street, it all felt logical.

He looked up and down Bourbon Street. Even with his training in martial arts, he'd never felt such a keen awareness of his surroundings. Everything seemed brighter and more vivid. Had the witch done this to him? This city of mystery. Is the feeling of excitement and edginess how life should be lived? The thoughts darted through his head, and his body was hyper-aware of every movement, sound, face, and voice.

Arriving at the French Quarter's address, he felt eyes watching him as he noted details in every direction. Thomas found Miss Pierre polishing glasses and whistling the French national anthem. Or at least, that's what he thought the off-key rendition was. As with the nurse at the orphanage, she seemed in no hurry to accept the envelope. When he pushed the envelope closer to her, she looked as muddled as the previous woman had. Then she looked at the writing, and her expression became masked.

"Ah, *bien. Merci.* Please tell your lady I will see her tomorrow, as usual, and—" She looked deep into Thomas's dark eyes and smiled. "*Mais oui*, she knows this. Just a word to the wise, never underestimate her, *mon ami.*"

Thomas watched her smile transform the weary barmaid into a woman of great beauty as if just touching the envelope changed her.

Is this barkeeper a seer, too?

"Please carry this message to *mademoiselle.*" She took paper from a box and scribbled *Le pot est en ebullition.*

After handing it to Thomas, she gestured as only the Parisians do, dismissing him with a flick of her wrist.

Le pot est en ebullition? Thomas squinted and whispered,

"The pot is boiling." *A code? It is the French Quarter, and danger is behind these doors. She must be a witch, too.* He thought of how her smile had beguiled him. *Is this entire bloody city full of witches?*

Back on the street, those he'd noticed before as possibly trailing him had disappeared, as had the two dockworkers. Yet the lady of the night was still at her corner on Bienville and Bourbon.

Thomas longed for cup of rich black French coffee but didn't dare. In panic mode after the bombs being dropped on Pearl Harbor, people in America would vent their anger and fear to anyone of Asian descent, except for those who worked in the laundries in Chinatown, and they knew not to mingle with the town's folk.

Perhaps I need to wear a sandwich board neon sign that says, "I am Chinese." He shook his head at the mystery in which he'd embroiled himself.

Having been given directions to the department store before leaving the tavern, Thomas entered Maison Blanche, picked out and paid for a suit that was his size and of the current style, along with shirts, ties, socks, and other necessities. It was enough for a few more days before he'd start the journey back to Britain.

When a clerk looked him up and down, Thomas said, "I am not the enemy. I'm Chinese, and an ally of the United States."

The clerk seemed leery of taking his money but packaged up the purchases and treated him with respect. However, in the distance, other clerks stared at the customer with a crisp British accent and demeanor of a diplomat who perhaps was from China if he wasn't a spy.

The walk took twenty minutes before he arrived at the rear entrance of the famed Windsor Court Hotel and the reason he was there in New Orleans. A burly man dressed in white, perhaps a sous chef, was hauling boxes of potatoes from the loading dock to the kitchen. He stopped when he saw Thomas.

"What'd you want, sir? You don't look like you belong

around here."

"My name is Thomas Ling. I have a message for Xia Kangnan."

The cook lifted his chin, and through clenched teeth, said, "Xia? Okay. You're one of her lot. Through there and ask the waiters. Good-for-nothing lot. They'll be lounging and smoking, as usual."

Thomas's presence in the kitchen didn't seem to startle the staff stirring kettles steaming with delicacies and succulent ingredients, waiting to be transformed into rich locally inspired French, Cajun, and Creole foods. The abundance, however, seemed obscene in a time of war, rationing, and worldwide deprivation. But as always, the rich ate well.

"Xia Kangnan?" he said to the general crowd of women, who stopped whispering as they polished silver, sorted dishes, swept the floors, and giggled behind their hands.

A tall Chinese woman with military posture and jet-black hair covered by a chef's toque flipped around as Thomas placed the parcels he'd been juggling in a corner near the door. She looked Thomas up and down, evaluating everything about him, and apparently did not like what she saw.

When Thomas didn't back down from the glare, she nodded and walked out to the loading dock, now empty of trucks and workers.

"If you are looking for Xia, then you have found her. I do not play any silly games, sir," she said in perfect, upper-class English as if she'd learned it from BBC radio, or like Thomas, was part of that class. "Why are you here, and what do you want with me? One scream from me, and there will be a dozen sous chefs here to wrestle you to the concrete, and I will make sure that if you plan to harm me, they will do much more damage to you."

Thomas was startled by her beauty, in contrast with the vile warning spewed from her perfect lips. Even with her chin jutting forward, should he somehow defy her, he could not stop himself as he blurted, "You, just a girl, are my contact?" he said in Cantonese.

"You are Ling from London, England? Please do not try to deceive me, sir. I was specifically told to expect an old, frail, gray-haired man—the courier. Who exactly are you?"

"I am a replacement courier, but the gentleman you expected, and I do share the same name."

He started to explain in chronological detail until she snapped, "Stop. Do you think I'm a fool? You do not have a Chinese accent, so if you are from the homeland, then speak to me in Pinghau, Ba-Shu, or the dialect of the Guangdong region. Any schoolboy can learn Cantonese. Or if those dialects are too difficult, Mandarin will do."

This time and in each dialect she had mentioned, Thomas said, "Are you questioning me? Will not the others here understand what we are discussing?" *I did not expect to be tested before giving up this message.*

He twisted his head and now looked toward the kitchen door, where the circle of women had followed them to see what Xia was doing with the foreigner or to have something new to talk about.

"Fine," she said. "Then at least you are from the homeland, even if you sound like all the stuffy British gentlemen who come to the hotel. My friends," she motioned to the gaggle of kitchen help, "speak a version of English mixed with Caribbean tongues." She whispered, "I cannot guarantee that there are no gossips here. I heard something on the radio today that said, 'Loose lips sink ships,' and kitchen workers are notorious for spreading rumors. Even that a suave gentleman came to visit me will be worthy fodder for their cigarette break," she said in a clipped version of the Pinghau dialect, a trade language in some areas of Guangxi, the south-central area of the country, bordering on what would someday be called Vietnam.

"Yes, well then, we should cut our meeting short," he replied. "Here you are."

And in Pinghau, he explained what his new employer had told him about the forthcoming battle in Burma. He said she was a *wu* and that there might be nothing to it, but, "Whether we believe it or not, please pass on the information about the loss of life and terrible battles that are to ensue in Burma."

Xia shook her head. "From a *wu*? And you believe her? My grandfather would tell me stories of their evil work, and then Grandmother would interrupt and say these witches only wanted the best for China and for everyone. Do you believe she has the power?"

"She ... she knows things." He thought of how Beatrix read his mind. "But this, I am not sure. Nonetheless, if I do not ensure that this information is passed onto the Counsel, and that the battles are vicious, I will share in their deaths. Please do as I have asked."

Xia patted his hand and placed the soiled envelope into her apron pocket.

"Then, as you wish," she said. "I will see that the Counsel knows this information and receives the document you've brought here."

He thanked her in Mandarin. "Have you been in New Orleans a long time?"

It was an inane question, but for some reason, Thomas didn't want to end their conversation.

"Longer than you," she replied. "I studied cooking at the Corden Bleu in Paris, but my family became frightened for me when Hitler's forces invaded France. They ordered me home to Hong Kong, but I disobeyed my father, and my mentor at the cooking school recommended me for this position. I do not know if I can ever return, with Japan seeking to invade that island." Xia stopped as if she'd told him too much, or it was too personal. "Will you be returning to England now that this work is done, sir?"

"No." He blinked at his response. "If the witch respects the bargain we made, being here will help our country." He hesitated, then said, "May I see you again? I mean, may I bring you more information about her visions?"

In Bah-Shu, she replied, "Sir, you may see me again, even if the seer is nothing but a *shă*."

While Thomas smiled at the concept of Miss Patterson being a *shă*, or fool, his smile was more about the woman in front of him. Unlike when Miss Patterson stared at him, he welcomed the scrutiny and smile from Xia Kangnan.

He walked through the maze of streets back to the office. *She had something more to say but did not. The wu's prognostications have me under a spell. Now I am doubting everything.*

When he returned to the office on Royal Street, the front door was locked, so he pulled out his key and opened the door.

"Miss Patterson? I'm back." Yet, he knew he was alone.

On the ink blotter centered in the middle of her desk was a gold wedding band. Perhaps it was the early afternoon February's sunlight streaming through the window, but the ring seemed to glow. As Thomas removed the packages from his arms, the glow followed him. Or seemed to.

What spells or powers has Beatrix placed into this ring? He moved closer but dared not touch it, although that required diminishing self-control. He was hypnotized by the pulsating colors of gold, never before knowing that gold was more than one shade, and he didn't hear the door open and close.

"It won't bite you," Beatrix said. "Touch the ring if you choose, Dr. Ling."

He flipped around and felt the hair on the back of his neck stand.

"No. No, it is possessed. You have put some kind of spell on it." He was shocked by his words, for he hadn't intended to speak them.

"The ring belongs to Flynn Howard, the police officer you compared to a canine. Sit and I'll tell you about my appointment, if you like." She removed the black cloche and patted down her hair.

Thomas had planned to say *No thank you*. He'd planned to nod politely and return to his room up the back stairs. This was the reasonable approach, and he was a logical and educated man. Yet the glow from the ring stopped him. Without knowing how he got there, Thomas was sitting in the guest chair across the desk from Miss Patterson, finder of lost things, and the ring throbbed as if it were trying to shout.

"Does it talk to you?" he said, struck with shame by this irrationality.

"Why do you think that is so absurd, Dr. Ling? Have you not at one time owned a valuable object you greatly admired?"

"I suppose so," he said, although nothing came to mind.

"Have you thought of the stories the objects could tell if they had but a voice to communicate with us? They hold secrets we cannot even envision. But imagine is what I do."

"In science, we—"

"Science cannot explain everything. Let's debate this at another time, unless you're not curious about the result of my appointment."

She said it with kindness, even though Thomas knew the supposed psychic thought his scientific mind to be that of a child.

"Mr. Howard's wife disappeared," she said. "He has hired us to make some inquires, which we'll do tomorrow. This is his wedding ring, and Veronica Howard had an identical one."

"Had?" Thomas said. "Past tense?"

"It's possible that that Veronica may have sold the ring. We could scour the pawn shops around the city, but that'd be a waste of time. If she sold the ring to leave New Orleans, then she does not want to be found, and I will not be able to discover her whereabouts."

"Then you're done with the case? You cannot find her if she doesn't want to be found? As a psychic?"

Thomas's eyebrows went up, and Beatrix duplicated the look.

"Has that been proven, Mr. Scientist? I assured the officer we would visit the Faubourg Marigny neighborhood, chat with neighbors, and visit the house to gather the psychic vibrations. Then we'll know the truth." She twirled the ring on her index finger. "We won't know anymore facts until tomorrow."

Beatrix stood, put the ring in a small blue velvet box, and moved the painting behind her desk. She felt Thomas's gaze on her.

"It's magnificent work, isn't it?" she said. "Are you a lover of art?"

"A remarkable copy of a Monet," he replied.

"You see flaws?" She chuckled and twisted the combination lock of the safe hidden behind the Monet to place the ring box inside.

She knew he'd seen the bundles bills, rolled documents, and something that glittered.

"If I were you," she said, "I'd wonder about what is in the safe, too. And it is because of the safe's contents that I need protection. I know you've memorized the combination, so you can have access to it and review the contents anytime you choose."

"But you couldn't see that I was looking at you. Your back was turned."

"True. But as you were focusing on my hand, you didn't notice that I saw your reflection in the wall mirror."

He fumbled in his jacket pocket, unable to decide if he should apologize or let her think he was unscrupulous. Then he decided it didn't matter and handed her the note.

"Miss Pierre wanted you to have this."

She smiled, knowing he'd read it, as she would have.

"Ah, so the pot is boiling. *Très bien.*"

"Furthermore," he said, "there were some unusual people in the French Quarter near the bar, and I had a feeling—"

"My friend, unusual is commonplace for the city. And if you plan to stay long, just accept it."

Thomas was going to snap; *You think I'd stay here?* But he didn't. As with other decisions that day, he didn't know what was truth or what was the spell put over him by the witch or by New Orleans.

Beatrix looked at the note once more, closed her eyes, and knew what it really said. Gillette was in contact with the French Resistance in North Africa and perhaps even with Charles de Gaulle.

It had been ten years since she'd been with her parents' good friend Uncle Charlie. She knew from their European visits, long lunches when she was in Paris, and year's back, his trip to her home in Santa Barbara. She remembered everything about him, as she did with all people. But he felt connected in a way none of her parents' other friends did. Tall and charismatic, Charlie was like a magnet to women and men, making strangers and even adversaries want to share his glow. She remembered his military bearing, strong views of France being the center of the universe, and how he made up stories to tell Beatrix, even when she was too old for fairy tales.

She looked down at the ruby ring and smoothed a finger over its silky, cold surface. He had given it to her when the family had stayed at his chateau on the Côte d'Azur.

Ah, Uncle Charlie, what weight you must have on your shoulders these days, knowing the Nazis have a price on your head, and even friends could be enemies.

She pulled sheets of paper from the desk, removed the typewriter from the cupboard behind her, slipped the paper into the cylinder of the machine, and started typing.

My Dear Uncle Charlie,

It is with a heavy heart that I write, knowing that the Nazi the savages who invaded France have stomped their filthy books through the Champs-Elysees, surrounded the Eifel Tower, and stolen the precious art from the Louvre. My soul mourns.

My late father confided in you something he was terrified of—that is, I have a gift.

Again, she felt the weight of the lie, as the *gift* was her memory and ability to connect people and situations. Yet, she was taken aback that she could lie so easily to Charlie. Was there justification if it gave him hope?

She curled her fingers over the keyboard and began typing again.

> I know the future, and please take heart, dear uncle. Your cause will triumph. Your liberation army called Free France will win, but there will be much loss of life.
>
> I have tears in my eyes, thinking of the anguish you must feel. However, if you believed in my father as the honorable man he was, then please believe that in the future, you will be the true leader of France. The war will end in 1944, and the people of France will rally again. Afterward, times will be bleak. But the outcome of the war is clear. You will move the resistance offices to Algiers, Algeria in North Africa, and become the president of the French Committee of National Liberation.
>
> Father told me that, at times, you become frustrated with your own inadequacies. Yet France will be released from the Nazi's stranglehold, and you will become France's hope and first president after freedom.
>
> Through connections here in New Orleans and my work, I promise to provide financial assistance to support the efforts. Vive la France.
>
> Your friend,
>
> Beatrix

She read the letter twice more. Satisfied, she withdrew it from the machine. She scribbled a B over her typed name and addressed an envelope to her father's longtime friend.

Tomorrow, I'll have Thomas take this to the tavern to be included in the next communiqué for the French Freedom Fighters.

Beatrix placed the envelope into the safe and twisted the combination to lock it. It would not be good to have someone break in and learn of her French connection to the resistance fighters or the extra thousand dollars she'd included in the envelope.

She glanced at her watch. It was almost time. Mr. Brockman said they'd have transport to the Higgins boat manufacturing plant, and the meeting with the Navy was just blocks from the office.

She called out, "Dr. Ling, our car is about to arrive."

She put on a snug black jacket, placed a light green, boiled wool hat on her head before adjusting her scarf and slipping a purse on her shoulder.

Thomas tucked the gun, once again, into the back of his trousers. *If the wu wants it loaded, she'll have to do it herself. I may be crazy to listen to the witch and carry a gun, but I'm not about to shoot myself in the backside.*

He dashed down the stairs from the bedroom above the office. The second they stepped outside, a black limousine pulled to the curb, complete with a uniformed driver. Fewer things now surprised Thomas Ling.

"Good afternoon, Mademoiselle Patterson," said the driver, a formidable man who could have played pro football if he'd been born in three decades later.

When he spied her Asian companion, he straightened to his full height, towering over the passengers, then crossed his arms, resembling a gladiator. He narrowed his eyes as if Thomas had personally organized the bombing of Pearl Harbor.

"Thank you, Henry. My Chinese friend, Dr. Ling, will be joining me today."

"Oh, um, Chinese, you say. I just thought ... sorry, ma'am," The driver stuttered, looked down at his well-polished shoes, and opened the car door, now unable to meet Thomas's eyes.

"These are complicated times," Beatrix said. "Dr. Ling and I understand." She patted the driver's arm in a consoling way. "Henry, may I offer my sympathies about the death of your brother Augustus. He was a hero, and you can be proud of Auggie. Never forget that."

Henry's face turned away from Beatrix as if he feared she'd see a tear, and then he inhaled and resumed the stance of a durable driver. When he turned, gone was any embarrassment, and he genuinely smiled.

"Mr. Brockman said you were a psychic," Henry said. "I've lived here all my life and still don't believe in that stuff, ma'am, even though I've seen some weird things, especially here in the Quarter and the Lower Ninth Ward. These days … heck, I don't know what to believe anymore. You called him Auggie. Nobody but Mama called him that, because he was bigger than me and would have decked anyone who tried. Guess you know he went down with the USS Arizona, right there in Pearl Harbor. But I never saw his name in any newspaper. You couldn't have known." He bent down. "Was his death painful? Is there anything I can tell Mama? Maybe a message from Auggie? Not a day goes by that she doesn't pray for him, worrying what might have happened at … well, at the end."

Beatrix's eyes softened, and she took the driver's hand. Another lie, but this one comforted the man.

While taking the trash to the bins one evening, she'd seen another of Brockman's employees gather the chauffeur in a manly hug and heard the words "Auggie" and "Pearl Harbor." Nothing psychic about it.

Of course, Thomas froze. If her gift was a parlor trick, this one turned his thoughts upside down. He wouldn't have moved for anything.

"After the bombs hit the ship," she replied, "a fire spread quickly. He was on the deck of the battleship, getting men into lifeboats, when yet one more Japanese plane swooped down. An explosion nearly knocked him overboard, and he grabbed the railing. Instead of jumping off the ship, as did a few sailors,

Auggie sped below. It was an inferno, yet he had to get his men out. Then more bombs were dropped, and yet again, he was knocked about. The smoke below was thick as he called to the men under his command, and then he heard their voices.

"Never once did he think of his own safety. Because of Auggie, who knows how many men did not go down in Pearl Harbor when the battleship sank. You might want to, after this war is over, contact the War Department so they can give you his Purple Heart. He lived as a hero, and died as one, too." She touched the ruby ring. "Auggie wants to tell your mother that he will be waiting for all of you in heaven, and do not grieve for him."

How the power of good lies helps soften sorrow, she rationalized.

The driver wiped a tear from his face, replaced his stooped shoulders with the composure of a warrior, and then gently closed the car door before getting into the driver's seat to start the engine.

Thomas whispered, "That was nice of you, consoling the man."

"Nice?" Beatrix turned to back Thomas.

Her eyes had lost all compassion and now held irritation as the anger she felt toward herself torched her words.

"There was nothing nice about it. It is what I know how to do." *Tell lies.* "It's what happened as certainly as we are heading to Lake Pontchartrain. Once there, we'll see boats in a warehouse. This is what I do, no matter what you might think of me."

Thomas shook his head and thought of chuckling but then gulped when he saw her face become clouded. Emotions he'd never acknowledged came to the surface when he pitted his academic education and philosophy against this woman.

He had never met a psychic or a witch and realized with a jolt that regardless of what he thought, the woman believed everything she was saying.

"I'm a man of science. You said this Auggie person spoke to

you from heaven, or perhaps some alternative universe, if there are such places, which 1 suppose one cannot know until after death, and then it is too late to report back to the living. Are you asserting that Auggie wanted to give a message to Henry, the driver?"

"Did you denounce Dr. Einstein's theory of relativity the first time you heard of it, well before you could conceptualize the concept, Dr. Ling? Isn't it against all that you hold dear, in your scientific world, to repute that what you do not understand?"

She smiled at him without any hint of frustration or sarcasm and tilted her head as if trying to communicate with a child.

With only kindness in her voice, she said, "If there is a time, Dr. Ling, when you would like to know about the future without conniving or waiting to eavesdrop on anything that might be told in your presence, you may openly ask me. 1 will tell you what is known and seen. Then you can make a decision if you believe it. 1 applaud you for accepting the visions of a *wu* and being brave enough to share them with the Chinese government. That, my friend, takes true courage, and 1 know of few men who, unaccustomed to being advised in this way, would have done so."

Her words were so convincing that she believed them as well. And that could be dangerous.

Thomas stared out the car's window during the half-hour drive through the city, past the churches and cemeteries, and then to the lake.

Am 1 brave enough to know the future? Will any of us survive this terrible war? What will happen to my distant family in China if the Japanese invade the land, especially since the Chinese and the Japanese have been mortal enemies since the beginning of recorded time? It will be bloody, and it is all hopelessly out of my hands.

He closed his eyes. *If 1 were to know the future, what would change for me? Or what would 1 change within myself?*

Thomas ached to know what would happen, especially with Hitler doing everything possible to destroy England, Scotland,

Ireland, and to invade even America through the mouth of the Mississippi. He refused to ask because, if he were to know the future, Thomas wondered if he could accept his fate as if it were all outlined with pen and paper ahead of him.

Beatrix touched the ring. It gave her comfort, and it was part of her act. She held it up to the window and watched the gentle February sun bring a sparkle to the facets.

Oh, Thomas, it's all going to be okay. She understood that accepting her predictions regarding the possible bloodshed in his ancestral homeland was one thing. It was quite another when it was personal.

She could guess, tell him he'd return to England, raise a family, become a leader in his community. Whatever she'd tell him, it would be good news. That surprised her, as the odds of a fairy-tale future seemed slim if one believed the news reports.

Yet, she'd had the oddest dream when she eventually fell asleep the previous night. It was of Thomas tossing a baseball to three teenage boys. They were teasing each other, but with love and admiration in their voices. At the side of the tableau was a woman in blue jeans, a striped man's shirt, and a bright yellow, wide-brimmed straw hat. She was kneeling in an expansive garden, with the grass stretching forever before it met with a comfortable craftsman-style home, reminiscent of the smaller houses found in the old Santa Barbara neighborhood where Beatrix's parents had built their mansion.

The woman of the rowdy boys was their mother, Beatrix was sure of that, and she knelt down, picking white and magenta cosmos, tall and willowy like the woman, and when she removed the hat, sunlight glistened off her hair. All around the scene was an aura of gold, much like often happens on late California afternoons.

A scruffy terrier dashed from the bushes and grabbed the baseball before one of the boys could field it. The woman's laughter rang out, and for a second, Beatrix thought she heard a familiar tone. *The sound of sheer joy. The music of unburdened happiness.*

Something sharp stung her heart, knowing her future would never include anything of the sort she saw for Thomas. *Once, as a child, I could laugh like that. But it's been decades, and I doubt I'll know that feeling of joy again.*

In her world of psychic forecasts, with so many lost hopes and dreams, there was little to laugh about.

She blinked, recalling the dream and imagining that this was the woman Thomas would marry and create a family with. She remembered thinking during the dream, *Just turn so I can see your face.* But the woman did not, and Beatrix felt certain that the woman knew she was watching her and choosing to ignore her. That alone made goosebumps race up and down her arms. *Never have I felt this way. Am I going mad? Am I about to die?* The thoughts frightened her, and she attempted to shrug away the confusion.

Instead, as she had since she was a child, Beatrix began creating entire life stories, happy-ending stories, about people she cared about.

What would happen after Thomas left New Orleans?

Throughout the drive to the lake, she told herself, *He will become a champion for conservation and lead a role in developing alternative energies. He will return to England many times and travel the world, lecturing, but settle in California, where ethnic diversity, after the war, is embraced. He'll focus his scientific work and become one of the leading minds of the world in his field. His hopes of seeing China will be realized just months before he dies.*

Beatrix could see Thomas walking on the Great Wall of China and holding the hand of a tiny girl, an adored grandchild. Ultimately, as an old and contented man, a grandfather many times over, Beatrix imagined that he would be honored with an international award for peace and technology. A lovely tale, but Beatrix's stories and the truth didn't always coincide.

Perhaps if Thomas had the courage to ask about his future,

these would be some of the lies she'd share.

Beatrix closed her eyes, clearing these images out of the corners of her head. It was time to concentrate on the work she'd been hired to do.

The car slowed in the grungy neighborhood that Beatrix knew would one day be transformed so much that locals wouldn't believe it when the lake would then be surrounded by palatial homes. Yet all that was there now were shanties and shacks, bars, and tiny snack shops. Next to the warehouse was a store advertising the best po'boy sandwiches in the city, although she could only smell greasy fried fish coating the damp afternoon air.

"Here we are, Miss Patterson." The driver opened the passenger door. "I'll wait for you and your, um … companion. Mr. Brockman drove himself and is just arriving now, ma'am."

As Beatrix got out of car, the bookmaker approached, hunched, his face puffier than earlier, and if possible, looking more stressed.

John Brockman has not gotten to be one of the most powerful men in Louisiana without being thorough with his business dealing. She saw him rub his temples. *Ah, yes, headaches. He's afraid the ailment could cloud his judgement.*

"Good afternoon, Miss Patterson," said the bookie and nodded to Thomas. "They're waiting inside, but do you have any intuition as to what they expect from me, other than agreeing to whatever they're proposing and investing a fortune? Do you have any hint yet whether their motives are patriotic, or greedy? I just don't have a good feeling about that Davies character." Brockman had lowered his voice. "If he came into the gaming hall, I'd have Henry keep a close eye on him. Just one of those feelings, which I bet you get all the time."

"I will know shortly, sir, what their motives are," she replied. "With that information, you can decide on the best approach to their proposals."

She slipped her arm through his to steady him as she could see a pulsating vein in his forehead.

Inside the warehouse, Andrew Higgins, Admiral Peterson, Major Davies, and three other naval officers stood looking at large, flat-hulled wooden boats lined up like soldiers. When Beatrix, John, and Thomas came through the door, their whispering stopped, and they started talking about the weather as if it required intense analysis.

Beatrix watched their eyes darting about, and they nodded to one another as if they were all part of a clandestine plan. Admiral Patterson and Major Davies both looked toward the ceiling and then quickly recovered their level of authority.

These two are not telling John the truth, and the major seems to think that the admiral and Mr. Higgins are too slow to see how much can be gained by convincing Mr. Brockman that he should invest in the arrangement. But was that the whole truth, and why were they hiding something?

"Good, good. You're here," said the admiral. "And you've brought your daughter and her, um … another person with you." He nodded and shook hands with Brockman but did not approach Thomas.

"This is Miss Patterson," said Brockman, "who is consulting with me on the proposal, and her associate, Dr. Thomas Ling, whose family comes from China."

Thomas felt the stiffness soften in his shoulders, as with that statement, he would avoid being considered to be a secret agent or terrorist for the Japanese government.

Major Davies came forward and shook hands with the group, including Thomas, smiling like he'd just won the best hand at poker.

"Well, this is mighty remarkable. I didn't know that you and Brockman worked together, Miss Patterson."

"Yes, we have known each other for some time," she replied. *He's trying to determine if I've been brought in to read everyone's thoughts.*

The major patted his pockets. "Oh, rats. No smokes again today. Trying to give that nasty habit up, especially since it bothers my, um … well, the people on my staff." He tried to joke, yet with a nervous obsession, continued to pat his pockets, attempting to find a cigar.

Andrew Higgins rushed forward to greet Brockman and looked like he wanted to snatch the bookmaker off the concrete and give him a hug. The scale of his booming voice nearly knocked John Brockman over.

"Brockman, you old son of a gun. It's mighty fine of you to come all the way to the lake to see these boats I've been making." He pumped John's arm and then realized that his enthusiasm could possibly injure his frail friend.

Higgins motioned to the three flat-bottomed crafts being constructed in the huge warehouse, each with a slightly different hull design.

"I hope after you hear more about it, you'll see the merit of the boats as the answer for a quick and risk-free way to get our GIs from the ships to the beach and onto the battlefields. It's an honor to share this with you. But please, keep it all hush-hush."

Beatrix watched Higgins swallow, and his eyes widen for the briefest flicker. *He's almost committed a cardinal social sin. He's forgotten to ask about personal matters before talking business. Is he just so excited to have John visit? Or is he feeling pressure from the military to swing this deal or bilk an old friend?*

Higgins quickly remedied his faux pas and relaxed, gaining his footing in the situation once again.

"Your health, John? You look fit as a fiddle to me. But we're both getting older, right?"

"Your family, Andrew?" said Brockman. "Doing well I assume?"

"The family keeps me running in circles, I can tell you. Gosh, I missed having our annual Mardi Gras parties this year. Damn war and all. But Mrs. Higgins and I will expect you to join us for the queen's supper next year, when, God-willing, our fair planet will be settled down enough that we can have the lavish parades and get-togethers again. Our daughter Ellen is going to be a deb next year. Can you believe that? Think you met her when her hair was still in pigtails. You'll get an invite, for sure, and it wouldn't be a party unless you were there."

Beatrix smiled at Andrew Higgins. *There is not one fraudulent thought in his mind. He's genuine, unusual in this group of men, and he's also someone John can trust.*

Higgins had started a lumber business in New Orleans in the 1930s, and it prospered through smart planning and a booming port trade. Always planning ahead, he began building lightweight boats that could navigate the swamplands around the mouth of the Mississippi for fishing and in the ever-constant need for discovering the oil deposits.

Higgins wore a blue-striped suit and red tie, and he kept running his index fingers around the collar of the stiff white dress shirt, unaccustomed to business attire.

"Mighty fine to meet you, too, Dr. Ling. Any friend of John's and all that." He turned and smiled broadly. "So, you are the famous Miss Beatrix." He took her hand and pumped it up and down.

Beatrix chuckled. "I have been anxious to meet you, Mr. Higgins. We have a number of mutual friends."

He leaned in and whispered, "That includes my bride. She told me how she consulted you when she lost her diamond engagement ring, and you helped her find it. She practically tore the house apart before I told her to call you."

Beatrix nodded.

Higgins was big, muscled, and loud, and his wife was a tiny slip of a woman. But like other females in the south, only on the outside was she delicate.

Once Higgins released Beatrix's hand, she saw his tentative smile and knew the truth. He was not happy.

Andrew Higgins does not want to work with these men. He inches away from them whenever possible. He does not believe that the federal government, as they have told him, needs to have the local bookmaker to bankroll the Higgins boats, regardless of how wealthy he is.

Beatrix moved closer to Admiral Peterson and pretended to flick a speck of dust off his blue wool uniform sleeve. She had explained, that she could gather the truth by touching people, which was all part of her act—the performance that inferred she was psychic, so it did no good to lie to her. Of course, that was a fabrication that Beatrix enjoyed watching take effect.

As the group circled the carcass of what would be one the crafts, Beatrix examined the men's eyes and microscopic facial expressions. Obviously, she could not read their thoughts, but their faces could tell her things.

Admiral Peterson boasted about how the vessel was needed at once to save lives of thousands of soldiers.

"The men will hit the beach, vanquish the enemy, and safely return to the ship." He patted the craft as if it were a faithful dog.

The clickity-clatter of high heels on the cement floor halted the conversation, and everyone turned to watch a woman deliver a tray of coffee and cups and place it on a table. She prepared one cup with cream and two sugars and offered it to the major before scooting back from whence she came, leaving a cloud of Evening in Paris perfume languishing in her wake.

The admiral ignored the refreshments. "Now, Brockman, we don't want you to feel rushed, but that maniac Hitler needs to be stopped, blast it all. It's going to take good old American ingenuity, like Higgins has here, to do it. You all might not be able to see how valuable and maneuverable these crafts will be, but they are. They are fast, they're light, and they're going to save lives. Yep, this is a whopping opportunity, and if I had the cash, I'd be investing right along with you. Or, well, we hope you will. Why, you're going to be the hero. You will certainly be remembered as the man who saved lives and money and preserved our American dream. Yes, future generations will thank you and credit you for turning the tide on this war. Why, I might even predict, if I were a psychic like Miss Patterson, that someday there just could be a museum that will honor all of this, and possibly you, too, Andrew."

Beatrix was about to pour some coffee, but the admiral's words stopped her. *A museum dedicated to the valor of heroes from the war. Yes, that would be appropriate to build in the city. Perhaps it could be called the World War II Museum.*

She offered a cup to Thomas, but he nodded a refusal.

The Admiral believes what he was saying, that this craft developed by Higgins could positively impact the war. Major Davies's eyes and rigid posture shout something quite the opposite. She finished pouring a cup of chicory-scented coffee and sipped it as she moved closer to Major Davies. *Now it's time to listen more closely and pretend I can read their thoughts.*

"Another cup of coffee?" she asked the major, who had gulped the creamy first cup in two swallows, as one might kick back a whiskey neat for false bravado.

Beatrix realized that it was possible that the major was scheming to use patriotism to lure one of New Orleans' wealthiest, but supposedly unprincipled, citizens to bankroll Mr. Higgins invention in order to make a small fortune when the boats were purchased by the government. While there were no laws against it then, Beatrix felt ill at ease about Mr. Brockman investing in the manufacturing process when Davies's true reason for making the deal was possibly to pad his pockets.

She put her cup on the table. "Gentlemen, it's quite warm in here. I need to get some air."

They continued to talk, barely turning as Beatrix left the warehouse.

She stepped close to Thomas. "Come with me to the office. I need some information."

In the distance, a flock of geese flew in a V-shape, clearly knowing their mission. Alas, Beatrix felt the supposed solid plans the military was presenting were the polar opposite to the fowl.

While they were inside the warehouse, the rain had turned to a heavy downpour; the gravel around the warehouses had absorbed the worst of it. Beatrix looked at the slate-gray sky, and after climbing three steps to the door marked OFFICE, Beatrix opened it, followed closely by Thomas.

"I had to come and thank you for the coffee, Miss ..."

The secretary slid a small blue bottle into the top drawer of her desk and stood.

"Cartier. Georgianna Cartier, ma'am." She stood, teetering on bright-red high heels and smoothing down the wrinkles in a serviceable, baggy woolen dress that had been the rage possibly a decade prior.

A fetching smile brought dimples to an otherwise forgettable face.

Beatrix removed her hat, placed it on a stack of what seemed to be invoices, and then surveyed the business office. Every flat surface was covered with files and rolls of blueprints. Trash cans overflowed with crumpled papers and greasy food wrappers. Behind the secretary, and opened on the desk drawer, were what seemed to be accounting books.

The secretary extended her hand. "Everybody around the yard here just calls me Georgie. Daddy wanted boys, so my older sis is called Willie, and my second sister was Bertie, because she's Bertha. But we haven't seen her in years."

Beatrix returned the smile and accepted the handshake, noting the local accent that was far from the upscale population that frequented her storefront business. She guessed Georgie's age to be late teens or early twenties and at once felt determined to make the young woman comfortable.

"Nicknames are funny, and I have been told we can't pick ours. When I was born, my parents said they were thrilled, and they chose Beatrix, which means, *She who makes happy*. I cried a lot, apparently, so Father decided BB was more appropriate. That is, for Bawling Beatrix." She laughed and studied the woman's face. "When I asked him about the nickname, he swore it was for Beautiful Beatrix. I'm just thankful BB didn't stick. Sounds like one of the dancers in the Quarter's strip joints."

The younger woman laughed, too, now relaxed a bit, and Beatrix continued.

"Georgie, can I be honest with you? I have just had a psychic feeling that you are worried about your boss. Is that right?"

The young woman looked down at her flashy shoes. "It's an honor to meet you, ma'am. I have heard about you, Miss Patterson, and your mysterious powers. Oh, Lordy, if I had them, I'd be betting on the horses. You can make book on that." She threw her hand over her mouth as if to stop more honesty and gulped. "Mrs. Higgins was in here after you helped her find that ring. She told me all about what happened." The words came in excited puffs. "Someday, I'd like to hire you to tell me about my future and if my sisters and I will ever get along. That Willie is so pushy. And Bertie ... well, you could never find a person in the world with a sweeter heart than our Bertie. I miss her."

"Back to my question, dear," said Beatrix. "You're worried a lot about Mr. Higgins? Or is there more that is troubling you?" She touched the secretary's shoulder.

Tears dotted Georgie's eyes, and she coughed with an asthmatic wheeze as words tumbled out.

"They hired me as a receptionist, Miss Patterson. Someone to file and make appointments, bring 'em coffee, and pull down the blinds at night. I was okay with that. Then the bookkeeper joined up and went to war. For a 'long time, we didn't have anyone to do the accounts, other than the boss, Mr. H. And he'd just write checks, never entering the amounts into an account book, and spent money like I could print it in the basement, if we had a basement, and if I could counterfeit anything, which I can't. I didn't know what to do, but Jimmy, the bookkeeper, had to make notes of the money that went in and out. That, I knew. I did okay with numbers at school, but oh, Miss Patterson, this is more than adding and subtracting. Mr. H keeps saying how proud he is of me. Why, he even gave me twenty-five cents an hour more, and promoted me to bookkeeper. If it weren't for the little help I've gotten provided by a helpful, um, friend, who, um, hired someone to, um, get things in order, well, um ..." Her words dwindled and became invisible as the sobs took over.

Beatrix moved to her side. "Georgie, these are tough times. Most of us have taken on jobs we are not suited. Bet you know women working in the aircraft factories and building boats in the harbor, right?"

Georgie gulped back a sob and wiped her face with a hankie.

"My colleague here, Dr. Ling, is a Chinese scholar all the way from England, and he is working with me now, doing a job he's never done before. You're not alone in this." Beatrix smiled.

Thomas frowned. *It does not take a clairvoyant to know what Miss Patterson has in mind. She's trying to gain the girl's trust. But what is she trying to convince the secretary to say or do? Get me to organize the office and bring the accounting books up to date?*

"My goodness, Dr. Ling, you have so many good ideas." Beatrix smiled as she watched his eyes focus on the open accounting books. "With the permission of your employer, Dr. Ling will help you here in the office. While he is not a trained accountant, I am certain he can update the books and help get the office organized. He's extremely organized and has already been more than helpful to me."

Georgie dimpled. "Oh, ma'am, and Dr. Ling. Oh, thank you. Would that be awful of me to ask for help? Money is tight, I think. At least, that's what Mr. Higgins says, and I'm afraid there isn't possibly any way that Dr. Ling could be—"

"Paid?" Beatrix said. "Oh no, Georgie. Consider having Dr. Ling here to help as part of the war effort." She smiled at Thomas. *And within a few hours, he'll know how stable this company is and what Higgins's reasons are for asking John Brockman to fund the manufacturer of the boats. Or if it was the Major's idea.*

"Perhaps, Miss Patterson," Thomas gave a slight bow, "if you do not require my services and will permit me to spend the rest of the afternoon here with Miss Cartier, I am certain we can organize the office by, say, five o'clock? Or six?"

Beatrix nodded. *A fine choice for an assistant. And if I didn't know better, I'd swear he could read my mind.*

She turned and left the two, along with her hat. "I believe there is a bus stop near the corner, Dr. Ling. But if you'd prefer, I'm certain Henry, the driver, would be able to come back here for you later in the day?"

"The bus will be an adventure, Miss Patterson. Thank you for your concern."

He lost no time diving into the paper chaos as if it were the best puzzle anyone had given him. *Unraveling facts and figures is something I do well, much more so than being a witch's bodyguard.* He sat down with the accounts' ledgers.

Back in the warehouse, John was circled by Admiral Peterson, Major Davies, and Andrew Higgins. Her client's face was flushed as if he were drinking whiskey rather than coffee, which she knew not to be true, as John rarely touched even a dram of alcohol.

She walked up next to her client, and the other men stepped back.

"This has been most instructive, Mr. Brockman," she said, "but I believe you have other pressing business this afternoon, is that correct?"

"Why, yes, Miss Patterson. I'd forgotten." He pulled a gold pocket watch from his threadbare vest. "The mayor doesn't like to be kept waiting. Y'all will have to excuse us." He placed the empty cup on the table. "Andrew, keep building these boats, and I will consider your proposal. Good day, gentlemen, I'll be in touch."

The major stepped closer. "Wait. We need a commitment, sir. The country needs your help. Are you willing to man up and make an investment?" He wrung his hands as if it was the end of the world should John refuse to say yes right then.

"Being a man, gentlemen, means that I sleep on big decisions." Brockman looked at the major. "I need to consult with Miss Patterson as well."

"You just give me a call, Mr. Brockman, if you need anything. Anything." The admiral slapped him on the back, knocking the bookmaker forward.

John stepped away to ensure that there would not be

another repeat of the friendly gesture.

Beatrix watched John flinch and then plaster on a smile. *Other than the major's possible get-rich-quick scheme, there may be nothing wrong with a wealthy citizen floating the boat-building company rather than the government funding it. But the officers, especially Davies, are far too affable.*

"I do want to talk with you, John," she said. "Are you ready to head back to the city?"

"Your assistant, Dr. Ling, won't he be joining us?" Brockman opened the limo door and turned to Henry. "Have someone come back for my car, would you. I want to ride to the office with Miss Patterson."

Beatrix didn't respond until he was next to her.

"I have dispatched Dr. Ling on a fact-finding mission here at the boatyard. He's spending the afternoon with their accounting books and the secretary. I already have information you need to hear, but there must be a full report. Would tomorrow morning be convenient? Shall we meet at Café du Monde at nine?"

He touched her hand with icy fingers. "The plans look solid, and I've liked Andy since we first met, working with a Mardi Gras krewe during the Depression. Both of us were younger then, as you can imagine, but somehow he stays young."

"Your health, John? Are you conferring with a physician?"

"How did you know? Oh yes, your powers." He smiled. "As well as can be expected for a man with ulcers. They've sent me to every quack in the South. You might as well know the truth. Or perhaps you know it already. The latest doctor says that I may not see it through the year. Do you have any physic feelings or readings on that, Beatrix? Tell me the truth."

"John, I do not know when your body will cease to exist and when your soul or spirit will be free. That is not my realm. However, I do know that what you have to contribute to the living is not over. Do not be afraid. You, like others who have crossed over, will find that the next existence—perhaps better termed, *Heaven*—is more splendid than our human brains can conceive. For now, sir, I hope you'll try listening to some music before bed. It will let you sleep better, and that in turn can make you feel less anxious."

"Thank you," Brockman said. "I know that will help, my dear."

"Thank you for asking me to be part of the meeting. After I confer with Dr. Ling, I believe you will be fully informed to make a decision."

As they arrived back on Royal Street, the driver held the passenger door open for Beatrix.

"We will meet then at nine." She watched as the black car turned the corner on Royal and disappeared into traffic, heading toward city hall and that meeting with the mayor.

Andrew Higgins was a reputable businessman and a patriot. *He believes that these boats must be built. Yet, inside, something's bothering him. That uneasy feeling is because it's unusual for the Army and the Navy to locate a civilian investor to fund this expansion. He doesn't seem to trust the major. That's good.*

Beatrix turned the key in the door lock, entered the office, and flicked on the lights. She moved to the safe and twisted in the numbers, then stared at the gold wedding ring that she'd placed in a box atop a six-inch stack of fifty-dollar bills.

She pulled it out. *What do you want to tell me?*

Beatrix slipped the man's ring onto the third finger of her left hand. She twisted it and examined the glow under the desk lamp. *You do have stories to tell me.*

Twilight had settled in early, as it did in February, and it seemed that she had been awakened from a trance. Beatrix slipped the strap of her purse on her shoulder and placed the ring on her thumb for safekeeping.

As she locked the office, she said to the ring, "Do not be shy, my little friend. I will keep your secrets if that is what you want. But you must reveal all to me. Let me help you find Mrs. Howard if she wants to be found."

By the time Thomas caught a bus back to Royal Street, the area had turned to a ghost town, and the light but oppressive mist had drenched him to the skin. He felt alone but strangely comfortable in this foreign city. All his supposedly important scientific work in England seemed pale to the adventures he'd had in the last two days. His mates at the local pub would never believe his stories—if he managed to live through another crossing of the Atlantic, now riddled by U-boats like sharks in bloody waters.

He turned the key to the office but didn't flick the light switch. He'd always had a keen sense of sight and hearing and found his way to the back office and then to the stairs that led to his room, but not before he snagged a bottle of Jack Daniel's and a stubby crystal glass from the cabinet.

"You are not the friend I would have chosen to spend an evening with, Jack, but you will have to do." He shrugged out of the wet suit jacket and trousers and placed them over a chair before pulling a blanket around his shoulders.

Thomas turned on the radio, which whined, sputtered, and came to life. A baritone voice gave the report: "*Little did the people of Saint Lawrence dream upon retiring Tuesday night, February 17, 1942, that on awakening, one of the worst sea disasters in United States naval history would have happened right on their doorstep. The disaster occurred when the twelve-hundred-ton destroyer Truxton crashed ashore at Chamber Cove on the outer side of Saint Lawrence, and almost simultaneously, the six-thousand-eighty-five-ton supply ship Pollux ran aground at Lawn Point, a mile and a half westward. Many sailors have been lost, and a source within the War Department leaked that this might be sabotage.*

"*Now, to news from Asia. Japanese troops are reportedly heading toward Darwin, Australia's Northern Territory, and President Roosevelt is preparing to sign the Exclusion Act, Executive Order 9066, keeping Americans safe by incarcerating all Japanese living in the US.*"

A radio commercial blasted about how Camay soap would help any woman to achieve that schoolgirl complexion, and

Thomas kicked back an inch of the amber liquid.

"Damn." He sighed and slipped down into the lumpy overstuffed chair. "Have the Americans lost their compassion and their minds? I thought Americans were the good guys, the ones who wore the white hats in cowboy movies?"

He'd read about the potential internment rules that the executive order would mandate but thought cooler heads would prevail.

The manly radio voice droned on: *"Sources close to President Roosevelt said that by tomorrow at this time, it will be the law of the land that Japanese Americans are to be rounded up and incarcerated for the remainder of the war. The War Department estimates there will be camps throughout the US holding one hundred thousand to two hundred thousand men, women, and children. According to our news sources, the camps for the Japanese are not prisons, but Japanese will not be able to leave either."*

Thomas snarled at the radio. "Next, they will start to round up other Asians, and I will be herded into a detention camp. Is this not what the Nazis are doing to the Jews, the gypsies, the intellectuals, and anyone who does not scream allegiance to their diabolical leader?"

But he knew that in England, the British government had interned Italian and German citizens.

When the telephone rang downstairs, Thomas jumped, fearful against logic that what he'd just said was about to happen.

He dashed down the stairs. "Hello. Thomas Ling speaking."

"Dr. Ling, it is I, Beatrix. I want you to know that nothing unforeseen will happen to you while you are in my employ, including being jailed in an internment camp."

"Why did you call now? You heard the radio report, is that correct?"

"No," she lied, glad she'd turned off the radio before making the phone call. "The images I see are clear, and there is worry in your heart and head about what might happen to you as a person from Asia. Be assured, those worries are unfounded."

"You can be sure of this how, Miss Patterson?"

"It matters little," she replied.

That was true, and she knew that the First Lady had the clout to intercede for her, if necessary.

"There is something more pressing," Beatrix said. "I called to get your report from the investigation at the Higgins boatyard."

Thomas flicked on the light inside the office. He had the strangest feeling that Miss Patterson was in the room with him, not across town in her home, and wondered for a half-second if she could see him standing there in an undershirt and boxer shorts, with a blanket covering his shoulders.

"The place was a mess," he replied. "That woman pretends not to be capable of being a bookkeeper, even less a secretary, but she's either a really good actress, or has other motives."

"Did you see the second set of accounting books?" she said.

Thomas felt as if a spider were climbing up his spine.

"You knew?" he said. "You knew that there was the chaotic and disorganized set, and another that was on the shelf in Miss Cartier's desk?"

"I did, but I couldn't compare the two. Were you able to do that?"

Thomas blinked. *Never in my life have I been so frustrated and curious at the same time. If Beatrix Patterson's visions and voices, and whatever, were some parlor trick, she could not have known this information.* He then felt stark naked, like his thoughts were exposed. *Can she read my brainwaves over the phone?*

"Yes, I can understand your thought process," she said. "and believe me, I never wanted to have this gift of knowing, Dr. Ling. It is mine, and I handle it with care. Shall we return to the matter at hand? Once Miss Cartier left with Major Davies, did you have the opportunity to compare the two sets?"

"Davies? Yes, he picked her up about a half-hour after I arrived. You knew? Of course, your psychic powers told you," he muttered.

"There were no powers required, Dr. Ling. It was the heady fragrance she was wearing. A woman who wears a shabby, dress that has not been in style for ten years could never afford a perfume that is all the rage. 1 assume you saw when the major leaned in to her, breathing in the perfume. Or when they touched fingers as Major Davies accepted a cup of coffee from her. She offered none to the other guests, by the way. Did you see her tiny smile before staring at the floor? Or the crushed-out cigars in the ashtray in her office?"

"No. No, 1 did not." Thomas pulled the wool blanket closer around his shoulders. *I must watch this woman and learn how she perceives even the slightest nuances that can reveal the truth. 1 cannot believe 1 missed all that.*

As if Beatrix knew his thoughts—which, of course, she did not—she said, "And the well-organized accounting ledgers filed on the shelf in back of the secretary's desk? How did they compare to the receipts and notes you looked at on the desk and tables?"

He could have thought the answer and not spoken, but Thomas wasn't rude, especially if Miss Patterson was truly going to help him alert his Chinese connections in the war effort.

"As 1 organized all the papers and made notes of the income and expenses," he said, "It became clear that the jumbled ledger was the correct one. Higgins Boatyard is indeed in financial straits. Nonetheless, the well-manicured set of books on the shelf showed that the yard is doing well. There is not a lot of profit, but there is some income."

"Two sets of books on the company," Beatrix said. "Did you recognize the writing on the false ledger, Dr. Ling?"

"Yes. There were three different styles of handwriting. The first ledger, the real ones, were in a tiny, neat hand. The second, which 1 compared to Georgie's from the notes on her desk, were of course hers. Then there was another person making more entries. The 'friend' she mentioned between sobs? An even more appropriate question is why would Mr. Higgins keep the real books in such a disheveled manner?"

"Perhaps Mr. Higgins didn't know anything about this, or Georgie and her friend didn't expect anyone to look through the bits and pieces that were on her desk," said Beatrix. "Or like a magician, she assumed everyone would think of her as a ditzy, disorganized creature, and not dive any deeper. Conceivably, she was anxious to leave on her date with the major and didn't think you'd compare the two. All the same, thank you. I have a meeting with Mr. Brockman at nine and will give him this information. How he should use it, and what I learned during the time at the boatyard, is entirely up to him."

"Good night, Miss Patterson."

"Good night, Dr. Ling. I will see you after my meeting, and we'll take the trolley to the Howard house. Please bring your pistol."

CHAPTER 6

February 18, 1942

BEATRIX LINGERED AT CAFÉ DU MODE after John bid her goodbye. He had taken the news of her report well, thanked her, and slipped into her hand another envelope containing $1,000. She had not told him her opinions. That was out of her capacity as an adviser. Yet she did know his thoughts after he sighed and said, "Poor Andy. He's so trusting and deserves my help."

A no-interest loan directly with Andrew Higgins is the right way to proceed, and without the red tape that the government might create. Beatrix nodded and had a curious feeling that this was what John had decided.

She dabbed a napkin to her lips. *All the officers believe what they are doing is right, even the major. Even if they set up a false set of accounting books to indicate that the boatyard is generating income, they believe our future is at stake and that the only way Higgins's boats can be ready for the warfare they fear will happen in the next twelve months is for John's financial support, along with the Army and Navy's decision to invade Europe. Had they merely come to the wealthy citizen and asked him to partner with Higgins, Mr. Brockman would have said yes, at once. But trying to hoodwink the affluent bookmaker had made Mr. Brockman unwilling to finance any other patriotic causes. Major Davies's possible financial dealings will never be exposed now.*

Beatrix walked toward her office and stopped to chat with a

street vendor.

"Three carnations, if you please." She handed the woman a dollar.

"No, madam, that's far too much. They're only a quarter, and I cannot take your money. I owe you my heart because of that day you foretold how my baby was going to die if we did not get her to the hospital. Because of your gift from God, you saved her life. They gave her medicine for the fever, and she is giggling again. We would never have dared take her to the hospital if you hadn't assured me that an angel would hear about little Monique and our bill would be paid."

"I only can tell you what I know," Beatrix replied.

"Oh, mademoiselle. The cost of the bill? It was over a hundred dollars. My flower stall has never made that much, and it's even less now that there's war. Our baby would have died."

The vendor wiped away tears streaming down her ruddy cheeks, twisted the delicate pink carnations into a sheet of the *Times-Picayune* newspaper, and kissed Beatrix's hand.

"Your baby will thrive now. I know you are a good mama." Beatrix pulled the cinnamon-scented flowers to her nose.

No psychic powers were needed to pay a bill. Just required some cash from her safe.

She breathed in the perfumed flowers. *Is this the scent my French mother wore?*

There was nothing otherworldly about her sense that she was not the biological child of her parents. Yet, she could never get the courage to ask, fearing she'd somehow damage her relationship with her parents or hurt their feelings. Then they died.

Beatrix walked toward the office, and for the millionth time, dug into her memories, trying to bring back some recognition of the woman who had carried her. This woman had kissed her, cuddled her, fed her, and loved her for two years until they were parted. But why? Why had her biological mother abandoned her?

On her aunt's deathbed, the frail lady said she'd heard one

doctor say, "The mother is too unstable to care for a child." This confirmed what Beatrix had heard in whispers about the secret adoption.

Without success or satisfaction, Beatrix attempted to unearth any fragile recollection but only got a wispy sense of a soft pink hand on her cheek. The remembrance dashed away, much like the street corner's litter as it was tossed in the wind. She touched the large ruby on her index finger, as she often did to impress a client of her psychic connections. *Perhaps what Auntie heard was true, and it's been so long that perhaps mental illness has taken my birth mother's life. But what if I could find her?*

Beatrix knew it was the ultimate irony. People paid her to find lost things, but she could not find out what happened to her own biological mother. The entire Patterson family went to their graves without revealing even the woman's name, although her aunt had revealed that the woman had returned to New Orleans. Sometimes, in a dream, Beatrix would smell carnations and wondered if her biological mother, now having passed over, was visiting her. But then she'd wake, shake her head, and realize that she was beginning to believe in her own lies. *That would be stupid and dangerous.*

She shrugged as if to lose the yearning for a mother she never knew, and again, as she unlocked the door, the office smelled of jasmine tea. Thomas was sorting the mail, slitting the envelopes but not extracting the letters.

"Miss Patterson, the tea is ready if you have time for a cup before we look into the Howard case."

Beatrix withdrew another white envelope from her purse.

"Thank you," she said. "I will have tea before we leave. It is chilly this morning."

"The envelope?" Thomas didn't know if he should ignore how plump it was or if he should just be bold and inquire.

"It is money," she replied. "And we will deal with this when we return from the Howard house, Dr. Ling. As with your last errand, you'll visit the asylum, Poydras House, and the Old Absinthe on Bourbon Street."

She placed the money on top of the desk and refilled her teacup twice more before disappearing to the back of the office, and then returned to the front as Thomas was just finishing reading the newspaper that he'd spread out on the desk in front of him.

"Do you have your pistol, Dr. Ling?"

"Madam, do you expect me to defend you with the gun? I am a scientist, and I gladly exchange my services as an errand boy, a secretary, and even a bodyguard for information you may choose to share with me about the aggression of the Japanese into my family's homeland of China. But if you expect me to kill someone, please be aware, I will not shoot because you have divined someone to be dangerous."

"You are right," she said. "I have no plans for you to kill anyone. But if you can possibly fire that gun toward the sky, or even wave it around while looking menacing, should it become necessary, then it might be useful."

His mind flashed to the laboratory where he'd spent years. Quiet, sterile, dull.

With a start, he slipped into the suit jacket, pulled the revolver from the top desk drawer, and placed it in a black leather satchel he'd found in the back of the office.

"Yes, it is loaded," he said.

"Did you read my mind, sir?" Beatrix suppressed a giggle.

She couldn't be sure if he was that gullible or overwrought with the tasks at hand.

Thomas was stopped by the comment and her smile. *This is what madness feels like. I have become the servant of a wu.*

If it had been one of those bright, spring-like days that happen even in a Louisiana winter, the walk beyond the French Quarter would have delighted Beatrix. And when she first came to the city to care for her dying aunt, she'd walk for miles. Previously, freedom filled the air, and the Crescent City oozed with Southern charm, making a stranger immediately like a friend one had yet to meet. The war changed that, and now dread was etched in countless faces. Even the mist felt heavy, and the occasional diversion of music or drink seemed to be distracted and agitated as if sewn tight into a nightmare. The city that had once been a balm to the soul now had a dangerous edge. Where flowers had once cascaded over balconies, now curtains were drawn, and laughter, genuine joy, was suppressed as if it was un-American to tell a joke or chuckle at one.

That day, with the biting wind whipping up more sprinkles and the proximity of the Riverfront streetcar to Frenchmen Street, it was impossible not to shiver and long for a cup of tea or something stronger, regardless of the hour. Surprising for many who didn't know the history of the city, this area was once the plantation of a wealthy Creole who introduced Craps, the game of dice, to America. He influenced the city of New Orleans with his *joie de vivre*—enjoyment of living—and utter extravagance. In 1840, his property was subdivided. The area of Frenchman Street in the Faubourg Marigny neighborhood slowly developed into a district that mixed shabby shotgun houses with opulent homes with European flair.

On that February morning, tormented black clouds lined up in military formation and threatened a deluge. The doors to the cafés were shuttered, and the owners and staff at the rowdy clubs knew they could snooze for a few more hours.

Beatrix noted it all, including filing away for future reference the faces of those they'd passed. Thomas stared ahead, checking numbers until they arrived at the Howard house, number 524.

The screen door flapped open and closed as if it were uttering diabolical warnings. Paint peeled from the siding, and the porch's roof sagged in the middle. Trash cluttered the front steps, twisting and turning in mini tornadoes, only to be lifted into the stiff breeze to seek freedom.

Beatrix stopped in front of the house to twist Mr. Howard's wedding ring on her thumb. Thomas had slowed, unsure if he should stand by her side or allow her to do whatever witches did. Then his mind went to the gun, somewhat safe in the satchel, and it suddenly felt too heavy to carry.

The breeze stopped. Beatrix was still, seemingly hearing

voices or waiting for a sign. Thomas couldn't tell and wouldn't ask.

She turned to Thomas and whispered, "Make a choice now, Dr. Ling. Either hand me your gun, or have it at the ready. Evil lurks inside."

Thomas gulped and hoped it was silent, yet in his head, it sounded like a clap of thunder. He reached into the bag and fumbled until he grasped the butt of the gun, feeling its weight, and with moist fingers, handed it to his employer. *I would give my life for king and country, but I cannot potentially shoot someone because this wu says there is evil inside.*

Now he was a good five feet behind her, forcing himself to take each creaking wooden step without breathing.

Upon reaching the porch, he shivered as Beatrix stood firmly in front of the wooden doorway. *Three weeks ago, I was naively sitting in my office at Oxford, reviewing the evidence of the potential components of an atom, attempting to fathom the work of Einstein in order to write an academic response to his latest theories, and looking forward to the end of the day to share a beer with a mate. Today, I am about to meet evil face to face, and there is a psychotic wu holding a gun and standing directly in front of me.*

Beatrix nodded to him.

Is she agreeing that I am as crazy as I believe? Or is she about to rush inside, guns blazing, as John Wayne would?

Thomas nodded back. There was no doubt in his mind what needed to be done, and his feet and body moved to do her bidding, even if his brain screamed for him to stop. She'd planted the thought, and his free will was gone.

He dashed to the side and tossed back the screen. Turned the doorknob and threw it back.

"Flynn Howard," Beatrix said in a voice that vibrated with intensity but not in decibels. "I know you are in the house, and I know why."

Thomas gasped. Had the burly policeman come back to the scene of his crime to wash away the blood of his butchered wife? If that were true, why hire Miss Patterson?

"*Unwise people will do unwise and bizarre things,*" his grandmother had once told him.

Thomas stood perfectly still, but his heart hammered against his chest, watching Beatrix entered the house. A beam of sunlight illuminated her as she stood just inside the door, and it seemed as if her image was glowing.

Flynn Howard bellowed, "Miss Patterson, put the gun down. I ... well, I thought maybe she would return. Maybe she left a note or something that I didn't see. Maybe I could find a reason why she just up and left."

As if he were a punctured balloon, he slowly deflated, and the bottle crashed to the floor, with Thomas's gaze flashing between the officer and his tiny employer, who looked huge and powerful.

"That is not true, Mr. Howard," she barked.

Flynn Howard snapped his gaze to her face.

"It does no good to lie to me, sir. You remember, I can read your thoughts. Your reason for being here is simple. You wanted to clear out the whiskey bottles, to straighten the house, to make it look like you were a happily married couple. Because you were not. Now, Mr. Howard, do I need this gun? It's loaded, and be certain, I can and will use it, if necessary, to protect myself and my secretary. Besides, Dr. Ling is right here, should I require someone to subdue you. He is a master of the ancient Asian martial arts, so do not underestimate him. With one quick movement, he can, and will, cripple you."

In fact, Thomas had managed to enter the ram-shackled house, even while his heart was in his throat. And while her confidence in him was admirable, he had never been faced with a life-and-death situation that required his hands and feet to become weapons.

He stood directly behind his employer. Over Beatrix's shoulder, he saw the man's eyes, and Thomas's gut reaction was to step back. Fast. If Beatrix had not indicated with a twist of her wrist for him to move forward and had not told him that he was there to protect her, Thomas would have run for his life. He had never seen eyes so enraged.

Who is protecting whom?

Beatrix turned and shoved the pistol into his hand before she stepped even closer to Flynn Howard.

"I know what happened, Mr. Howard. The puzzle is why you hired me to trace your wife?" Beatrix touched Howard's sleeve and guided him to a brocade-covered chair so worn that tuffs of cotton stuck out all along the arms as if it were a flock of sheep before shearing.

"I didn't like you, ma'am. Didn't want to hire you. Our priest would excommunicate me if he knew I'd hired a spiritualist. I'm ... well, I'm desperate. I want her back."

Flynn Howard teetered and grabbed the edge of a table, which crumbled under his weight. He looked down at the rubble and sobbed, frustration and anger dissipating, until his voice turned to the wail of a frightened child.

"Are you sure?" Beatrix said. "I am not questioning your heart, sir, but your head."

Flynn Howard flopped into the chair. Particles of dust and grime sprinkled down on his feet as he rubbed beefy hands over his puffy cheeks, and his head dropped forward.

He gulped and whispered, "It's my fault."

Thomas surveyed the filthy room and on into a kitchen, which was strewn with garbage and empty whiskey bottles, and stacked with pots, and he felt anger well up in his throat, powerful and bitter.

A drunk. A drunk and abusive husband does not deserve to have his wife back. He is guilty. Any man who touches a woman in anger or for power is truly not a man. And to do this against a wife, the woman he supposedly loves, deserves no sympathy. It should be a criminal offense, and God-willing, it will be someday. What is wrong with Miss Patterson? Why is she patting his arm? Why is she taking pity on him? Must I beat him as he did his wife, who had to flee her home, this filthy pen not fit for a pig, in order to save her life?

Thomas swallowed hard and shuttered. Where had the violent notion of beating Flynn Howard come from? He had not been in a fight since he was in school, and then he'd been tossed around like a wet rag. Thomas didn't even know the man, but he despised everything this bully had done.

It seemed longer, but in the second, Thomas swallowed back the vicious taste of repulsion. He longed to hear what foolish excuse Howard would give Miss Patterson for forcing his wife to live in abject squalor.

Thomas took a step closer, fists clenched, but stopped short when Beatrix said, "Mr. Howard, why do you think this is your fault? It is not, you know."

Thomas felt as if someone had thrown icy water at his face. *Not his fault? He beat his wife, and he is innocent?* Thomas wanted to yell it and grab the domineering oaf off the chair.

Beatrix sat on the armrest and turned to Thomas. "Please get Mr. Howard some water."

Thomas obeyed his employer, but anger made the water slosh to the scarred linoleum as he handed it to Beatrix.

Beatrix passed the glass to Flynn. "Alcoholism is a disease. Your wife is sick."

Flynn Howard blinked and shook his head, obviously incredulous to what Beatrix had just told him.

"Disease?" He blinked again. "I don't understand what kind of sickness this could be."

Thomas wanted to grab the miscreant by his shirt collar and tell him what he thought of that theory. *Sick lowlife. Now his justification for beating her is that she's ill?*

Beatrix looked up at Thomas. "You are a man of science, Dr. Ling. Perhaps you have studied the sciences of the mind, such as psychiatry or psychology, no? The newest research is showing that alcoholism is a disease. This is beginning to get the attention of the medical community. There are groups and doctors making strides in helping those whose addiction is to alcohol."

"I need not hear a lecture on what this man did to his wife, Miss Patterson, whether she had a drinking disease or not." Thomas huffed and had to turn away from their client for fear that hate's nasty taste might somehow make his hands connect with Flynn Howard's throat.

"Dr. Ling, your attention for one moment please." Beatrix stepped close to him. "In Akron, Ohio, just seven or eight years ago, Bill Wilson and a doctor colleague started Alcoholics Anonymous. It's a program to help those with a dependence on alcohol, and it will, I foresee, become so accepted that the organization will spread throughout the world and become the cornerstone to helping those with cravings of both liquor and dangerous drugs."

"Help the likes of him?" Thomas spat at the thought of assisting the scoundrel.

"Please listen, Dr. Ling. You have made a grave error and misconstrued the situation entirely. It is not Mr. Howard who is consumed with the need for liquor, but his wife."

"But the house, this mess. What does this mean?"

"Your eyes have told you something that is not true. There is a lesson here, Dr. Ling. Perhaps a more cautious approach to jumping to conclusions is in order, but that is something you must ponder. Veronica Howard has been obsessive in the growing need to destroy her loss, and she has turned to the only emotion-dulling substance that is readily available." Beatrix looked at the police officer. "Mr. Howard, the ring has told me that you and your wife were expecting a baby. After long hours of labor, and Veronica's screams to let her die, your first child, this baby boy, was born dead."

Her mind flashed on hearing of the tragedy, to when she visited Touro Hospital to pay the flower seller's medical bill.

Flynn gulped. "What? How? No one at the police department knew it. None of our neighbors even nod hello. And just the midwife came here to the house and then dragged Veronica off to the hospital, saying it was the only way to stop the bleeding." He wiped the tears with a handkerchief and then blew his nose loudly.

Thomas steadied himself against a cabinet. He knew she could read his mind, but to have a ring tell her these things was beyond belief. It didn't seem logical or possible. Did Beatrix have a network of informants in the city that reported the local gossip? And further, how could she know for certain as she hadn't met Flynn Howard before the day Thomas had taken refuge in the storefront business.

"As I said," Beatrix replied. "I know things. After weeks, when she still refused to leave the house to attend mass or confession, you suggested maybe a wee dram of whiskey would help her sleep. You could not have known that she would become addicted to the substance as a way to numb her broken heart."

The policeman cleared his throat, making a croaking sound.

"When Veronica asked for more, I thought it was a good sign. Back when I was a boy, my granny from County Kerry always believed a drop of whiskey, or a few fingers of moonshine, could cure about anything. My wife kicked it back like she'd been drinking for years, which wasn't possible, and our world crumbled because a little was never enough. Veronica stopped eating and spent grocery money at the tavern." He pointed. "I would plead with her to come home, to share supper with me, to come to church, but it was like talking to the wind. She stopped caring for herself, wore the same soiled dress, day after day. I didn't know what to do."

"It is an illness," Beatrix said.

As if he could not hear Beatrix, Flynn Howard continued.

"Night after night, when the bar closed, I was there. Outside. Even when I worked the extra job as a night security guard, I made sure I'd be there. Outside. Waiting. I helped her home, but—"

"She became violent. Isn't that right, sir?" Beatrix whispered. "She did this because you constantly found her stash of liquor and poured it out when she was at the tavern."

"You could not know this. I've never told a living soul. Here I am, a big old Irish cop, and my wife threw things at me, beat me with the broom handle and that iron pot over there." He pointed to a corner of the chaotic living room. "Well, she flung it at me, spewing insults as if I were the devil himself. Is she possessed? Does Satan have her soul?"

All the facts slowly came together for Thomas, and as he heard the confessions and the heartbreaking questions, it was as if the interior of the filthy house nodded to confirm it all.

"Mr. Howard, can you hear me?" Beatrix whispered.

The man's head snapped toward her as if she'd slapped his tear-stained cheek.

"Yes, ma'am."

Beatrix stared into his eyes, ringed with exhaustion.

"Again, as I've said, this is an illness. She is not possessed. If I were to reunite you and Veronica, would you take her to a clinic I know that can help people with her illness?"

"I would give my life for her. 'Sides, it's all my fault. She didn't want babies. Her mama had died giving birth to her. I was brought up Catholic, and we all got these big families. Oh, Lordy. Why did God take that baby's life, and why did I give her alcohol to soothe her nightmares? If I hadn't—"

"Mr. Howard. Stop that. If it had not been you, it would have been something else. Look at me. Veronica needs special help. She may have been addicted to alcohol long before the baby's death and kept that secret from you. When I find her, I will talk with her. But she needs you to be a good husband, and an even better friend. Can you do that? If you are able to, then I can help you. If not, our relationship is over. Is this clear, sir?"

CHAPTER 7

BEATRIX, THOMAS, AND FLYNN HOWARD WALKED to the corner and hailed a taxi to take them to the police station near the docks.

"When we arrive, please wait on the street," Beatrix said.

At the station, it took just five minutes before she returned with two concerned fellow officers and Howard's supervisor.

She turned to Howard. "They understand now, Flynn, and they will help you find a place to live while I find Veronica."

Thomas could see in the men's eyes that they had been placed under a spell, or they would have glared at the Asian with the almond-shaped eyes, bristling that he was the enemy.

Beatrix and Thomas watched as the police embraced their fellow officer.

The group escorted Flynn back into the old stone building as Beatrix said, "This is far from the end of the Howard's relationship. I fear more hurt will come."

Then she climbed into the waiting cab.

"Do you mean you won't find his wayward wife?" Thomas said. "Or she will batter him with a skillet again? I thought that was your deal with him, and you were working out the details by twisting the wedding ring."

She chuckled. "Dr. Ling, honestly, I already know where Mrs. Veronica Howard is, and you would too, if you'd concentrated on your mission when you were visiting Poydras House yesterday."

"The nun, who could be a nurse there, was bewildered,

and spoke with what I'm sure was a fake Parisian accent as she thanked me for the envelope," he replied, after giving the taxi driver the address of their office. "Was that woman Mrs. Howard?"

"Wait, what?" Beatrix said. "Stop, please."

The driver started to slow.

"No, please continue, driver. I'm talking to my associate." Beatrix looked at Thomas and shook her head as yet another copper curl escaped her wayward bun. "You met Mother Adelina?"

"That was not the policeman's wife, then?" he said. "Why, yes, of course, that could have been her name, and she was called Mother. Does that make her a supervisor of some sorts, like a head nurse or teacher, perhaps?"

Beatrix smiled. "Mother Adelina only believes she's a nun, as she had a grave loss in her life, and it stopped her from thinking clearly. Or so I've learned. She insists on wearing a habit and walking the halls of the refuge. I've never met her, and wonder if she's an apparition, or is playing a cruel joke on me when I seek her out."

Thomas felt his back straighten and hoped the shiver wasn't visible.

"She's odd, and quite real," he said. "However, if she is untrustworthy, she's probably destroyed the money by now, doing whatever ghosts do with money. And that was a lot of money."

"Thomas—if I may use your Christian name—she'll turn the envelope over to the real headmistress at the home, and all will be right. So do not be concerned. As for Mrs. Howard, I learned she has taken exile at Poydras House a few days before you began your employment with me. She is in the care of the doctor at the home, and I understand that she wants nothing to do with alcohol."

As they returned to Royal Street, Thomas got out of the cab and walked around to open the door for Beatrix.

"But Beatrix, if I may also call you by your first name ..." a hint of a smile played on his thin lips, and he waited while she paid the driver and then nodded.

"Yes. We're going to be working together for a while and calling me Beatrix makes it easier."

"So here is the question, Beatrix. What will you tell Officer Howard?"

"Why, the truth."

"That will settle it all? Everyone will live, as in a children's story, happily ever after?"

Beatrix entered the office, removed her hat, and shrugged out of the wool jacket that came just to her hips.

"Not quite," she replied. "She refuses to see or talk with her husband. She's devastated at her behavior and how she broke the vows of her marriage."

"That is it? They get a divorce?"

"Will you kindly make some tea, Dr. Ling—Thomas? Catholics do not divorce. But some believe there will be a time when their faithful will be able to annul a marriage. For now, Mrs. Howard will participate in group therapy, like psychological counseling, which will someday replace most of the one-on-one sessions you may know about. I believe that with time, she will accept that Mr. Howard loves her and only wants to help her."

"Does he?" Thomas said, from the tiny kitchen just in the back, behind the curtain that concealed him two days earlier.

He stopped pouring boiling water over the fragrant black leaves and looked out at Beatrix.

"I had the distinct feeling that the blustery and angry policeman felt he should have chosen a different wife," he said. "Perhaps one who would bare him son after son."

"Frankly, I had much the same feeling," Beatrix said, "so the outcome is hard to say. I will ask him, but not until he feels better. I am most assuredly not ready to tell him where his wife is now living, or he would storm into the home, waving his shiny police badge, and turn the entire situation into something the residents would never forget. Hence, I'll take a gentler approach. Wouldn't you?"

"Then you are a psychologist, and not a *wu*—l mean, a psychic? Or what term do you prefer for what you do?"

Beatrix accepted a steaming cup of jasmine tea.

"Thank you." She took a sip and smiled. "I have studied psychology with some of the most fascinating experts in the United States and was planning to go to Germany for more in-depth education, until that fanatic Hitler came into power. Now the world is not safe, and the work of those like Frieda Fromm-Reichmann, who fled the Nazi genocide, has been halted. The work will bloom again, which is a marvelous thing."

"Is that your psychic prediction?" Thomas said.

Beatrix laughed, and he noticed how her green eyes crinkled, and her face became rounder, gentler, nearly girlish, and he realized with a start that he'd guessed wrong. She was much younger than him.

"No, Thomas, it is clear that's the future, and one that I plan to embrace. There's far more challenging and intriguing work for someone who studies the inner workings of the mind and helps people cope with sound medical methods such as hypnotherapy, which I hope to learn more about."

"More than for a *wu*?"

"Definitely more of a mesmerizing and challenging future for a psychologist than a *wu*."

Major Davies burst through the office door. "Have you found the Nazi cell that is about to give the order to invade the city, Miss Patterson? Has that old coot Brockman made up his stinking mind?" He removed his cap and slapped it down, his face grim and his cheeks blotchy.

"Tea? Coffee? Come in, Major, and close the door. These things take time," she whispered, but looking at the major's face, she could have been screaming at him.

"We're at war here, in case you didn't know, madam, and I have little patience for a sideshow psychic to tell me the things that our intelligence community should be doing." He huffed and patted his pockets for a cigar that never seemed to be available.

"I am in agreement with you, sir. I believe in the United States and her allies. But I refuse to let you bully me. That is how I work, so you can leave right now." She rose, crossed the short distance, and opened the office door.

The frigid February wind blasted into the room. The officer did not leave. Beatrix twisted the ruby ring, and Thomas could see his employer's mind calculating what do to next.

Beatrix looked up. "Take your choice, Major. Either confess to the illegal manipulation of the accounts you've created at Higgins Boatyard, and stop pressuring Mr. Brockman, or I will explain your deceptions to him, Mr. Higgins, and to the First Lady of the United states. When I'm satisfied that you are no longer attempting to misappropriate funding from Mr. Brockman, I will tell you where you can locate the spies you are seeking."

"Whatever are you talking about, woman?" he barked, but the fire had gone from his anger. "I have done nothing wrong. You are a typical, hysterical female. Why, you should be locked away."

In a slice of a second, Beatrix saw a micro facial change, just a quiver in his grimace, and she knew she was right.

"If that's your decision," she said, "and you do not want to tell the truth, then I will tell you exactly what Mr. Brockman and Mr. Higgins will learn about you. You have been manipulating the secretary, Georgie, and have convinced her that if she does your bidding, you will marry her. That gift of perfume, the scarlet high heels, and the smart woolen jacket casually draped on the back of her office chair were your way of convincing her to do whatever you wanted. She's not stupid, Major. Georgie knows a lot more about manipulation than you might suppose. What will your wife think of this affair?"

"My wife? I'm not married—"

"Please do not patronize me, sir, or lie to me. I have the gift to know things. That's true, or you wouldn't have hired me, right?"

"This is ludicrous."

"No psychic abilities are necessary, Major. Just the power of deduction. I have seen you touch the base of your left hand's ring finger, right where a wedding ring would rest."

Major Davies's gaze flicked to the floor, and when he looked up again, guilt had replaced the previous bravado.

"Whatever you tell that ditzy blond can't matter. Girl's nuts for me. And besides, she won't believe you. If I asked her to find enough snow to make a snowman, even in July, the girl would do it."

Beatrix clapped. Thomas jumped, and the major flinched.

The curtain separating the front office from the rest was ripped open, and there was a wheezy gasp before Georgie Cartier pounced on the officer.

"You rat. You stinking scumbag," she hissed. "You never even hinted that you were married. You tricked me."

Her long, red nails would have connected with the major's face if not for Thomas. He pulled her back and clamped his arms around her waist. She screamed and fought, all the time trying to regulate chronic asthmatic breathing.

Screaming, she kicked the air when she didn't get to kick the major, as she was no match for Thomas's strength. With her arms flaying, he allowed Georgie to come within inches of the military man, then pulled her back as she screamed a string of expletives. Only Beatrix noticed a satisfied smirk on Thomas's face as he contained the woman.

"Georgie, control yourself." Beatrix clapped again, and the drama ended at once.

Georgianna Cartier froze as if she'd been shocked by an electric current. Thomas held her limp body and folded her into one of the guest chairs, all fight drained out of her. She covered her face in the skirt of the navy-blue polka-dot dress. The whimpers were loud and sounded like the clanking of a cracked bell. Thomas produced a fresh handkerchief from his jacket, and she grabbed it.

"Major." Beatrix stood over him. "Your conniving days, at least in New Orleans, are over. I believe your scheme to raise the value of Higgins Boatyard has just been destroyed. Please leave now. Once you have explained the two sets of books to Mr. Higgins, without blaming his secretary, we can resume our conversation about the spy cells here in the city."

"I will do no such thing. I've done nothing wrong," he sputtered.

"Nothing wrong? You have lied to Mr. Brockman for your own financial gain, attempting to buy into a company at an inflated price so that you can pocket the difference, thanks to Georgie and how there are two sets of books. Besides, you've been preying on his patriotism. And you've used the backing of your uniform and the Army to do it. That's wrong. And what of Georgie here?"

"What of her?" He frowned.

Georgie stared at the major but didn't move toward him.

Thomas couldn't imagine how she could contain herself until Beatrix said, "Or would you prefer that I clap my hands once more? I would rather enjoy seeing your beloved here, the ditzy blond, again attempt to gouge out your eyes. Oh, and if I do that ... Thomas, stay right where you are, please."

"Yes, Miss Patterson. Anything you say." Thomas clenched his teeth, stunned and awkwardly pleased that the milquetoast personality he thought he'd become had a threatening side.

The Major growled, "Why are you playing Miss High and Mighty, madam? I've heard about you and how you target wealthy matrons and dupe them into thinking that they're speaking with their long-departed loved ones. It is you who should be arrested and thrown in jail. If I could, I would do just that."

Thomas's eyes widened. *Does Beatrix victimize the brokenhearted for money? Is she truly a seer, or is she simply good at understanding and reading people? Dare I ask when we are alone?*

"Here are two witnesses who would testify that you are attempting to use your position as an Army officer during wartime to inflate stock prices for your own financial gain," Beatrix said. "Do you really think your word has any credibility, sir?" She moved to the front door and opened it.

The Major stormed out.

Once more, Beatrix clapped. Georgianna Cartier blinked and looked around the room.

"That's odd." She shook her head, focusing only at the handkerchief she was crushing in her fist.

She placed the soiled kerchief on the chair and stood.

Her forehead wrinkled. "Were we going to have some tea? Mighty kind of you to leave the front door key under the mat and invite me to visit and have afternoon tea when I had to come into the city to do the banking. When you returned for your hat, I was thrilled to be invited, and if I had that pretty hat, I wouldn't want to misplace it either. What a treat this is to be in such a fine office. Oh, I hope I didn't leave the kettle on in the little kitchen. I'm so forgetful at times, like just now ... I didn't remember even sitting down here." She looked to Beatrix and then Thomas.

"Do you need a bit of air, dear?" Beatrix said.

Georgie shook her head.

"No? Then shall we see about that tea?"

Beatrix took the woman's hand and pulled aside the curtain, and the two women headed to the tiny kitchen.

Thomas stepped out of their way. *Georgie was under an incantation. That must be it. One cannot do anything they don't want to do while hypnotized. This is something stronger. Something only a wu could do?*

Beatrix returned and whispered. "The tea will be ready soon. And you're right, Thomas. I could never make Georgie say or do anything she didn't want to do. Apparently, she was already savvy to the major and his games. I don't think she's as naïve as we'd like to believe, but please keep your own counsel on this. I would prefer the major confess to Mr. Higgins. And if the officer is any sort of gentleman, he'll avoid Georgie, especially now that he has seen how violent she can be."

"What of Mr. Brockman?" said Thomas. "He hired you to find out the truth, right? He's considering investing a fortune into a company that's nearly bankrupt—or so it seems, by the true set of books—unless the second set has also been altered."

"The second set of books are the true financials." Beatrix put a finger to her lips as Georgie came back to the office with cups and the tea. "There you are. This is lovely."

She accepted a cup from the bookkeeper. Thomas took one. And Georgie sipped quietly as if it were just another gentile ritual in the Crescent City.

Beatrix tilted her head to the side, touched the ruby ring, and circled the saucer's edge with a finger, all the time staring at Georgie.

Beatrix nodded. "Thomas, would you kindly escort Georgie back to the shipyard? Please take a taxi, as with the rain and wind, the buses will all be running late." She handed him five dollars.

"Yes, of course, Miss Patterson."

Thomas picked up Georgie's tattered rain slicker and helped her into it, then slipped into his coat and pulled an umbrella out of the stand near the door.

Beatrix waited until they were gone, then locked the front door and walked through the back offices to the alley. From there, she knocked on the next door.

A man, as tall as he was wide, with food clinging to his mustache, opened the door. He looked her up and down and then smiled.

But whatever he was thinking vanished when Beatrix said, "Mr. Brockman is expecting me."

"You're that fortuneteller lady from next door, right?"

He put out his hand, and Beatrix turned it over, studying it, then the cuff of his shirt, and then his eyes.

"I don't read palms, sir, but if you want advice, I suggest you stop smoking cigarettes, especially in bed."

"Um, what? H-how did you know that?"

"It is a parlor trick, my friend. You seem to be a man who indulges in sensual pleasures, from the drops of whiskey on your shirt cuff to the yellow tinge of nicotine on your fingernails.

Someone who also loves food might relax in bed and smoke."

In her mind, Beatrix could see his rotund intoxicated body surrounded by flames but knew it would be of no use to tell him this. Perhaps her warning might change his ways.

The bear of a man laughed and opened the door wider.

"The boss said you were sharp. Parlor trick? Sure, that's it. Just last night, my old lady said she'd skin me alive if she saw me smoking in bed again. Mr. B's in the office." He motioned to the glass-enclosed room on the far side of the illegal gaming house, as bookmakers and poker players, who'd stopped when she came in, resumed their diversions.

Mr. Brockman slowly rose when he saw Beatrix sliding a fat ledger into the top drawer of his desk.

"Please don't get up, John. I have news."

"From your face, I have a feeling it's not good."

"You are an astute man." She sat across from him at the immaculate desk. "Major Davies is scheming to cheat you and Andrew Higgins."

"Along with the citizens of the United States of America?" Brockman said.

"Yes. And to line his own pockets in the process. There are two sets of accounting books, and you were shown the ones indicating that the boatyard was prospering. You may hear, through the grapevine, a version of the truth. But I want to explain all that transpired."

"Higgins in on this?" Every word coming from his wrinkled mouth made him look as if he'd just tasted bitter fruit.

"No, John. Andrew Higgins's fault is that he hired a young woman who was down on her luck and allowed herself to be manipulated by the major."

"She's at fault?" Brockman said.

"I believe Georgianna Cartier didn't mean for this to happen to you. You were not her target."

"I have a mind to call the governor right this moment and get the state police to drag that traitor Davies to jail."

Beatrix stood and leaned across the desk to touch John's hand.

"Please say, *I can wait*. Miss Cartier made a mistake by falling for lies told by a dashing Army officer. Other mistakes were made that are worth finding out about."

"I can wait," he repeated in a monotone voice and then quickly shrugged. "I can wait, but I'm going to call Andrew right now and set up a meeting. I like that boy. Always have. Good spunk in him, and I want to help him. No damn reason not to get him the money today. You are much appreciated, Beatrix."

She walked three paces toward the door before turning.

"I have a question, John. And since you know more about the happenings in our city than anyone, I hope you'll be honest with me."

"Haven't any reason not to, Beatrix. Especially since you have the gift."

"Is there a contract out on my life?"

"What?" Brockman rose with a swiftness Beatrix had underestimated, and before she knew it, he was at her side, looking into her eyes. "You? Because you've warned someone against something? Who would do this?"

"Do not be distressed," she said. "It's been less than a year since I've since learned that I was adopted as a toddler. I was born in New Orleans, and that's my reason to be here."

"You've come to find your heritage, and perhaps your inheritance? Your birth parents?"

His brow knitted. *How can someone want to kill a woman for seeking her kinfolk?*

"No, it's not that I want to find long-lost family," she said. "Rather, I am simply seeking answers that must come from my birth mother, if she is alive. Such as, why she thought she needed to give me up. I do not blame her. The most courageous thing a woman can do is attempt to give their child a better life."

John pulled a flask from a closet and offered it to Beatrix.

"Don't often touch the stuff myself, but you look a bit pale."

She shook her head. "I rarely confide in others, John. But

you have been honest and helpful to me."

He returned to sit behind his desk, and Beatrix lowered herself into the visitor's chair again.

"I was not quite three when Jennie and William Randolph Patterson adopted me from Poydras House," she said. "Unfortunately, they died some years ago, without ever revealing my adoption. But on her deathbed, my aunt gave me a christening certificate. The place of birth was here in the Crescent City. I have a strong intuitive feeling that my mother is alive, although I've been wrong before. But if there are still people here who may have known her, perhaps they will have the answers to my questions."

"Why not use your gift, then, to find her," John said.

"I cannot find people with it unless they want to be found," she lied.

"She does not want to be found, then. Is this true of anyone looking for her? Or is it you, my dear, whom she is avoiding?"

"Exactly. I do not know."

John's thin lips became invisible, and his boney chin jutted out.

"Inquires will be made. Nobody in this city does anything without one of my men knowing about it."

"I just want information, John. Is this understood?"

"It's not like I'd have her kidnapped and brought to you in shackles or anything." He smiled.

Beatrix knew that was exactly what John wanted to do, and misguided as that might be, she appreciated his friendship even more.

She stood, and John followed suit.

"The harm that is intended for me may have nothing to do with my birth mother. But as much as I've tried, I cannot unravel this mystery or figure out why other situations have changed my future."

He patted her hand. "We'll get to the bottom of this. As for that secretary or bodyguard you have ..."

"Thomas Ling."

"Yes, Ling. Do you trust him?"

"With my life."

"I hope you are right, Beatrix Patterson. If what you say is true, you could have, instead, put that conviction to a test and hired the man trying to kill you. Be careful."

CHAPTER 8

AT FIRST, BEATRIX DISMISSED the feeling that she was being watched. Yet, for a sliver of a second, she considered if she should take John's caution to heart.

The late afternoon clouds suddenly disappeared, and the city, for the first time since Beatrix had arrived in the summer, seemed to be breathing again. Rather than heading to the office just next door, she walked toward the river, now cluttered with warehouses, trucks, and workers lifting supplies and moving materials all meant for the war effort. The air felt free, and she stood at the base of Canal Street and looked over Eads Plaza, dedicated to John Eads, an engineer who cleared the silt out of the port city.

She walked the promenade, trying to stop the constant wrestling match in her head about who would want to harm her. *Not everyone is happy when learning their truths. Should I have told Thomas about the threats? Or John? The police?*

The thoughts tangled more, and the knot tightened. Then she felt eyes on her, boring in, even as the sun warmed the back of her maroon wool jacket.

"Penny for your thoughts, lady?"

She jumped and swung around. "Ohhhh. Thomas."

"I've been trying to send you telepathic messages to see if you want to share some dinner with me." He smiled.

It was the first time she'd seen him genuinely smile. It relaxed his entire face.

"My apologies," she replied. "I was deep in thought."

"About Mr. Brockman and his circumstances?"

"No. Rather, it's a personal matter. Shall we walk further?"

Thomas pulled the black wool fedora a bit lower to cover his eyes, bone tired of being suspected as a Japanese spy by every second citizen.

"I have been told that I am a good listener," he said.

"As am I. So tell me, Thomas, about your family, and do they know that you've become a courier for the Chinese government?"

"Beatrix Patterson asking me a question when she can easily read my thoughts?" He laughed and nudged his shoulder against hers.

She nudged back. "I dislike knowing everything about everyone. We all deserve to have secrets and you ought to keep some to yourself."

Beatrix found comfort in Thomas's closeness, even if she didn't want to pursue that concept at all.

"I cannot even imagine the things you have heard, come to know, and can tell about people," he said. "Are you often shocked? Does it ever overwhelm you?"

They reached the warehouses and a federally restricted area, so they turned and headed back toward the French Quarter.

"I don't sleep well, if that's what you are asking," she replied.

"I did at one time," he said. "It seems eons ago, rather than weeks, back when I was merely a physicist at Oxford. Although, then I felt sleep was a waste of time. I understand Dr. Einstein sleeps ten hours a night, and even takes naps during the day. Often, when working on an especially problematic equation, I'd walk through the city, getting lost in the towers and my thoughts. It wasn't unusual for me to realize I was in Market Square, oblivious that I was standing right where the vendors were attempting to put out their stock."

"You gave that up to become a courier?" she said.

"My ancestors came from the Canton region of China, and some distant relatives still live there, but I have never been. Its people are my family."

"The errand you completed was done because you are a patriot?" she said.

"If you had not told me you were no longer reading my mind, I would accuse of you of ridiculing me. No, I felt anxious to do my part for the war effort. Of course, I thought of joining the British Army or Navy. I tried, and was shocked when a kindly enlistment officer said, 'With your face, young man, you will have written your obituary the second you put on an English uniform.' He told me to get out of his office and not to come back. Then a colleague, twice my father's age, told me he was asked to transport a document to New Orleans and pick up another in an appointed spot only then to be transferred to another courier. He'd had a mild heart attack and begged me to take his place. I still do not know why, but I snapped at the opportunity."

"Too many Humphrey Bogart movies?" she said.

"That is simply unfair, as you are now reading my mind." Thomas laughed. "It's true. There is little adventure in calculations and formulae. And as for social contact? Even less. Although, I do mentor and instruct graduate students, and teach basic mathematics in order to see the scholars of the future. I am hoping, when I return to England—if there is a safe way to manage that—that the work I began with developing alternative fuels from atoms might find interest with the War Department. It sounds like madness now, but there will be a time when fossil fuel such as oil will be scarce, should countries who become the main producers recommence their religious wars, once this confounded war ends. Unless the planet is destroyed in the process, that is. I have the utmost respect for a fellow scientist, Cedrick Klein, who is now living in Venezuela and working on similar theories as I am, on how there could be a time in the future when wind and sun power will be harnessed. It is one of the most exciting technologies of this decade. If I were to predict the future, Beatrix—which, of course, is your area of expertise—I would say sun power will someday provide more than enough electricity to light even cities like New Orleans."

"Dr. Cedrick Klein? You met him in Berlin when you studied there?"

Thomas gazed at a group of servicemen heading toward the bars on Decatur Street. The area smelled of spicy gumbo, jambalaya, and crab etouffee, And somewhere, a trumpet played a soulful Dixieland medley. The city had suddenly embraced Thomas in a way he'd never expected, and he felt as if New Orleans was much like an aunt who was wild and crazy and wore too much make-up, perfume, and rouge, but he wanted to be with her, no matter what.

"Thomas? Dr. Klein? Do you know him?" Beatrix stopped and turned to him.

"I'm sorry. I must be more fatigued than I realized. We scientists often drone on and on to others in the field, but not like I have just submitted you to. It is probably because we rarely wield guns, break into houses, and do the work of forensic accountants. Yes, Cedrick and I, before the war, encouraged each other with our findings. It was an intense and exciting time in my life, and I believe in his also. He, his wife, and their youngsters fled Berlin when the Nuremburg Laws were instituted in 1935. Do you know much about this terrible time?"

Beatrix shook her head.

"On September 15, 1935, the Nuremberg Race Laws were instituted in Nazi Germany," said Thomas. "Since Hitler's rise to power in early 1933, Jews in German society had been subjected to increasingly discriminatory legislation, which mainly restricted their public rights. The Nuremberg Laws, however, went further still in alienating the Jewish population from mainstream society, and even dictated on private matters such as relationships. Under these laws, a system was devised that defined whether a person was Jewish, according to their ancestry, rather than their religious beliefs and practices. Anybody with at least three Jewish grandparents, or with just two Jewish grandparents, but who was religious or married to a Jew, was deemed wholly Jewish under Nazi law. Everyone categorized as such was stripped of their German citizenship, disenfranchised, and forbidden to marry or to have sexual liaisons with non-Jews. An extension of the laws in November 1935, also made it illegal for Roma, or people of black ethnicity, to have relationships with gentile Germans."

Thomas realized he'd stopped walking and then looked directly into Beatrix's eyes, which seemed to understand, even when he wasn't clear to his own self.

"A vicious time to be an academic, an internationally recognized scholar, or a Jew," he said. "It still is, as I am tragically aware."

Beatrix watched his face.

"Oh, my goodness, I am lecturing to you again. Forgive me. You are the woman who can know the minds of anyone. I have just been using my professor's voice to talk with a *wu*."

"Thomas." She touched the sleeve of his gray gabardine suit jacket, expecting that he might flinch since he'd just called her a witch, but he did not. "I do not know how it is to live in such fear, as many Jews have. I cannot imagine how they risked their lives to flee the Nazis and travel the Atlantic, which is filled with U-boats and submarines, to settle in Central and South America with their family."

"As you said, it is a terrible time," he replied.

"It is becoming worse, Thomas. How well do you know Dr. Klein?"

"We met for tea a few times, when I did my doctorial work in Berlin in the early thirties. But we have continued regular correspondence—as limited as the mail is between Britain and Venezuela—during these last few years. Why?"

"Through a contact, I have just gotten word that your friend and his family have been rounded up and deported here to New Orleans."

"Here? In the city?"

"In the now refurbished Army camp across the Mississippi that they are calling Camp Algiers."

"This is lunacy. Cedrick is an academic, a great man of

science, and a Jew. I thought—no—I heard on the radio that only the unfortunate American Japanese were being incarcerated."

"My contact has been informed that the United States is so frightened that Hitler's Nazis may invade and overwhelm the governments in countries like Venezuela, Nicaragua, and Honduras, that the FBI has been called in to expose German-speaking immigrants who supposedly have Nazi connections. This is true, especially for the Jewish immigrants who fled Nazi Germany or escaped the horrors of the concentration camps and simply wanted to live at peace in a new country. My government is calling it the Enemy Alien Control Program."

Thomas slammed his fist against an iron lamppost, swore, and yelped from the pain. Not one person in the French Quarter even looked his way.

"That is the most asinine approach to keeping America safe that I have ever heard," he said. "God help us all if we resort to this type of discrimination. It seems no better than what the Nazis are doing in Germany, and we Brits and the Americans are fighting against that cruel bigotry and unspeakable intolerance."

"I felt you should know." Beatrix took a lace-trimmed handkerchief out of her clutch purse and wrapped the cotton around Thomas's bleeding knuckles.

He barely noticed, his face stony with anger.

"Listen, Thomas, there is something we can do."

"We can do? They are in a prison right across the river. I am certain armed guards are locking them up at night and doling out indecent food not fit for rats. The only thing missing here, as opposed to those trapped in Germany and the countries Hitler has invaded, is that, God willing, the people incarcerated there will not be slaughtered or sent to gas chambers for their religious beliefs."

"Absolutely not," she said. "Breathe for a moment, please. There is something we can do."

He tilted his head and looked at Beatrix. "You are willing to help Cedrick, and you do not even know him?"

"Is he not your colleague? Your friend?" Her brow was knit

as she led him into a small café on Decatur Street. "Come, we will have a meal and a glass of wine. But alas, the wine will not be from France. I want to talk over a plan."

Thomas pulled out a wrought-iron chair at a tiny table inside the café and sat across from his employer. He looked around, suspicious of the eyes on him, an Asian, about to share wine and dinner with a woman of Beatrix's beauty.

He blinked. Had he not noticed her smooth, pale white skin or the freckles sprinkled across her nose and cheeks? Had he missed the glistening auburn hair that sparkled with red in the lights of the restaurant as she removed the black cloche hat, her curly bog now slightly flattened to her head?

"You are staring at me, Thomas?"

"You must know why, if you can examine my thoughts."

He felt a warmth around the collar of his starched white shirt, and while he should have, and normally would have, been embarrassed, he simply couldn't stop looking at Beatrix.

The lie came out before she could stop it. "I should have told you. It is like a faucet in the kitchen. I can turn on my ability to perceive thoughts, and then turn it off."

"That is silly." He laughed, and to his ears, he sounded like a schoolboy talking to a girl for the first time.

"Yes." She laughed with him. "There's much of my gift that is downright ridiculous and trivial, but it can also be dangerous."

It felt as if someone had thrown icy water on him.

"Dangerous?" he said. "You mean, like that bully Howard about to attack you when we entered his filthy house?"

"And sometimes because people believe I know things about them or others, that can be useful for their own benefit."

Conversation stopped as the server took their order for the house red wine, bread, and the soup du jour. When it arrived, Beatrix broke the hot, crusty French bread and handed the loaf to Thomas, then breathed in the soup's steam.

"My Uncle Charlie—you may know his name, Charles de Gaulle—always made bouillabaisse better than this when my family and I stayed with him at his vineyard in the South of France, near the port town Marseille, and later, just for me, when as a teenager I stopped in Paris."

"You are related to the freedom fighter? *The* Charles de Gaulle?"

"The *uncle* is a term of endearment. I fear for him now, Thomas, and know absolutely no way I can help, except to assure him that Hitler and the enemies of freedom will eventually be defeated." *Could hope mixed with tears and lies produce truth?*

Thomas had been lifting a spoonful of fragrant broth to his mouth but stopped in midair, and then the spoon clunked to the bowl.

"You know the ending of the war?" he said.

"Yes." Beatrix looked away as tears sparkled in her green eyes, as this is what she told herself would happen so many times that it felt like the truth.

"Hitler's forces are overpowered?" Thomas said. "The Japanese surrender?"

"The future will see heavy casualties, I am afraid, and countless soldiers will never forget the horrors of the war."

He gripped her hand that lay on the white tablecloth.

"If words matter," he said, "I am so sorry."

She shook her head, snapping it as if coming out of a trance, and pulled her hand away.

"To keep my sanity," she said, "I spend time each day meditating on the decent, uncomplicated joy that can still be found in the world."

"Good in the world?" Thomas said.

"With people like you. You risked your life for the good of a country you have never set foot in because you belong to it in your heart. Now you want to do something to help your colleague. Let us pretend we are old friends, just for this time together, and we will finish this soup, eat more bread, and have another glass of wine. Perhaps we can laugh. Or merely talk about the weather."

"I would like that." He smiled. "The British are obsessed with talking about the weather. But let's start with my family, instead." He told her their names and gave a snapshot story about each that made her laugh. "I do not know if my large Chinese family resembles other Chinese families, but we always talk on and on about how the four of us children gave my parents premature gray hair. My grandmother—oh, you would like her, I am sure—lives with us, and she always tells outrageous stories of when she was a girl. My father continues to be shocked by it all, or he pretends that he is, and Mum just laughs. And we talk about the weather a lot."

"Let's get right to your confessions on the terrible things you did as a boy. Once we are back at the office, I will tell you what I have in mind."

The evening was unusually mild as they strolled from the café. Beatrix unbuttoned her suit jacket, revealing a lacy white blouse that seemed in total opposition to her no-nonsense suits.

"I can almost pretend we're walking in Paris," she said.

Thomas tried to concentrate on anything except the blouse.

He said. "It won't ever be the same, will it, now that the Nazis have invaded that jewel of Europe."

"She will survive," Beatrix said.

"There are times when I truly long to believe your words as the absolute truth. And then other times ... well—"

"That I am a witch or a liar."

"Yes. But then, perhaps—like in that story my grandmother read to me, about the wizard and a place called Oz—you are the good witch, and your lies somehow help people."

"I like that image much better than someone who must wear a tall, pointed black hat and fly around on a broom stick," she said.

Thomas laughed, and Beatrix joined him. They slowly quieted until they simply enjoyed the tranquility before reaching the office on Royal Street.

Thomas flicked the lock and turned on the lights.

He closed the door. "Now, tell me about your plan to find Dr. Klein."

"We will go to Camp Algiers and ask for the scientist."

"That is your plan," he snapped, eyes wide and mouth agape. "We waltz in there and ask guards—who would chew me up and spit me out for looking anything like a Japanese enemy— to simply take us to someone who has been accused of being a German sympathizer?"

"My dear Dr. Ling. That is the only thing to do. But if you will remember, Major Davies wants me to locate the supposed Nazi cell here in New Orleans. What better way to gather information and psychically evaluate the truth than to interview those in the internment camp? First thing in the morning, I'll arrange for us to have a military pass sent by Major Davies, to the offices at Camp Algiers."

"This for Dr. Klein and his family?" said Thomas. "Do you suppose that he could have information on potential Nazi sympathizers within the dormitories at the camp?"

"It's late, Thomas. I believe the information we gather tomorrow will be useful on many levels, so please do not trouble yourself. My goals at the camp are to ascertain how Dr. Klein is being treated, and to see if there can be a way to free him and his family. But you will have to see that he trusts me. I am a *wu*, after all."

"The Torah speaks of such things," Thomas said, "but Dr. Klein is a man of science. I doubt he will be concerned at all with your reputation or worry that you might cast a spell or hex him and his family."

She nodded. "Still, Thomas, after all they've been through— being seized in Venezuela, arrested for nothing except that they were speaking German in a Spanish-speaking country, and taken captive, forced on a ship, and manhandled into the barracks— he will need your assurance. He will be frightened, as will his wife and children, and will believe no one but you. I want to talk with some of the other inmates at the camp. Perhaps pretend to read their palms, as a way to gather information."

Beatrix knew he deserved an explanation because what she was going to do tomorrow was sheer trickery.

"You see, most people prefer that I *see* something when

I'm predicting their futures, and the palm is simply a vehicle to let me do it. It is far less frightening than me twisting this ruby and telling someone, like you, that if you finish drinking that whiskey you have in your room, you will have a terrible headache in the morning."

Thomas shook his head. "You've been in my room and saw the bottle?"

"But if you get the whiskey now, we can have a nightcap before I leave."

"Right. But from your carnival act, how will you gather information from people at the internment camp for Dr. Klein and his family to escape, and even more, about the Nazi cell here in the city?"

"I will. You don't doubt me, do you, Thomas?"

"Doubt a *wu*? I imagine that would be dangerous. I will retrieve the bottle, if you will get the glasses, Beatrix."

They stood in silence, sipping, gazes meeting and then darting away.

Thomas said, "Should I walk you home? It's getting late. You asked that I provide security for you."

"No, no thank you. But would you kindly hail me a cab. I will return at ten, Thomas, and everything should be arranged by then." She placed the empty glass on the tea table. "Whatever I tell people tomorrow, you must agree as if you already know this. Do not look surprised."

"I will be detached and unreadable, like the impenetrable people of my race are said to be."

Beatrix was still chuckling as she climbed into the taxi.

"You might want to practice that very skill this evening, Thomas. So far, even without my gift, you're pretty much an open book when it comes to emotions. Look in a mirror to see if you can be the inscrutable Asian you hope to be."

With Beatrix safely in the taxi, Thomas took the stairs to his room, leaving the whiskey on the tea table. For the hundredth time, he thought, *Why does Beatrix need a bodyguard? I understand she'll need me tomorrow to speak German to the immigrants, but when we met, she specifically said I was to protect her. From what?*

He paced the rooms, straightened the clothing now in the closet, and then switched off the light. But still, he wrestled with these thoughts for hours.

Beatrix reached her address on Audubon Place in the Garden District. The current housekeeping staff, as instructed, had left a dim porch light on and drawn all the curtains since the blackout was mandated to protect the city.

Walking up the broad front steps, Beatrix felt eyes on her back. She flipped around and heard a rustle in the bushes.

"I know you're there," she called out. "I know what you want." But that was a lie.

It won't be long before they act, and perhaps I should be the one keeping the gun, not Thomas.

CHAPTER 9

February 19, 1942

MAJOR DAVIES GRUMBLED when he stubbed a toe after getting out of bed, again when he cut himself shaving, and once again when he was discovered by his wife having yet another cigar. She had forbidden him to smoke.

He snuggled the cocker spaniel more affectionately than he did Mrs. Davies, who only got a perfunctory peck on the cheek, then reluctantly returned to his early morning phone call with Beatrix.

"Madam, if you want to ask me to do something, you do not need to call the wife of our president to get my attention."

"Eleanor said she would pass my request on to you. I simply wanted to make sure you knew exactly who I'm connected with, and that I was honest about the clout I possess. As you know, I'm planning to visit Camp Algiers this morning. And while it is a fact-gathering opportunity, frankly, there are those in the city who would like to see me incarcerated. I do not want any surprises."

"You can be assured that you and Mrs. Roosevelt will not be troubled by anything of that sort," he ground out.

"I know already, sir, that you are not above letting money become more important than your patriotism, and this is in regard to Mr. Brockman and the Higgins boat. It seems to me that perhaps your motive for asking me to locate a Nazi cell here in New Orleans could be a ploy to have me disappear."

"Hogwash, he yelled.

"I'm glad it's hogwash, but that's confusing, Major, because from what I've learned from Eleanor, the entrapment of German immigrants in Latin and South America is real and was a sift and unconstitutionally worked-out plan created by the State Department. I also know that you have close colleagues in that department who consulted you on the entrapment."

"I have no idea about what you're speaking." His voice rose higher to a squeak at the end.

"Oh? Then let me inform you about what our government is doing. You see, Major, there is a secretive program called the Enemy Alien Control Program, that is being run by the State Department, and it is illegal. It is against the law for the US to seize individuals outside the country. Consequently, it was dreamed up by some overzealous bureaucrat to get around this by refusing to issue entry visas for Latin and Central American deportees. More so, countless low-ranking minions from the FBI have gone into Venezuela, Honduras, Panama, and other countries, and offered money to anyone who outs a Nazi. To get the US money, unscrupulous people have dashed forward, turning in anyone speaking German or Yiddish. These mostly innocent people have been herded like the Nazis are doing to the Jews on their way to the gas chambers. But in this case, the immigrants are forced on ships headed to America. And upon arriving at the port of New Orleans without papers, they are denied visas. Of course, they don't have papers because they've been arrested in their homes and their businesses, and not given a chance to retrieve any documents. They have been abducted against their will. Entire families taken. Then they are arrested on the grounds that they attempted to enter the country illegally and are then subject to internment."

"This is all news to me, Miss Patterson."

"Nevertheless, humor me, Major. Imagine you amazingly manage escape from a concentration camp, try to enter the United States, are denied entry, so you go to Latin America instead, and are then kidnapped and sent to the US, only to once again live behind barbed wire, and face harassment, and even beatings, at the hands of real Nazis in a New Orleans internment camp."

"The president's wife told you this?"

"I am not to be toyed with, and I expect full access anywhere in the camp. I thought we understood this, sir. Believe me, Major, I have left a letter of instructions with a colleague that is to be sent by courier to Mrs. Roosevelt, unless I contact my friend by the end of today when I safely return to my office."

Silence on the other end of the phone.

"Do we understand one another, sir?"

"Your passes will be at the front gates of the camp, and an escort will help you navigate the quarters."

The telephone line clicked off, and Beatrix finished typing the letter that would be given to Mr. Brockman for safekeeping, as insurance perhaps, before she and Thomas left for the internment camp.

She put the letter for Eleanor in an envelope, then slipped that into a large one with a note to Mr. Brockman: *Please send the enclosed letter by courier or special delivery to Washington if I do not contact you by nightfall.* Then she dropped the letters in the bookstore's mail slot before entering her own office.

"You look like someone who is part of the Roma people, the gypsies." Thomas entered the front of the office.

"That's what I want the detainees to think. Those who see fortunetelling as blasphemy will shy away from me, which is telling in itself. Those who come forward to have me read their palms will already be ready to tell me about things in their past and problems with various inmates at the camp."

Beatrix took off the flowing, theatrical green velvet cloak with its oversized rhinestone buttons, flopped it on a chair, then removed the sensible purple scarf tied around her neck, revealing the lowcut lacy neckline of a peasant-style blouse. The scar she'd received when her parents died was even paler than her skin and just above her collarbone. She saw Thomas wince.

"An old story," she said. "And like you, some of my scars are visible, and others are kept in here." She patted her heart. "No need to be alarmed."

"That scar? Does it have anything to do with why you need protection?" He stood still, afraid that if he asked too much, she would mesmerize him, and he'd never learn about her.

Knowing her suddenly mattered.

"I suppose, in a way, it does," she replied. "You already know it is not possible of me to predict things about my own future, but that does not stop me from attempting to do so." She touched the indentation, preparing to tell Thomas the secrets that came from eavesdropping and not clairvoyance. "No, this happened when I ignored my ability and feared retaliation for using it to save others. When I look in any mirror, even when wearing a scarf around my throat, as I always do, I see it. I cannot forgive myself for failing to insist Mother and Dad make other plans instead of taking their regular Sunday drive."

Thomas rushed across the room but stopped before he touched her.

"They were killed," he said. "You were with them?"

"The executor of my parents' trust sent me to European boarding schools and summer camps in New Mexico and Maine, and a dozen other places, possibly as a way to shake my fragile self-confidence. I'll never know. Rather, I learned to keep my own counsel, depend on no one, and accept the kindness of strangers when that rarity happens."

"I am so sorry," he said. "My family is close, and I have more sisters than I can often endure."

Beatrix laughed. "I just had a fleeting image from what you said last night, about your sisters forcing you into some living-room theatrical performance. They didn't make you dress up and dance, did they?"

"They also captured the moment with a photo and teased me that they would show to my mates as a form of blackmail if I didn't help them whenever they needed it. It proved useful to them once, when they sneaked off to see some risqué production in London and missed the last train home. They had to call me at Eton College, my prep school. Either I could somehow find a way to get them home, or they swore they would show the photo to all of my mates."

"Your dignity was saved. Girls can be ruthless at times, Thomas. I always wanted to have sisters, to be part of a large family. There was lots of laughter in your home, is that right?"

"As the *baby*, it was often at my expense, but ..." He looked away, remembering. "Mother keeps that photo of her dressing table. She took it with them when they evacuated to the Lake Country."

Whether Beatrix was reading his mind or not, it no longer troubled him. But what did was how their friendship had grown in just three days. It was as if they'd known each other forever.

He looked out toward the street at the crowds of servicemen and women.

"It is a terrible time now, this war," he said. "It has made good people afraid of anyone who looks or sounds different."

"I fear those are the reasons that Dr. Klein and his family were kidnapped in Venezuela," she said. "They were probably heard speaking German or Yiddish, that beautiful language used by Jews in Central and Eastern Europe before Hitler's wrath came down in his attempt to obliterate those who weren't *ethnically correct*." Her voice became like steel. "Today, we will make a difference. At least for a few. Let's go gather information."

Thomas stood a bit straighter as they left the office and walked the few blocks to the Algiers Point ferry, which had carried pedestrians across the Mississippi since 1870. The mornings would find factory workers, household help, and dock hands going from Algiers to their jobs in the city. And in the evenings, drained, sweaty, and tired, they crowded back in the boat for home, only to repeat it all the next day.

Thomas and Beatrix stood in the front of the ferry, watching the river move along the black silt that once was part of the farmlands in the North, now being churned up by the growling engines before it made its way to the sea. Neither spoke, especially after seeing a few police officers get on.

With the Mississippi's swift current that day, it took nearly twenty minutes to cross the quarter mile.

"Do not expect any special treatment when we get to the camp," she said. "I will check in with the warden, show our papers, and briefly confirm our mission, which Major Davies supposedly has explained."

"Will I be able to move freely around the camp?" Thomas said as they headed east on the two-mile walk to Camp Algiers.

"I can't see why not. Your German is excellent. Mine is rusty. I will have to depend on English and the interpreter that they've assigned to me. Don't be fooled by anyone they assigned to us, Thomas. This person will be watching us so that should we choose not to tell the major everything we learn, then that will be reported to him. Therefore, our best bet is to split up."

He bent his head toward Beatrix. "If this wasn't real, it would be the plot to one of the Hollywood movies I often saw back in London."

Reaching the foreboding walls of the internment camp, both looked up at the rings of barbed wire, like a million sewing needles sticking out in all directions and circling the entire facility as if cunning criminals lurked inside. Guards were posted every twenty feet, with rifles swung across their chests.

At the steel gates, Beatrix said, "In every way, it is a prison, except there are saboteurs, spies, Nazis, and pro-Nazi sympathizers here among the innocents. Can you imagine being Jewish and knowing you could spend the entire war in a place where a flag with a swastika is proudly waving on US soil? Knowing that your relatives in Germany potentially have been exterminated because of their faith, and inmates here support that regime?"

Thomas and Beatrix did not have to call attention to their arrival. A woman in a drab, oversized green uniform hurried to open a side gate.

"Miss Patterson, welcome. I'm Willamina Jones, deputy warden here at the camp. Major Davies has assigned me as your liaison." She kept her gaze on Beatrix, who sensed what she was thinking. *This can't be the mind reader. She's a gypsy fortune-teller. Has Major Davies gone stark-raving mad?*

"This is my secretary, Dr. Ling, from China. He's fluent in German, as well as a host of other languages. So you will be accompanying me, Deputy Warden, while Dr. Ling interviews some other people of interest."

"But Miss, Major Davies told me explicitly to accompany you both, and the ... well, the ..."

"If this is a problem, please call the major and get his permission. I doubt that with the fine law enforcement you have in this internment camp, that a man of Dr. Ling's facial appearance will be seen and heard everywhere he goes, so nothing will be in secret, I can assure you."

The deputy warden gulped. "Yes, I suppose if you both talk with different people of interest, then you'll require less time here."

"Exactly." Beatrix turned to Thomas. "Thank you, Dr. Ling. If you have any questions, please come and find me. You have the list of people to talk with and can begin the investigation."

She nodded, and Thomas started his mission as she strode toward what she knew, from the signage, were the women's and children's dormitories.

"My gypsy guise, Deputy Warden, is a tool to help those who want to know their future to reveal things in the present."

The young woman's face burned. "I really didn't mean to interfere—"

"Now, introduce me to a few who are seemingly in charge."

"No one is in charge except Uncle Sam's Army, and the warden, and me." The retort came in a series of huffs.

"It's truly commendable, in our current sexist society, that you have become a deputy warden of the camp. I appreciate that you're in charge. Nevertheless, do not offend me with this twaddle. We all know that in captivity, bullies who want to lead, rise to the top however they can."

"Yes, ma'am, you're right." She seemed to be placated by

Beatrix's compliment and swung back the door to a room the size of a barn, with cots every two feet and scores of women huddled in small groups, waiting.

But for what?

"Listen up," the deputy warden said in a high German dialect, which Beatrix had studied while in a boarding school outside Geneva.

It wasn't used by most people, and the clusters of women most likely only understood a few words. Yet, the young woman didn't seem to notice the quizzical looks on the detainees' faces.

"This is a visitor who has volunteered to give palm readings. The warden says that in your homeland, you like to have gypsies, fortune-tellers, visit you. So the US government arranged to have this lady come here today."

Beatrix greeted them first in conversational, basic German. She smiled, and there was relief on many faces. Then she continued in English.

She turned to the warden. "Is there a quiet place where a few of these ladies and I can sit? Then you can arrange for the next group to come to me when the first ones have had their fortunes read."

The deputy warden was going to sputter, but she heard from the major how Beatrix could read her thoughts and now experienced it.

"Give the psychic anything she wants," had been the order.

So she replied, "There's a small classroom at the back of the dormitory that can be used."

Throughout the day, Beatrix met with the female detainees, many with babies nursing at their breasts. She held their hands, telling the majority that they would see their families again. For some, they realized being reunited meant Heaven, and Beatrix was honest as they cried and hugged her. For others, she assured them there was always hope, perhaps even to return to the Fatherland, or perhaps back to their adopted Central or South American homelands. She did not tell them that the Germany they'd once knew would be in ruins or that there could still

139

be animosity toward them in the Spanish-speaking countries they had escaped to before being rounded up by the State Department.

Sometimes the news was better. And with one young girl, Beatrix felt an immediate connection with the child, perhaps because she'd seen a worried look in her own eyes at about that age.

"Tell me, Zoey, do you enjoy reading?"

"Reading fortunes?" The girl's English was nearly accent-free, and she looked at Beatrix with bright brown eyes as if she were a puzzle as she tucked a thick book under her arm, hiding the title.

Beatrix laughed. "Oh, you're teasing me. I meant, reading books."

Zoey replied, "Oh yes. In the library is a lovely set of encyclopedias, and I can sit for hours and read. That makes me happy." She revealed the book, and it was the volume marked *K*. "I am alone here, so it isn't like at home when Mama would scold me for reading, and I had to do chores. We still have chores here, like scrubbing everything and keeping the grounds raked, but a few of the ladies, not the angry ones, tell me to go have fun. They insist that they will do my work." A smile cleared the worry from her freckled face, and then she frowned. "I miss Mama and Papa. I even miss the boy who lived next door to us in Berlin. But once the government said Jews were bad, we were not allowed to play, or even talk anymore."

"I am certain you are missed, too, child, including by that boy you lived near." Beatrix held her hand." I have lovely news for you. This might not make sense right now, but please continue to read and study science and be brave." With her index finger, she drew lines on the child's palm. "I see you attending a great university someday, and achieving a prestigious degree, especially with your ability in languages. You speak impressive English, and of course, German—"

"I also speak Polish and Russian. My parents wanted to make sure that I could live anywhere I wanted after the war is over.

They did not expect that to be this place called New Orleans."

"Since you speak so many languages, you will be of a great help to this country. You will be reunited with your parents, too."

"Mama and Papa? How can that be? I do not know where they are. Everyone was shoved into big, ugly gray ships. I was dragged one way, and they were pulled in another. I have cried every day since we were separated, and I can still hear Mama's screams when the police pulled us apart."

"Write down your full name and where you lived in Germany, and your parents' names. Let me see if they can be found. I have many friends who like to help me when I ask."

Beatrix felt certain that the First Lady would come to this child's aid. And if not, there were others who felt indebted to the psychic.

The girl wiped tears from her eyes. "I have been praying for them. May I tell you a secret?" She looked both ways and then whispered, "I am afraid here. Some women are mean, and they hurt the sweet ladies who are so gentle and kind to me. I do not know what to do."

Just as the deputy warden returned, reeking from her cigarette break, Beatrix took the girl's arm, "The child and I are going to walk to the restrooms. You will prefer to stay here rather than hear us use the facilities, and then you can enjoy whatever gossip you can learn from the women, or perhaps have another smoke."

"I do not need to visit the toilet," Zoey whispered in Beatrix's ear.

"Quiet, please. I need to ask you something." Beatrix led the girl into the washroom, bent down to make sure all the stalls were empty, then put her body against the door so no one could enter. "Of the women in your dormitory," she whispered, "and those you know from eating in the mess hall, can you write down the names of those you are afraid of?"

Zoey wrote five names, then pointed at the one on the top.

"She hurts some of the ladies when they do not pledge their

allegiance to the Third Reich, to their 'Fatherland,' although it is against all the rules of the camp to do so. This is done in secret. I am fifteen, but they think that I don't notice since I'm small and short for my age."

"Have you seen these women talk with any of the men at the camp?"

"The guards, you mean?"

"Yes, the guards. Do you know the names of any of the guards that the women especially talk to?"

Beatrix had seen a few of the women primping their hair and smoothing what looked like silk stockings, a day's wages even in New Orleans' black market, and definitely not for the incarcerated.

"Not the guards," Zoey replied, "but another man. This one has gray hair and is round. Too round to be a soldier."

"What of the German men? Do they like to talk with those men?"

The girl looked around. "A few, but they are like boyfriends and husbands. They don't do the visiting in secret."

"Please believe me. No harm will come to you in this camp, or when you are transferred to another camp where your parents are, probably. It may be in a place called Mississippi, which is also America, but you will be treated better. Thank you, my dear young friend. You have been incredibly helpful to the cause of freedom."

"You are a pleasant lady. I hope what you say is true." The girl was quiet for a moment as she looked in the distance. "May I tell you another secret? I want to be a scientist and invent things, and maybe even travel to the moon, or at least help people do that. Papa always told me it was a silly fantasy."

"Your dreams can come true. I promise you. You must not give up. Mr. Roosevelt is the president. I bet you know that. Do you know his wife's name?"

Zoey slowly shook her head as the two left the washroom but stood quietly in the shade of one of the wooden buildings.

"She's a smart and well-educated lady," said Beatrix. "Her

name is Eleanor. She once told me something that reminds me of you. Mrs. Roosevelt said, 'You gain strength, courage, and confidence by every experience in which you really stop to look fear in the face. You are able to say to yourself: I lived through this horror. I can take the next thing that comes along.' You've lived through a lot, and you're a warrior now."

"Don't you want to visit with other prisoners—um, I mean detainees?" said the deputy warden.

"I have done well so far," Beatrix said. "I believe it's time that this young woman returned to her reading."

Zoey dashed off.

"I would like to interview the warden. Or do you call him the commandant."

"Impossible." The woman huffed.

"On the contrary, you may recall that Major Davies said I was to have access to everyone."

"I'm sure he's too busy to meet with you." She moved backward as if she could get away from Beatrix's eyes.

"Let's ask him together, then, Deputy Warden. Is there something you'd like to tell me about the things that are happening in the camp? Like known Nazis being housed in the same buildings, in the same rooms as Jewish immigrants they persecuted and attempted to exterminate when they were in Germany? What of the events where the staff turns their backs when there is known bullying, abusing, and torturing of the Jewish detainees? Is that what you're going to tell me about?"

CHAPTER 10

"WHATEVER DO YOU MEAN? Everything is run by the book. Why ever would you think there's a problem with intimidation and mistreatment in the camp?" The deputy warden's face became blotchy, and she stiffened, once more giving herself away.

Beatrix stared long and hard into the woman's eyes.

"Tell me what you know about the women who are browbeating the Jewish detainees, especially the frail older women and their children. If I touch you like this," she laid a finger on the deputy warden's green wool jacket, "you cannot lie to me."

A lie, but the woman believed her.

"We can't help it. There's not enough room in the camp to separate the Jewish people from the Nazi sympathizers. We have to house them all together. Even the warden says this has to be, in order to save money for the war effort. He and the German ladies like to visit, and they visit a lot. I sometimes believe that one big blonde you saw in the dormitory is blackmailing the warden. But that can't be. It would be so wrong." She darted her eyes darted in each direction as if she might be overheard.

Beatrix said, "He visits with the women who are Nazi sympathizers? The blonde one is a particular *guest* of the warden? Does she get special privileges?"

"Yes."

"Tell me about that, Deputy Warden. Remember, I will know if you're lying, and I will report that to Major Davies."

"Yes, ma'am. Please be quiet about this. The warden works late, telling all of us on staff that he has mountains of paperwork to do. But one night, when taking over a shift for another officer, I could hear music coming from his office."

"Everyone likes music. What else did you see? Please tell me. I know there's more."

"I left my duty station and peeked in the window through a crack in the blinds. The warden and the woman were drinking and dancing."

"Everyone likes a good time. Is there more?"

"Yes. The warden was just wearing a T-shirt and boxer shorts. And that woman, the one you asked about, was in her slip. I felt dirty after I snapped a photograph and turned at once to leave. I was going to give it to the warden's superior officer with the police department. That's when someone hit me. A brick or a pipe, right here." She removed her hat and touched the back of her head. "Hurt like the dickens, I can tell you. When I came to, the camera had disappeared and there was a huge lump on my head."

"Your truth has helped me. Why do you suppose the warden turns his back on how the sympathizers are persecuting and tormenting the Jewish women and children, who through the fault of the FBI, were kidnapped and dragged to the US? Has he turned a blind eye to the pro-Nazi detainees hanging a flag with the swastika there in the dormitory?"

"I, um ... he says that's what has to happen to keep peace here at the facility."

"He's being controlled by whoever has those photos," Beatrix said. *No need to be a psychic to understand that.* "What special privileges does the warden give that woman and others? Are the detainees allowed to leave the compound?"

Somewhere close, she could hear Thomas's voice.

"One or two," said the deputy warden. "And most of the Nazi women leave on Friday evenings, all dressed up, lots of perfume."

Beatrix snapped her fingers, and the deputy warden,

although not hypnotized, immediately became all business again. "As I have been trying to tell you, Miss Patterson, the warden is far too busy to see you."

"I have enough information now. By the way, is that Evening in Paris perfume you're wearing?"

The woman sighed. "A gift from my sister. At my paygrade, I can barely afford the basics."

"Yet it seems you have sheer stockings."

Thomas, as expected, turned the corner, and the deputy warden looked relieved that she didn't have to alibi how her sister could have afforded such luxuries.

His face was pinched, and his dark eyes jetted from one direction to another.

He said, "It's urgent that we speak privately, Miss Patterson."

Beatrix turned away from the deputy warden and stepped out of earshot.

"Cedrick Klein is fine," Thomas said. "As fine as can be expected in captivity. He's most worried about his wife and daughters, as there are strange things happening, including making the weaker detainees in that group swear allegiance to Hitler, along with being harassed or abused. We did not have a chance to discuss that because an Asian and a Jew talking drew too much attention."

"I learned of detainees coming and going," Beatrix said, "seemingly on their own schedule, and being brutal to the Jewish women as well." She scowled. "Why in the world didn't I just ask John Brockman if there was anything odd going on at the camp?"

"I assume that is rhetorical question," Thomas said. "However, since I do not read minds, do you think your Mr. Brockman is involved in the Nazi spy cells here in the camp?"

"He is not *my* Mr. Brockman. And the answer is definitely no."

"You sound sure."

"Mr. Brockman may be many things, from political kingpin and influencer of city officials to bookmaker and money launderer, but he has ties to his Jewish family members in New York. Without a doubt, he will know or be able to find out specifically who, other than the warden, has turned a blind eye to the power of the spy cell. This is no longer simply a misrepresentation of justice—like the FBI kidnapping people in foreign lands and transporting them to the US—this has potential to allow for the US to be invaded by Nazis if the Enemy Alien Control Program continues. This camp is a hotbed of coercion, sex trade, and active Nazi infiltrators gathering data to pass to a pro-German underground, and then on to officers sailing the U-boats in the Caribbean. The warden is nothing more than a pawn."

"To quote your famous American mystery writer Poe," said Thomas, "'The inmates are running the asylum.' But my colleague, Cedrick, has never been a spy or a secret agent. This is ludicrous. I have failed you."

"Thomas, you have done well. Believe me. We know where Cedrick and his family are, and we will rectify matters. You've told him that I will help?"

Thomas stared at the ground. He couldn't mention to his learned colleague that the person who possibly could help him was a *wu*.

"We talked of work, and he mentioned briefly about slim batteries that he was trying to develop that could hold current to be turned into electricity."

Thomas shoved his hands deeply into his jacket pockets. The afternoon air had turned colder.

"Suppose Major Davies is in on this?" he said.

"If he was, I doubt he would have let me come here, even though I threatened to expose his scheme for making a profit at a cost to the Higgins Company. He knows I will use my gift to stop him. The warden? Well, he has been caught with his pants down, literally." She explained how the deputy warden had snapped the compromising photos, only to have the camera snatched. "Now the photographic negatives are out there somewhere and being used to extort special treatment. It does not take a psychic to know that the warden believes he has no other options except to go along with whoever is in charge of this. I believe it goes much higher than the pro-Nazi women detainees who are now running the camp."

"We have to stop this." Thomas looked around to make sure no one was close. "It is wrong. Who do we report this to?"

"No one here in New Orleans, Thomas. I do not know who is to be trusted. I have contacts in Washington. I must talk with Mr. Brockman to assure him we have safely returned, and then from the office, make some telephone calls."

"Do you suppose these spies allowed themselves to be apprehended in South America and transported here as a plan to create saboteur cells in the city?"

Beatrix buttoned up her cape. "*You* are now reading *my* mind."

That Monday, Hitler's vendetta continued to cripple Europe, and the Pacific rim trembled with Hirohito's proclamation to conquer Asia and the United States. Widows mourned their husbands, mothers worried about their sons and daughters in war zones around the world, and orphans wailed, alone, cold, hungry, and afraid.

New Orleans, with all of its swagger, was hardly immune to the agony. Yet, underlying the dread and hopelessness the city felt, the spicy food, flowing liquor, and flashy music made it possible to carry on, despite what tomorrow might bring.

At the office, Thomas removed his jacket and sat back against the settee.

"You know you can trust me," he whispered after he'd been surreptitiously studying her for some time. *If I offer to help, will she shove me away?*

He then realized that he wanted to take his employer in his arms, and his contemplations of what might happen after that were not respectable at all.

Beatrix stared toward the door as if she expected someone to fling it open at any second and began rubbing her temples with her thumbs.

Thomas put the *Times-Picayune* newspaper next to him and was ready to spring up when her shoulders sagged, and she placed her head on the desktop.

"You *can* trust me," he said, louder this time.

"Just give me a few moments," she replied.

"Tea? Something stronger?"

She looked up. "Thomas, you asked why I hired you. I wasn't truthful."

"Will I need to get the gun? I have now learned how to load correctly, thanks to Henry, Mr. Brockman's driver."

He wanted to make her smile, which she did for an instant, and then it was gone.

"No, you will not need it right now," she replied. "Perhaps in the future."

"Are you ready to tell me why you need a bodyguard?"

Thomas got up and moved to the guest chair directly in front of Beatrix. He ran a hand over the oiled walnut wood and settled into the cushion, but his muscles stayed tense.

He said, "Is it something to do with the money you had me take to the Old Absinthe saloon or the Poydras House? Was the money for the French struggle? I assume the code words the chef wrote, about the pot boiling, meant that things were heating up in France, or with the fighting in North Africa."

"Yes, that money does go to my uncle and the French Resistance," she said. "It is so little, and I long to do more. Unfortunately, the people who run the trust for my late parents' estate, which is significant, will not release any funds to me. If I had the money, be assured it would go right to Uncle Charlie and the French freedom fighters."

"You have this." Thomas motioned around the room, indicating the antique furniture in the snug office and the good reproduction of a Monet on the wall behind her desk. "And your grand home in the Garden District? I assumed—"

"It all belonged to my aunt, before her passing. And yes, there is enough money to keep up the house and pay the lease here at the office, but for little else. You see, for the last few weeks, people have been following me."

"Who are they? Can we call the police?"

"To say what, Thomas? The local psychic, who most consider a nuisance, thinks someone might be stalking her? In these desperate times, all the law enforcement officers out there are trying to keep our country safe. And here in New Orleans, they're worried about an invasion. They're not going to have time to discuss theories with one of New Orleans' colorful characters. That's what they would think, I'm certain of it."

"Let me gather my things," Thomas said, "and I will move into your house to protect you. You should have told me before, and I would never have let you go home alone last night."

"I think that might be best."

She was about to continue with a lie about how she could read thoughts and knew something was going to happen, but it refused to come out.

Instead, she said, "I have heard from the vendors out on the street corners and those who run the shops, like the lady who sells flowers on Canal Street, that there are two or three men taking turns following me and watching me."

"Will they harm you?"

"Are you naïve, Thomas? You said you watched years of American crime movies before the war. I assume they're local thugs, but something the flower vender said has me terribly troubled."

"Do you care to explain?"

"You see, after university, I left for France and began getting letters from the trustees of the estate in California, saying that my money was gone. But that's not true. And while I have no proof that the men following me have been hired by the trustees, I know they might definitely do me harm for the millions of dollars tied up in my parents' estate."

"Again," Thomas said, "I think we should inform the police,

which is what one might do in Britain."

"Is Britain much more civilized than America?"

"You are not taking me seriously, but you must do so before you force me to use the gun against some intruder or kidnapper." Thomas hopped up to dash to his room for the gun.

"Wait." Beatrix said. "I've missed something. Oh, how stupid. My friend who sells the flowers gave me a description of one of the men."

"Good. That'll make it easier," he said.

"The opposite, actually. One of the men who has been following me for a month fits the description of Flynn Howard. The flower vendor saw him enter the office for an appointment the other day. As he lurks around in the shadows, he always wears the same worn brown suit and black wool hat he had on when he came here. He mentioned he did private security. How did I miss that?" Beatrix stared at the street.

"Oh," Thomas said. "That complicates the matters. But Howard is just one copper. You aren't implying that the entire police department, or its officials, are on the take, as they say in movies, and being paid to keep you under surveillance?"

"I've always speculated that the trustees paid someone to weaken the brakes lines of my parents' car, hoping we'd die in a fiery *accident*, so they could control all of the wealth. I cannot understand why my father trusted these men. Although, the trustees had worked for my grandfather, and that may have been the reason. The interest alone is sizeable, Thomas, and I wouldn't put it past these men. I can't prove it, and I'll never know the truth. Since I survived, there have been quite a number of other *accidents*, from being knocked into the street by a man on a bicycle, to returning to the house here in New Orleans, only to discover that the gas oven was on, but the pilot light was out. Gas had started to fill the kitchen, and if I hadn't smelled it but had simply flicked the kitchen light switch, we certainly wouldn't be having this conversation. The incidents are getting more frightening."

"Murder?" Thomas said. "Are there not better, less violent

ways for them to get the money your parents left to you? This is, after all, 1942, and not the American Wild West."

"The trustees have tried," Beatrix said. "My degree is from the University of Southern California, in the arts, a lovely pastime for a rich girl. Yet Father schooled me about finances when I barely started to read, gearing me to take over the business someday. He and Mother agreed a woman should be independent, as Mother always handled her own investments and did quite well, which I have since learned. I assume Father never told that to the men handling the trust, because after the accident, and with my parents gone, these people treated me like a recalcitrant child, a spoiled trust-fund teenager. They continued the lies that our entire estate had all been lost during the Great Depression. I hired forensic accountants who were able to tell me just where the money had been invested. The trustees did extremely well when most of our country was standing in soup lines, begging for bread, as happened in Britain. Now, the estate is significantly larger, but they're keeping the funds out of my reach."

Thomas swore under his breath.

"That brings you to the current situation," she said, "and a long answer as to why I need a bodyguard."

"Nothing can be resolved then, until, as they say in movies, you are *out of da picture*."

Beatrix laughed at Thomas's attempt to sound like a gangster.

"My attorneys in California have subpoenaed the trust's books," she said, "and they tell me it could be just a few more months for the resolution. The war has slowed things, and I wonder, at times, if they're working for me or the trust bankers."

"It is all about greed," Thomas said.

Beatrix nodded. "Money and love are civilization's greatest motivators and biggest down falls. Speaking of money, I was going to drop off some cash at Poydras House earlier today, but our errand at the internment camp took more time than I anticipated. I must write Uncle Charlie a letter, so could you kindly hail a cab, take this over to the home, and by the time you have returned, I'll be ready to leave for the day."

"Shall I leave the gun here with you?" he said.

Beatrix extended her hand. "I'll place it here in the front desk drawer. Although, if one of the men is Flynn Howard, frankly, Thomas, I don't know if I could shoot him after all he's been through with his wife. He's greedy and controlling, but I do not think he's truly evil."

"Then fire straight at his leg," Thomas said. "I will not let anything happen to you on my watch."

"Is that a quote from one of the crime movies?" Beatrix gathered some papers from the safe and withdrew another, smaller stack of money.

"Yes, and I have always wanted to use that line. But as a scientist, when not being a potential spy, little happens on my watch. The only watch I have is this one on my wrist."

The joke seemed to fall flat as Beatrix looked out the window.

"Thomas?"

He was nearly at the door but felt the pull of her voice and turned.

"There's one more thing you need to know about me," she said. "While my aunt laid dying, she told me a truth I should have always known, but never faced it. I do not know who I am."

CHAPTER 11

"YOU ARE BEATRIX PATTERSON, psychic, patriot, helper of the underserved and undeserving, amateur detective, and finder of lost things," Thomas said, trying to lighten his employer's somber mood, which looked like a gray-green cloud, the color of the sky before a massive thunderstorm.

He blinked, but the ghastly color still encased her.

What has happened to me? Why am I suddenly trying to make her smile? He refused to delve further into that perturbing notion, hiding it in a compartment of his logical brain.

"Up until Auntie laid dying," she said, "that is what seemed to be the obvious. Then she told me that my parents were not completely truthful to me. Yes, they loved me like their child, but Father was a giant of a man with sandy hair and blue eyes. Mother's family originated in Spain, and they established a huge hacienda north of the Santa Barbara area, before it was Santa Barbara, and a few came and settled here in New Orleans. My parents met here when Mother's family, from Barcelona, decided that they wanted to build a stronger American connection, and so she had her debut here in the city. Yes, it was to build a business empire, but that was how these things occurred then, apparently. Mother was lovely, with classical Latin looks, much like a model in one of Francisco Goya y Lucientes paintings. She was delicate and mysterious."

Thomas said, "Your hair is brown—no, wait—it is more auburn, and you have green eyes."

Beatrix touched her hair and had always thought it was lackluster. She'd never heard it described that way. "It was always obvious that I was not their biological child, but I never pursued the truth. It didn't seem relevant until the time came when it became clear the trustees were swindling me. I began to fight back and had to provide that the adoption was legal." She looked at her hand. "Yes," she replied. "Auntie gave me this ring and would only tell me briefly a bit more. She was in tremendous pain at the end. Even hypnotism did not stop it, and the drugs that the doctor gave her caused hallucinations. It was impossible to tell if she was conversing with Mother in Heaven or if she was just under the effects of the medications.

"Could you not have simply touched her or put her under a spell to get all the information you needed?"

"Oh, Thomas, I am able to locate things because of keen and intentional observations and I put my observations together. People typically reveal what they know. They just don't realize it."

It was the first time in years that she had explained her *gift* honestly, and a weight fell from her shoulders.

"My parents made my aunt swear she would never tell me any details, and even the small amount she shared ..." Beatrix took a deep breath and hesitated, "was what I have come to accept, because I may only think that vast Patterson holdings are mine. What if it was never official?"

"What?" Thomas said. "This is nonsense."

"Her last words, as agony distorted her body, were, 'If you want to find yourself, help the orphans.' I vaguely remember Mother talking about Poydras House. And once, when we visited Auntie here in the city, there was a party in Mother's honor, which I believe had to do with a significant financial gift she had made to the home."

"You've been through their files for foundlings and formal transfer to new parents?" Thomas said. "They must keep adoption records, right?"

"They are all sealed. Even as the daughter of their largest

contributor, I have been denied access to them."

Thomas kept his hand on the door. "Why not simply break into the records room and steal the information one night?"

"Oh, Dr. Thomas Ling," Beatrix said with the flair of a B-movie actress auditioning for a part, complete with a hand on her forehead, pretending to look aghast. "I have corrupted you completely."

"Not completely," he said. "Or as an alternative, petition the courts to allow the asylum to release the records, if there are any. If that doesn't work, then I could use my considerable Asian charm and persuade the ladies there to leave me alone in the file room."

She smiled. "Go and deliver the money. And on the way back to the Garden District, and my nearly empty house, we'll have dinner."

"Empty? Of people, I hope, and not things?"

"I have been quietly selling off the antiques to supplement the money I make from clients like Mr. Brockman."

It seemed a waste of Beatrix's money to take a cab every time he needed to go out. But as a lone Asian hurrying along the dark streets of New Orleans, the alternative could have been fatal.

The large wooden doors at Poydras House were locked, as Thomas expected. *The kitchen should be busy this time of the day.*

He walked around the building. Even with the endless wind of the night, the windows were open a bit, and laughter rang from one of the rooms where lights illuminated children playing games and dashing around as piano music bounced out.

Thomas climbed the steep back steps, and as expected, the kitchen door was open. Two women of considerable size were at a rough wooden table, shelling peas and whispering. He didn't want to frighten them, so instead of knocking or just barging in, he waited until they looked up, smiled, and spoke.

"Good evening, ladies. Miss Beatrix Patterson has instructed me to deliver an envelope to whoever is in charge."

"Miss Patterson? Oh, I remember. She's that kind lady who comes to play with the wee little ones," one of the cooks said in a lilting Irish accent that reminded Thomas of his childhood nanny. "You'd best come in from the cold, young man. The tea is there, in the pot, and I'll fetch the head mistress or her assistant."

The tea was black, and he added cream and sugar. The second cook continued to ready the vegetables but kept peeking at him.

With a crooked smile, she said, "You're a strange one."

"I suppose that is true."

She finished shelling the peas, and a practiced motion, from three feet away, tossed the shells in the trash before plunging the little bright-green spheres into a pot of boiling water. She didn't move and spoke with her back to Thomas.

"My Mama always said, a few bad people can make all people look bad. I reckon Japanese people aren't all wicked, even with what they'd done to our boys in Pearl Harbor. Can't say I never met one before you."

"Your mum was right," Thomas said, "and I suppose there are many good, kind Japanese. I am Chinese, ma'am, and like your Mama said, there are good and bad types in all races."

She went to the cupboard and took out a plate of sugar cookies, each the size of a saucer, and turned back to Thomas.

"You are too skinny," she said. "Bet you get too busy to eat, right?"

"My mum tells me the same thing every time I visit her and Dad."

"What'cha doing here?"

"At Poydras House, or New Orleans?"

"Here. Don't see many folks like you round here. Never saw any. I don't leave this neighborhood much. My family been here for a long time."

"My family is from China, but Mum and Dad and my sisters live in London. Or did, until the bombs started dropping."

"You eat cookies in China?" She pushed the plate toward him. "See, those cookies are tasty with that tea you're drinking. You drink tea in China?"

"I am a man of Chinese heritage, but I was born in England. That's why I have this English accent instead of talking like someone from the country of China. I do speak a number of Chinese dialects, and could impress you, ma'am, if you want that."

"Well, boy-oh-boy, just learned something new. I thought maybe all Japan—um, Chinese folk talked funny. You come here often?"

The lady kneaded bright white dough that would soon become biscuits, and once every few seconds, she plummeted her index finger into the mound on the breadboard. Then she smiled with satisfaction.

"Here, to Poydras House?" Thomas replied. I've been here twice. Once, Mother Adelina met me. She was kind to me." He took another cookie and saw that the cook's smile broadened. "In England, we call cookies biscuits, and the biscuits like you are making are called baking soda biscuits."

"Why, that don't make no sense. Lots in life makes no sense, and some people here just talk gibberish most of the time, like Mother Adelina. She's the oddest old lady, saying things about the future and telling everybody stuff, just like she was a voodoo priestess or something. I think she frightens the ladies. But, oh my, she be kind to the kids. That's what counts, don't you know."

"Are you saying that Mother Adelina predicts—well, tells things that will happen in future?"

Is being psychic, or even a voodoo wu, part of the culture here in New Orleans? Thomas wondered if the cook would offer to read his fortune in the tea leaves swirling at the bottom of his cup.

"Told me my old man was stepping out," she replied. "Out of the blue, she said that. You know what I did. Soon as I got home that night, I pulled out Granny's cast-iron frying pan and was at the ready when he come strutting in the front door, all polished up and in his Sunday best. Before 1 could swing that pan twice, he yells, 'I'm taking dancing lessons, honey pie, to surprise you so we can dance at our wedding.' She almost had my man's killing on her conscious. Stepping out?"

She laughed, and every ripple of fat jiggled, and Thomas couldn't help himself. He laughed long and hard and wiped away a tear.

"1 haven't felt this comfortable since before the war, since '39," he said. "I have forgotten what a home feels like. 1 miss eating biscuits—um, cookies—and being fussed over. 1 miss sitting at a kitchen table. 1 miss laughing."

He was shocked that he'd admit these thoughts to a stranger. And even more, so that he'd never realized how lonely he'd been before coming to New Orleans, and this burst of longing made him feel somehow happier, even if he was now under the spell of a witch.

He rubbed his hands together and put them around his teacup, which was being refilled.

"Perhaps it's just as well," he continued. "1 am able to focus on science. A wife and family would take away from all that."

"Honey, you might talk fancy," the cook said as if she'd known him forever, "but it makes no sense. Everybody needs a home. That's why 1 work here and make good food for the kids. They might never see their mommies and daddies again, but they know this food is made with love."

"You are an extremely intelligent woman, ma'am. You are correct. 1 am a fool."

"First, you say you're not Japanese. Then you say you're Chinese. And now you say you're a fool. Make up your mind, young man."

Once more, laughter echoed in the cozy kitchen until a shrill voice rang out in back of him.

"Dr. Ling?"

It was Veronica Howard, the alcoholic and runaway spouse of Flynn. He'd seen her photo on a cabinet in the Howard house. Her hair was tied up in a checkered scarf, and she was dressed in denim overalls, much like the Rosy the Riveter posters Thomas had seen displayed against buildings. She looked happy, unlike the stoic wedding photo.

"I'm sorry," she said, "but the head mistress and I are in a bit of a *challenge*. One of the children was acting out and decided to stop up all the toilets on the second floor. That's probably way more than you need to know, but she asked me to see if I could help you." Veronica looked down at the fresh stains on her overalls. "I'm in charge of the maintenance around here, and an old house like this always has something wrong with the plumbing."

Thomas stood up. "Mrs. Howard."

"Did Flynn send you to drag me back? I don't know what he's said he'd pay you, but he won't. He just lies and uses people. Used me. I beg you, don't tell Flynn I'm here." She grabbed his hand. "I didn't think anyone would find me or recognize me. Especially dressed like this. You won't tell, will you?" Her face grew pale, and with trembling hands, she grabbed the table.

"Miss Beatrix Patterson sent me. Not your husband. You are safe here. You are that afraid of your husband?"

After the story her husband had spun, this was a shock.

"Yes. I am ill, I know it. Some women might jump off the Huey P. Long Bridge, but I used alcohol to try to kill myself. It nearly worked. I'm not proud of what I have done, but here, I am safe. If you say anything, he'll bring the police here, or some of his buddies, and drag me out, I know it. Here, there is no time for me to feel sad for myself, and everyone is so good and kind to me. Besides, I love being with the littles."

"We want you to stay right here, too, missy." The cook grabbed her in a bear hug and then walked into the pantry.

"Is Flynn a dangerous man?" Thomas said. "I have to ask, as my employer, Beatrix Patterson, is alone in an empty office on a main street that is only busy during the day."

"Yes, when things aren't going his way. He's rough when he gets angry and frustrated." Veronica pulled up her shirt sleeves, displaying scars caused by being bound. "One night, when he came home from his second job as a security guard at the docks, he exploded. He lashed me to the bed, saying it was the only way he could stop me from drinking. But I tore at my skin and the rope with my teeth in order to escape. That was my turning point. He would have left me there forever rather than help me. I got away."

Thomas's face grew stiff. "I have no time to waste, Mrs. Howard." He withdrew the envelope from his breast pocket and handed it to her. "Miss Patterson asked that this to be given to the head mistress." He was at the door and then turned. "Can I return, if possible? Perhaps tomorrow? There are some old adoption files I would like to examine. Could you allow me to do that? It is for something Miss Patterson and I are working on."

"Yes, anything. But please don't mention that you've seen me, except to Miss Patterson. One of the ladies here always says how kind she is." Veronica tried to smile.

As Thomas flew out the door, she called. "Don't wear a nice suit. That old file room hasn't been opened in ten years." Then whispered, "Except for about a week ago, but that can't matter."

Night settled into the city like an unwelcomed houseguest, with clammy fog gripping and sticking to everything. The streets were deserted. In the distance, a siren screamed. Then dogs barked, setting others off, relaying unseen fears.

The safe house was miles from the rowdy music and lights of the Quarter, and with the blackout curtains drawn on the dilapidated houses, the district felt as appealing as cold oatmeal.

Thomas sprinted through the streets, barely looking out for cars, dashing and weaving until he eventually reached Broad Street and spied a taxi. He jumped out into the street to stop it. The cab swerved and then squealed to a halt. Yet, once the driver looked at Thomas, he spewed a string of racial expletives about Asians, then sped away, splashing mucky water all over Thomas's trousers. Thomas threw his arms in the air, adding a few Cantonese terms for uncouth human beings of disgraceful birth, and sprinted toward the office, weaving in and out of the traffic on the main thoroughfare as horns blared and drivers cursed. By the time he threw open the front door of the storefront, the shock in front of him took away what ragged breath he had left. His knees buckled, and only by grasping the door handle did he keep from tumbling to the floor next to where Beatrix was face down on the Persian carpet.

"No, no, no ..." he repeated twenty times as he knelt by her, smoothing back her auburn hair to reveal a scorching red-purple welt on her temple. "Beatrix, Beatrix, wake up." He touched her neck to check her pulse. "Thank God."

Her eyes fluttered open.

"Ouch," she groaned. "My head hurts."

Thomas turned her slightly and gingerly propped her torso against his chest.

"Do not try to talk. You have been injured. Who did this? You have to know." He could feel anger constricting his breath, souring in his belly. *It is my fault. I should have merely handed over the money and immediately returned.* "I am so sorry. Oh, my dear Beatrix, so terribly sorry."

She tried to steady herself, but the pounding in her head made her dizzy.

"Why are you sorry? Don't be silly, Thomas. Whoever did this was watching for you to leave."

"Howard? Was it Flynn Howard? The coward. I am not surprised, Beatrix. He is despicable human being."

"I don't know." She sighed. I was putting the typewriter back into the credenza, and that's the last I remember."

"Did you hear the door open?"

"No. That's strange, because I should have. Though, I did have the radio on as I typed a letter. There was more news about the Japanese families being interned in California and the government confiscating their business, shops, homes, and farms. It's getting worse. These families—most, American citizens—have done nothing, and they're being treated like criminals." She pulled away slightly. "Thomas, help me get up."

He lifted her as delicately as an infant and settled next to her on the brocade settee.

"Water? Brandy?" he said.

"A small glass of port, please. And a damp cloth to wipe away the blood."

He jumped up and did as she'd asked. "Let me clean the blood off. I think you should be seen by a doctor, Beatrix. The welt looks horrible."

"Let me rest for now and sip the drink. Get yourself one, Thomas. This has been a difficult evening."

He poured a half-inch of bourbon and then slowly dapped her head wound.

"I am not the kind of doctor to give a diagnosis, but I do think the gash needs to be stitched."

"It was not the blow to my head that caused me to black out. Someone knocked me down and then put a rag drenched with chloroform to my face. It has now evaporated, but I remember the sweet smell before I blacked out."

Thomas then told her about meeting Veronica Howard and how she'd begged to be protected from her husband.

"I knew he was violent," Beatrix said. "I felt his pain and anger." She froze. "My ring. My ruby ring. It's gone."

Thomas grabbed her outstretched hand. "That is what this thug was after. Could it have just been a random act of violence? Are your powers as a *wu* gone? Did the ring assist you in reading minds and stopping time?"

"It's okay," she said. "It was given by my birth father to my biological mother. When my parents adopted me, my aunt told me, before her passing, that it was to be given to me on my twenty-first birthday. But when they were killed, the ring came to her, and I've only had it a short time."

"Whoever attacked you was either going after the ring, which is worth thousands, or perhaps thought he would then have your supernatural powers. Who would do it?"

Instead of lying, which had become second nature, Beatrix said, "I do not know. Most likely, the intruder assumed the ring could tell the future."

"We must call the police," he said. "Report this to the authorities and let them handle it."

"When we were with Flynn, he barely kept his eyes off the ring. I would not put it past him, Thomas, to steal it, thinking it would help him find his wife. Is she okay there, at the Poydras House?"

"Yes, it seems so. And they are sympathetic to her. Make no mistake, Beatrix, she is terrified of the brut Howard."

"We have to protect her and not call the police," she said. "Please get my jacket. It's time we get some rest."

Thomas helped her into the sleeves and then straightened the shoulders as Beatrix swayed.

"We can stay here longer," he said. "You should not move yet. Or shall I carry you?"

"I need to walk." She teetered a bit and grabbed Thomas's arm, then let go in an instant.

He felt it, too. Her touch was warm through his wool suit jacket and crisp white shirt.

Both avoided eye contact.

"The letter on my desk ..."

"Yes, Beatrix. You want me to mail it? If we can hail a cab on Canal Street, there is a postal box on the corner of Saint Peters Street. I saw it yesterday."

"No, it must be given to Gillette Pierre, at the Old Absinthe House," she said.

"We have to get you home to lie down."

"The letter is too important." She straightened her spine and tucked strands of auburn hair behind her ears. "My Uncle Charles. He must flee to London and be on guard, as there's a plot by the Nazi SS to assassinate him."

"Can you not simply make a long-distance telephone call and tell him this?"

"Oh, Thomas, it is not that simple. And I am sorry to say, but the British government finds my uncle to be a thorn in their side. Many of the Parliament members have even spoken out that Uncle Charles is not welcome in England, as they're afraid the Blitzkrieg will increase their relentless bombing of London once it is known that Uncle Charles is being smuggled into the city."

"England and the king certainly would not turn him away?" Thomas said. "He is the leader of the freedom fighters for France."

"If members of Parliament thought anything could slow or stop Hitler's vengeance against England, including handing over Uncle Charles's head on a platter, they would do it."

"I do not want to believe you, Beatrix, yet it is plausible. You have not been there night after night, when the sirens scream, the German airplane engines roar, and the city is rocked by bombs. You venture out of the shelter, and the buildings you were just in are now rubble, the shops where you regularly buy food have disappeared, the sidewalks deeply pitted from the explosions. And the people? Shell-shocked—suddenly homeless and hurt emotionally and physically."

"Killing my uncle will not halt the spread of Nazism or contain Hitler. But it could gravely shift the outcome and length of time to rebuild Europe, especially in France. If he is murdered, France could easily plummet into a financial depression even greater than what was experienced in the early 1930s, pulling in the Netherlands, Belgium, and perhaps Germany once it is free of its maniacal leader. The repercussions will be felt worldwide."

She had gleaned this information from economic reports, and it seemed to be the truth.

"The fate of one man as important as your uncle, can have this effect?"

She looked at Thomas. "Haven't you ever wanted to know your future?"

CHAPTER 12

THOMAS FROZE.

What if she used her psychic gift and told how he'd die trying to defend her from some thug attempting to swindle her out of the millions tied up in her estate? What if she informed him that he would eventually make passage on a ship endeavoring to return to England, only to have the vessel torpedoed in the freezing Atlantic by a Nazi submarine? What if he did make it back to England, only to discover that previous his life was tedious and monotonous. What if he found out that science was no life at all?

He tried to mask the fear he felt from staying in the normal human condition of darkness called the future. He chuckled, but it sounded tiny, even to his ears.

"You know what will happen to me in the future, should I live through being a bodyguard to a *wu*? No, I do not want to know. Although, now that you have told me, your question will eat away my resolve. Therefore, even as a stodgy, overeducated man of science, I am, from now forward, going to accept your gift and attempt to forget your offer. But what have you told your uncle in that letter you have just finished typing, if I may be so bold as to ask?"

Beatrix sighed, not from Thomas's refusal to hear his supposed future but because she didn't need to lie to him. She'd been asking about knowing what might happen, but it had not been an invitation for a reading. Yet that's what it sounded like.

"The letter?" she replied "It is a caution. I fear this warning will not stop Uncle Charles from meeting with British officials and the French Resistance, or those who pretend to be against Nazism. But I had to warn him about a paid German assassin, because right this moment, a hunter of men is readying himself to be parachuted into England to track down and kill my uncle. If nothing more, I pray it will alert Uncle Charlie to be vigilant and to not trust some of his advisors, who I have named. I need to tell him what is at stake, should he be foolish enough to ignore my counsel. I cannot change the outcome of other's actions, nor could you. I simply want him to be on guard. It is the best I can do. Please tell me you agree, and that if you had come by specific information that could alter the events that were to come, you would attempt to give it to someone you love. It is all true, Thomas. I can't lie to you." Her voice cracked, and the truth bubbled out with so much emotion that Thomas longed to encircle her with his arms.

What a coward I am when it comes to Beatrix. She is unlike any other woman I have known. Or has she just mesmerized me into thinking that?

Thomas's doubts had to be put aside as he slipped the envelope into the breast pocket of his coat.

"Then it shall be as you request, milady." He bowed deeply as if he were addressing royalty.

"Thank you, kind sir." She smiled. "We will stop at the Old Absinthe House on Bourbon Street before making our way to my home in the Garden District. A contact at the bar will see that the letter is delivered to Uncle Charlie as soon as possible. Every moment counts, as I know the plot to assassinate him is being formulated right now. There's no need to worry about my health. I am feeling fine now, Thomas."

She may think she is not lying to me, but she is lying to herself. Being attacked—viciously clobbered on the head and then drugged—cannot but have lasting effects. It is impossible that she feels fine.

He chose to say nothing and instead guided Beatrix out the

office and watched in awe as a taxi driving by squealed to a stop, even without Beatrix signaling for it.

"This is part of your supernatural work? The last time I tried to hail a cab, I nearly became ... what do Americans call it? Oh yes, roadkill?"

"Goodness, you have watched a lot of American movies." Beatrix smiled.

Getting into the waiting taxi, she told the driver, "The Old Absinthe House, but not to the front. Drive to the back alley, and I'll tell you when to stop."

They reached their destination minutes later. With the heavy blackout curtains now mandated by the government, pulled shut on the second-floor apartments above the cafés and restaurants in the Quarter, the streets felt haunted—at least to Thomas, and his now budding sense of otherworldly things.

With the errand completed, Beatrix directed the driver toward the Garden District. In just a matter of days, it became the law to have streetlights dimmed, and any cars that were driven at night had to have slotted headlight covers to reduce the chances of enemy airplanes loaded with bombs, to spot the city.

Unlike in the past, now there were no mellow, welcoming lights to beckon Beatrix and Thomas as the taxi slowly pulled in front of the Patterson home at Audubon Place. The storm's pelting rain turned to drizzle as they got out of the cab, which somehow felt worse than a raging storm. The neighborhood was still, as if residents were frightened of the night, something unheard of in New Orleans, and all this since the Japanese bombed Pearl Harbor and the Nazis rampaged through every corner of Europe.

America, for the first time ever, was afraid, as the war touched every citizen, and millions of breakfast tables were without a father, mother, uncle, brother. Would they ever see their loved ones again? And if they returned, how great would the toll be of seeing the horrors of war?

"The Allies will succeed, and this terrible war will end,

Thomas. But not before even greater tragedies happen, l just know it." Beatrix walked the cobble stone walkway to the house. "Good will prevail, but the world will be changed forever. America will always be in a battle someplace in the world to help the underdog achieve freedom."

"Will the United States be attacked?" Thomas said. "Invaded? Will England be lost?"

Beatrix turned the key to the front door, then reached inside and flipped on the light to the front parlor. She looked around to make sure they were alone.

"England will triumph, l feel certain," she replied. "America will survive."

Thomas entered the Victorian-style estate first, scanning the room, and then released the breath he hadn't realized he'd been holding. A warm glow from two gilded lamps illuminated the foyer, the parlor, and through to the front room.

"You weren't joking when you told me about selling furniture," he said, "but l did not expect your home to be empty."

"Don't be frightened. l haven't had to liquidate the upper floors yet. You'll find any of the ten different guest rooms ready for a good night's sleep in a fine old bed. The master bedroom is at the top of these stairs. l do not sleep well. Therefore, if you hear footsteps in the night, it is me pacing, and not some ghostly phantom. I'll leave my bedroom door open, should you continue to worry, and I'm comfortable having you check on me, if you need to in order to sleep."

"Madam, you may know my future, but as for my worrying nature, indulge me. l will not be dissuaded from a bit of fussing, especially since, in the last two days, l have become quite adapt at it. Would you care for something to eat or drink before l turn in, once l double-check that the doors are locked, and windows are bolted?"

Beatrix shook her head. "You are the finest bodyguard I've ever had."

"l thought as much. You frighten all the rest, or sent them to an early grave, agonizing over your welfare?"

"Goodnight, Thomas." She patted his arm.

He stood there for a long moment before he saw that his hand was now on the spot that Beatrix had touched.

February 20, 1942

The shrill ring of a telephone startled Thomas out of the finest, dream-free sleep he'd had since before the war began. When he heard Beatrix speaking, he jumped out of the cocoon of lush bedding and into a drafty February morning in a big, cold house.

It is not my business. But he still he opened the bedroom door a few inches to listen.

"Thank you, Eleanor. That is kind of you. We will expect Dr. Klein and his family shortly, and this house will be safe for them and their military escorts for the rest of the day. Early afternoon? We'll expect their transportation then."

Thomas leaned out into the hallway to see Beatrix speaking into a phone on the landing.

"How marvelous of you to have found that scientific community in New Mexico for him to continue his work," she said. "It will be much safer for the family as well, instead of being returned to South America. The events in the future will agree with your kindness to help the war effort and provide a home and protection for Dr. Klein. I know Thomas, my colleague, will be relieved that there will be a generous salary as well for the work to be done there. As you can imagine, Cedrick and his wife lost everything when they were abducted in South America and transported here to New Orleans."

Another silence, and Thomas realized that Eleanor was the First Lady of the United States.

"Eleanor, please give my best to Franklin, and suggest to him that exercising in the hot thermal springs at Warm Springs, Georgia, will help the paralysis caused by his polio. Yes, peace be with you as well, and God bless America."

Thomas stood by the opened door. He wanted all the news but could not dash out in his undershirt and boxer shorts. His white dress shirt and woolen slacks were tossed on a chair, and he was about to slip into them when he saw a blue terry bathrobe in the open closet. He pulled it on and then noticed plaid pajama bottoms on a shelf next to suits and shirts.

He replayed in his mind what he'd heard. *Beatrix was chatting with the First Lady of the United States as casually as a childhood friend. Who is my employer that she could be associated with such high-ranking people?*

Giving up on his wild, spiky hair, which refused to be patted into place, he left the bedroom, only to bump right into Beatrix.

"Dr. Klein has been liberated?" he said.

"Look at you." Beatrix straightened the cuff of his bathrobe. "My, nicely filled out. It's a good fit on you, just as when Great Uncle Joseph wore it. Sorry, that's probably more than you wanted to know about my relatives. Let's go to the kitchen. The coffee is made, and I'll tell you everything."

Beatrix's hair lay loose on her shoulders, and the welt on her forehead was now a pale purple rather than scarlet. She was dressed in an identical terry bathrobe, although smaller than the one Thomas was wearing, and even the pajama bottoms that showed around her ankles were the same.

"I find it adorable," she said, "but some might not. Great Uncle Joseph and my great aunt often dressed alike or coordinated their outfits to match."

"Do you suppose your uncle might be generous enough to allow me to use some of the clothing in the closet?"

"I can't see why not. And I don't think he's going to need any of the wardrobe in that room, as he's been dead for about ten years.

Muffins popped up in the toaster, and the coffee smelled rich and strong. The warm oak dinette table was set for two, and a small plate of butter—rumored to be the last in the shop because of the war—and a pot of peach jam were placed in the middle.

"I apologize for the absence of a *good English breakfast*," she said. "I wouldn't know how to cook it, if it were possible to get all the ingredients, and I definitely do not stock lots of food here."

Thomas sipped the coffee, an American habit he now embraced.

"Tell me how you arranged to have Cedrick released from that prison?" He bit into the muffin, and suddenly it was gone.

He hadn't realized the last food, the only food he had had yesterday were the sugary cookies at Poydras House.

"I prevailed on the First Lady, and she agreed that a brilliant scientist like Dr. Klein would be more valuable to the war effort if he were at the new military base in the West, than if he were submitted to bullying by pro-Nazi supporters in a Louisiana internment camp."

Thomas grabbed her hand, the hand that was about to put a heaping spoonful of peach jam on the muffin, and the confection flew into the air.

"You have done a marvelous thing for my friend and his family. Thank you, Beatrix." He looked down at the lump of preserve that had flipped to the tablecloth, scraped it up with the spoon, and put it back on the top of his muffin. "Now, you will never invite me back to your home, knowing how uncouth I am. You must not blame all Englishmen, or my mother, for my bad manners."

"Think no more of that," she said. "Soap and water were made for spills, and I think your mother did a fine job raising you. She must be a marvelous person. I have also arranged for that young girl, Zoey, whom I met at the Algiers camp, and her family to be reunited. And they will be sent to another facility in Mississippi that, God-willing, is only for Jewish detainees. Their horrors should be over later today, as should the other Jewish prisoners in the camp. Eleanor, Mrs. Roosevelt, is sensitive to our diverse American culture."

They finished the toasted muffins and pot of coffee in silence.

"I know that you must have a terrible headache," Thomas said, "and it is cheeky of me to ask, but have you received any psychic information about the Chinese plight in my homeland against the invading Japanese forces?" He dotted the corners of his mouth and then refolded the linen napkin. "I heard on the radio report a few nights back that hunger in the Henan Provence was becoming desperate."

"The news for the immediate future is not good, Thomas. Do you want to know?"

He nodded.

"I believe there is nothing we can do to stop the horrendous series of events."

She picked up the cups and walked to the sink, unsure if Thomas wanted to know of the tragedies to take place in his ancestral home.

"Tell me," he said. "It is better to know the truth than allow doubt to fill one with fear."

The words were stiff, as he already knew that with her reluctance to share the information, it would be heartbreaking.

He gathered the plates from the table and stood next to his employer. She turned on the faucet and then turned it off, watching a robin bounce around the garden, dip into the birdbath, and splash water in sheer delight.

In another month, the azaleas would be dressed in their spring finery of bubble-gum pink flowers. The dogwood trees would sparkle in glowing white, and the hydrangeas would stun visitors as their pompoms of blue and pink flowers danced in the spring breeze.

On the visits she'd made to the house as a child, it was the oak tree in the middle of the sloping lawn that she loved the most. Memories of spreading a blanket beneath the oak to read or talk with her dolls played in her head, and yet she had to relay what the future would be for China and her people.

Beatrix watched a female robin join her red-breasted mate in the bird bath and wondered if her vow to never get close to another person, for fear they'd abandon her or die, was wrong.

What's happening with me?

She stared at the playful couple for a long moment and was shocked when she realized that it was no longer possible to contrive a story, wind up a lie, or even sugarcoat the truth, as she'd done while being the Robin Hood of psychics, especially now with Thomas.

She said, "A growing number of environmental scientists in Australia and Asia believe there will be a great drought this coming summer throughout China. I understand they're using models in a way that hasn't been done before, which is calculated by the temperature of the ocean. If drought occurs, there will be crop failure, Thomas. And starvation, as well as disease, could spread, creating an epidemic of misery, along with the constant threat of Japanese occupation of the weakened country."

Thomas's knuckles were white as he pressed harder against the porcelain kitchen sink.

"It is hopeless, then, to tell any of the officials there in China, or even America, about the forthcoming famine?" he said.

"It is never hopeless if just one person can be helped, Thomas. Tell the Chinese Embassy about the probable starvation, and here, I'll write down the names of these scientists who are delving into the theories. If they don't believe you, and if they can stretch resources away from the effort to protect mainland China, there is a possibility that hundreds of thousands will be saved through food storage and distribution. We can alert the British and Canadian Red Cross, and church organizations, but the danger of Japanese conquest is of far greater threat than a possible drought. I am so sorry."

"Thank you. I needed to know this, Beatrix, even as terrifying as the news is." He longed to hug her, something foreign for a stiffly indoctrinated Brit.

What if she rejects me? We hardly know each other. Or even worse, what if the feeling is far from mutual?

He stepped back. "I realize Dr. Klein and his family will be arriving shortly, but might you excuse me for a few hours. I must get word through to the Chinese Embassy about the starvation and crop failures. I hope they will take heed, but I cannot ignore your foretelling of the future, Beatrix. There is, however, much corruption in my ancestral homeland, and since many of the provinces were once individual kingdoms, often there is still grave animosity between neighboring states. The local governments may choose not to listen."

Thomas returned to his room, and after finding a pen, paper, and a large white envelope in the desk near the window, he wrote Beatrix's visions for China in all the detail that he could recall. He sealed the multi-page document, and after readying himself to walk the few miles to the hotel on St. Peters Street, where his contact Xia Kangnan worked, he left without seeing Beatrix.

She said she would not read my thoughts, but she knows what I am about to do, I'm certain.

Beatrix stood at the nicked porcelain sink, lost in thought and scrubbing nonexistent spots off the dishes while allowing the warm water to warm the chilling predictions.

"The war will destroy so many lives in China, and yet this dreadful famine can be avoided if the government takes heed and stores food for the lean times. If only the greedy hearts of the local governments would soften, history might tell another story."

An hour later, in an unmarked car, but definitely of military issue, Cedrick Klein and his wife, with their two young daughters, were delivered to the mansion on Audubon Place. The family and their escorts settled in for the day while Beatrix visited the local grocery store and used her ration coupons for three packages of vanilla wafers and a small bottle of milk, convincing the grocery that visitors were three and five years old.

"Just this time," the grocer said, allowing her to get milk even though she wasn't registered as having children.

Once Thomas returned, his face said that his mission had failed. But he instantly brightened as he hugged Cedrick. Chatter was warm and friendly, and they both spoke a hodgepodge of English, German, and French. The Klein family eventually settled into a large bedroom with a private bath on the second floor—palatial, after the dormitory rooms at the camp.

Thomas said, "Beatrix, may I have a word? Xia is gone. There was no one at the restaurant who even wanted to talk with me. Are they fearing for their lives? Is it that they thought I was the enemy?"

"Thomas, that's what I thought might happen, and I will try to find out if Xia is in the city, or if she has left the country. Perhaps Major Davies, or even Mr. Brockman, might have intelligence on this. Your letter? Did you take it personally to the Chinese Consulate? Let's walk into the garden so you can tell me."

"They refused to let me in," he said. "To be certain, I explained at length that I knew Xia. And while the guard took the information and the letter, he would not let me speak with his superior."

"You have done everything possible right now. Be at peace. Let's hope your message will get into the right hands."

"There are times when I truly want to believe you, Beatrix, and others. Like now, when I cannot imagine anything happening to that letter but being ripped up and tossed in the fireplace. You did not see the guard's stony face. He peered at me as if I were the enemy, and not a fellow countryman."

"Now it is my turn to share information with you," she said. "I want you to know this because, should you hear rumors and speculation from those in your scientific community, you'll know the truth."

"About Dr. Klein, then?" said Thomas.

"He's been hired by a group called The Development of Substitute Materials. This is a war effort, but they will be working on breakthroughs that will help humanity, even if they are not aware of it during the research and testing. This is fantastic, really."

"Why, that is marvelous," Thomas said. "You have told Dr. Klein, I assume?"

He watched the robins take flight as a plump, ginger cat sauntered through the bushes to settle in a spot of sun.

"No, because this has been classified, I realize," she replied, "and it would be far too dangerous for him to know. Once something is known, it cannot be unknown."

"They'd be safe in New Mexico, without threats? They're Jewish, Beatrix."

"I have learned that Dr. Klein will be assigned to work with Dr. Robert Oppenheimer, a nuclear scientist for the top-secret mission that will eventually be called the Manhattan Project."

"This feels like ... what is that American slang ... the other shoe is about to drop? I do not know what that means, but there is more, right? I may not like what I am about to hear? Is that what you are about to say?"

"I don't want to keep anything from you. Do you want the whole truth?"

Thomas nodded. *I must know.*

"Dr. Klein's concepts could just change the world as we know it. Many will criticize what he'll be doing, but please know, the result will be more beneficial than anyone can predict."

"Tell me everything," Thomas said.

"The American government has hired the greatest minds in the country to develop new energy sources, much like you're studying the atom in your labs. The Germans, I have been told, are also working with atomic energy. It's hugely controversial, as you know from the work you're doing. Things can go terribly wrong. If you choose to assure Dr. Klein, then you can explain that while he's working for the war effort, the discoveries could save countless lives, too."

Thomas rubbed his forehead. "This is a lot to understand, even as a scientist, Beatrix."

He sat at the patio table again, suddenly weary from just a small portion of what Beatrix must constantly carry on her thin shoulders.

"I understand he must not know," Thomas said, "especially if he is given a polygraph test when he arrives in New Mexico."

"I didn't want to overwhelm you, Thomas, yet I don't know what will happen to me in the future. You need to have this information."

He jumped up and grabbed her arm. "Have you seen someone lurking in the garden? Do you sense that you are unsafe? What if you hide out at Poydras House, or even leave the city? We could hire a guard—not the violent copper Flynn Howard, but someone else to protect you."

Beatrix was about to tell Thomas that he was the finest guard she could have when the shrill ring of the hall telephone stopped her. She dashed to answer it.

Thomas caught the end of the conversation.

"Thank you. Yes, I will be there. I understand. If you want me to come alone, then that's how it'll be." She replaced the receiver and scribbled a note on the pad next to the black telephone, with its large, numerical dial.

She then ripped off the page and placed it in the front pocket of her gray trousers. By this time, Thomas was at her side, close enough to grab her if he thought he could stop Beatrix.

"Whatever this is about, it's dangerous," he said. "You are not going anywhere alone." *Who am I to tell this woman what she can and cannot do?*

"So you have the gift now? Do you know if something untoward will happen, Thomas?"

"Well, no, but you've said, time and again, that you have reason to fear for your life. I believe there's cause for caution since I found you drugged and with a welt on your head last night."

"This was simply an invitation to have a cup of tea at Le Petite Patisseries, the little bakery and tea shop next to our office."

"With whom, if I might inquire?" Thomas took a step back, as the closeness to Beatrix was making him anxious yet more alive than he'd ever experienced.

"You may," she replied. "It's Georgie Cartier, Andrew Higgins's entire office staff. She said she has some additional information for me and asked that I come at once. She seemed quite agitated, even for Georgie."

"Then I will go with you," Thomas said.

Beatrix placed a palm on his chest, and her warmth penetrated the buttoned wool suit jacket, the stiff cotton dress shirt, down to his skin.

"No, Thomas. There are some things that women must talk about alone. And there are some women who will not be honest, even with themselves, if they're in the company of any male. Growing up with sisters, you must have seen them whispering and not wanting you or your father to hear, right? You have seen how unwise Georgie was getting involved with the major. If it's a delicate topic and she still feels like a fool, she will not reveal that with you an elbow's length away."

"With your consent, I will keep my ear to the thin wall between the bakery and our office?" he said. "Do you suppose she is working for the trustees of your parents' estate, or has a vendetta against you for some unknown reason? Shout; scream my name, and I'll hear you. And I will also leave the office door open. Should I be wrong, and she has a gang of assailants—you say, goons with muscle—I will be close and come running. You must call me. Yell my name."

"Goons and muscle? You are sounding more American by the hour. Like an American from Chicago, but with this upscale British accent. If the situation weren't this serious, I'd be chuckling." A sly smile ticked the corner of Beatrix's mouth. "Have you been wrong about women before, Thomas?"

"Deplorably. More times than I will comfortably admit. My sisters attempted to school me in the fine art of communicating with females, yet each lesson failed."

"Georgie seems harmless enough to me," said Beatrix. "Did

you learn anything else that you may have forgotten when you were with her in Mr. Higgins's office?"

"No. Other than, she is not particularly discerning in affairs of the heart. But you knew that."

"That can be said of women as well, Thomas, even smart and well-educated ones."

"I will take that to mean you are speaking from experience, Beatrix. Nevertheless, Georgie was easily swept off her feet by Major Davies, who has proven to be devious, dishonest, and dubious in character."

Beatrix quietly chuckled while grabbing her suit jacket from the only chair in the empty parlor. She slipped into it before tying a scarf around the scar on her neck and swung a black leather purse over her shoulder.

"Kindly inform the Klein family that a military escort will arrive in the next hour to accompany them by train to New Mexico," she said. "There will be two males and one female guard, but they will be in plain clothing and will show their credentials to you when they arrive. Mrs. Klein and the children are afraid, so please assure them that they're safe. As for your comment, it's refreshing to have discovered you have a poetic side I've not seen, Thomas. That was a fine alliteration with devious, dishonest, and dubious."

"I can alliterate with the best of them." He smiled. "Please do your *wu* magic and make a taxi appear in front of the house so we do not have to walk all the way back to the French Quarter." Out on the wide front veranda, he pointed to the sky. "I have never been in a place where the weather changes so quickly. Those clouds look ominous, and I would rather not be caught again in the rain."

A taxi pulled to the curb of the mansion, which took no magic powers, as Beatrix had ordered one.

She arrived at the café before Georgie, which suited Beatrix well, as she had never been inside Madam Flambeau's Le Petite Patisseries and wanted to select a table facing the front door, with a good view of the street. The café was twice the size of

Beatrix's office, and because the walls were far too thin between tenants, she'd heard enough of the drama to believe the owner was Parisian and had a temper, proven by the constant hysterics as the woman fired one novice baker each week.

By the time Beatrix sat down, the morning crowd had left, and the luncheon patrons had yet to arrive. The smell of white chocolate and peppermint Neapolitans, apple tarte Tatin, and cherry clafoutis brought back long-ago memories of Paris. She stood near the door and peered through the lacy curtains, attempting to snatch the joy of the city that was no more—not since Hitler's troops invaded the City of Light.

Madam Flambeau peeked out from the kitchen and saw Beatrix. In a squeaking French accent, the proprietor scolded two giggling waitresses before rushing to the dining room and greeting her neighbor in a calmer manner.

"*Bonjour*, Mademoiselle Patterson. How kind of you to visit my humble café."

"You are so kind," Beatrix replied. "You have a marvelous shop here, and it reminds me—no—it makes me long for the Paris of the old days. Days before Hitler sullied the city."

"Merci. Then you must visit me more often, if for nothing but to remind you of Paris. Now, perhaps some coffee or tea. A plate of macarons?"

"Tea, thank you, as coffee will be rationed shortly, and we all must do our duty."

Beatrix noticed that Madam Flambeau didn't seem crushed that Paris now was not the Paris that they both knew. *It's probably denial. If we don't talk about something bad, like the Nazis overtaking the City of Light, then it isn't real.*

"Will you return to France once the Allies win the war, Madam?"

The baker huffed as if she'd tasted something bitter, then shrugged and frowned.

"Table for one?" Madam Flambeau squinted at Beatrix as Georgie Cartier walked in, teetering in red high heels, perhaps a size too large. "Ah yes, you were expecting a friend. Then tea for two?"

"If you please," Beatrix replied in French, then greeted Georgie.

"I am so sorry to be late. Mr. Higgins was crazy-happy this morning. Something about how he's gotten enough money to float an entire armada of crafts. Where he gets the lettuce—um, cash—is beyond me. Looks like I'll have a job at least for a few more weeks. He even forgot his raincoat when he dashed out tell Mrs. Higgins some news. I haven't seen him happier ... well, in ever."

That day, as with their first meeting, Georgie reeked with the expensive perfume gifted by her former lover. Or had she bought it? *If only I were psychic, I wouldn't have to wonder. I'd know.*

Would I still wear a pricy fragrance given by a lover who lied to me? Yes, she would with delight.

Georgie was rambling on about how awful it had been to get to Royal Street and their meeting, and Beatrix realized she wasn't listening to anything the woman had said.

"I stood in the rain, and when the streetcar came, I realized I didn't have a dime. But a kindly old lady gave me one after I begged the driver, who has known me for years, to give me a break just this time, and that I'd never ask for another favor in my whole life. Oh no, that geezer just told me to get off the streetcar and out of the way of others. That lady, smelling like carnations, handed me the money. Bless her, wherever she is."

Georgie looked like she wanted to run away, but took a deep breath, pulled out the chair, and then pushed it back in. She gulped and joined Beatrix at the table.

"I like you, Miss Patterson. I really do. I can tell you've got a kind heart. My Mama always knew those things, and maybe I get the feelings from her. I hope so. If it weren't for you, I swear, that two-timing scumbag Army officer would have strung me along for another year."

She flicked open the clasp on her purse and then closed it a half-dozen times.

"Georgie, what is that you want to tell me?" Beatrix watched as the young woman's hand quaked. "Tea first?"

"I wrote it all down because I was afraid of forgetting something. I have to get this right."

Georgie pulled a hanky, a lipstick, a toothbrush, and a small address book from her purse and then fished out a crinkled note. She pushed it toward Beatrix just as the tea arrived and then snatched it back as the baker looked down at it.

"May I pour, and then you can share the note," Beatrix said. "Try to relax. We're alone here. Look, there are no other customers. You can tell me what you want me to know." *Because I cannot, for the life of me, read her mind or pick up any clues, except that you're frightened to death. But why?*

Beatrix lifted the cup toward her mouth just as Georgie waved the note in front of her eyes. With quaking fingers, she got the dainty cup back in the saucer and shoved the message at Beatrix, which she read in a whisper: "Unless you go quietly with Georgette Cartier, you will never see your mother alive."

Georgie's gaze circled the room, avoiding Beatrix's.

"Whoever you work for, Georgie, they have got this all wrong. My mother died when I was twelve, in a car accident, along with my father and our chauffeur. That's how this happened." Beatrix took off the silk scarf tied around her throat, exposing the thick, white scar.

Just as Georgie gasped, the shop door swung open, and the deputy warden at Camp Algiers darted to their table.

"Have you told her yet?" Willamina Jones glowered over them, no longer simply a sly women's warden but a force who would harm anyone standing in her way. "Why aren't you in the back room by now?"

"Sis? Willie, honey, please," Georgie said. "It doesn't have to be this way. We agreed to just ask Miss Patterson to go with us, and I'm sure she wants to help the war effort. Why, I'm certain she wants the war to end soon. Don't you, Miss Patterson?" The words came out in a rush. "Why do you always have to bully people?" she told her sister.

"How can you really be my blood relative, you silly, stupid girl?" said Willamina. "I knew I couldn't trust you to take her. To make her go with you. That's why I showed up. Now, Miss Patterson, if you want to see your mother, you'll go with us." She grabbed Beatrix's arm.

"Madam Flambeau, please come here," Beatrix called out toward the kitchen.

"No use making a scene," said Willamina. "The baker believes as we do, and maybe even more so because of her involvement in the effort. She always says, 'We must win the war at all cost.' Looks like you're part of the cost."

"Please, Miss Patterson. Please come quietly," Georgie whimpered from behind.

Willamina snarled. "Go on, Miss Patterson. Scream if you want. It's useless. We will have you locked away at Camp Algiers, in solitary confinement, and we will send a telegram to your precious Charlie, demanding that he turn himself over to the Third Reich's puppet Vichy government. The sooner he complies, the sooner you will be released."

CHAPTER 13

THE DEPUTY WARDEN MUSCLED BEATRIX out the back of the bakery, but not before taking a napkin from the café table and shoving it into Beatrix's mouth.

"Don't try to scream, or so help me, I'll shove this down your throat to shut you up. Baby sister here tells me that you and John Brockman, the weird old coot, are as thick as thieves. Or lovers, which is even more disgusting," she spat. "With his bookie hall just over there, it wouldn't do for him to rush out here. Then there's that pretty boy toy of yours—Teddy, or Tommy or something. He'd probably do a hero act, too, because I saw him making goo-goo eyes at you. You know, I'm not afraid to use this gun on anyone who stands in my way—in the cause's way." She patted the military-issued pistol holstered on her hip. "You can be sure of that. Our mission it too great to let the likes of you to get in our way."

Less than twenty feet from the kitchen door, in the back alley, sat an armored military police vehicle, drab green, with a uniformed driver at the wheel, a man Beatrix didn't recognize.

She fell forward, and the napkin tumbled from her mouth. Chest down on the damp cobblestone pavement, she flailed around, attempting to toss her purse as far as possible beneath the vehicle, and screaming for Thomas, but the cries were muffled by the truck's throaty engine.

Willie sneered, "I should have handcuffed you. What a stupid trick to try to leave your bag here as a way to find you.

Georgie, get down on your stupid hands and knees to grab the pocketbook. Oh, don't look at me like that."

"These are new stockings," Georgie whined.

"Get it now, or you'll make me do something I will not regret."

The deputy warden wrenched Beatrix's arm, forcing her into the truck.

She yelled at the driver, "Once we're inside, I'll slam the door. You just gun the engine and drive. You're not being paid to ask questions, soldier. Do as I tell you."

"People will miss me," Beatrix said. "You've underestimated my worth to whatever group it is you're working for. Just ask me to come. Don't threaten me or my long-dead mother. I can assist you. I find lost things. Whatever it is, I can be of service. Let me help you. I can predict what might happen, tell you things about the government that can help your cause." Her lies tumbled out as her voice got louder. *Thomas, please listen. Help me.*

Back doors of the businesses along the alley were often open to catch a breeze, but not that morning. Everything was far too quiet. Beatrix assumed the deputy warden had paid off the shopkeepers to stay inside with threats of violence. Was the bakery's owner part of the Nazi organization, or had her captors frightened her?

"Quiet down now, or you'll wish you had," Willie growled through clenched teeth, just as the back door of the gaming establishment flew open.

Through the front windshield, Beatrix saw John Brockman dash toward the vehicle, and then the driver closed the window separating the front and back.

"Beatrix, what's going on?" he shrieked. "You need to let her go. You can't do this."

Before she could cry out, Willie shoved her even harder into the military truck and slammed the door. Then she grabbed Beatrix's wrist and shackled her to a steel bar welded around the back of the vehicle.

John beat at the passenger side of the truck. "What's

happening in there? What are you doing to Miss Patterson? Who are you? Where are you taking her? Stop this truck at once. Stop and get out. Beatrix, I'll get help."

He scurried around and put his arms against the hood of the truck but was forced backward as the driver slowly accelerated.

Willie opened the sliding window behind the driver's head.

"If he doesn't get out of our way, drive over him. We are at war, and he's the enemy. He'll tell the police, and we'll all go to federal prison. Do you want that, soldier? Don't you want to help the cause?"

"Deputy Warden, I can't do that. That's murder."

"You are an idiot," Willie growled. "Just drive."

The soldier stared at her through the rearview mirror.

"Do it, or I'll shoot you and drive this vehicle myself."

The van twisted, and there was a horrifying thump.

Beatrix thought she might faint as terror coursed through her body. *Dead. They have just killed him like he was some foul rodent, just for attempting to stop me from being kidnapped.* Beatrix gasped with an image of John's lifeless body.

Tears tumbled down her face. She fell forward as sobs got stuck in her throat.

"I need air," she gasped. "I'm going to throw up. Open the window, or I will, and I'll make sure it gets on you, Deputy Warden."

Then she felt anger boil and erupt, and she wanted to beat the deputy warden to death. If she hadn't been shackled to the side of the van, she would have.

Georgie and her sister screamed at each other, and Georgie, gasping for air, slid back a slit of a window.

"Miss Patterson, I am so sorry." She pulled out a crumpled handkerchief and placed it on Beatrix's lap—the same hanky that Thomas had given the bookkeeper. "Willie, did you have to do that? You've had an innocent old man killed. What's wrong with you?" she screamed while crying and wheezing.

"What?" Willie said. "You two are nuts. That old geezer didn't get killed. I wanted the driver to scare the guy, but the idiot behind the wheel here just hit a pile of dirty laundry cluttering the alley, waiting to be picked up. Now shut up. You're both getting on my nerves. I knew it was a mistake to have you help me on this, Georgie. You've always been more trouble than you're worth. And all your yammering and complaining ... well, that's exactly why that loser of a husband of yours found himself another woman. I've a mind to shackle you two together and drop you from some bridge out in the Bayou Country, where the alligators will dine on you with gusto."

Beatrix wanted to believe the woman that it wasn't John's body smashed by the truck. But with the crazy look in Willie's eyes, there was no doubt that John was lying broken in the back alley, regardless of what the deputy warden said.

When the French Quarter's cobblestone streets became smooth blacktop, Beatrix knew hope was lost. *There's no use in struggling. Will they torture me to give away military secrets they believe I have? Should I tell them I have no insight as to what the US government is going to do? That I'm a fake, a fraud, and it's all a racket to make money from the rich to give to the poor?*

"You are all Nazis," she blurted.

"I took you to be smarter than that." Willie smirked. "Thought you'd get the reason why we grabbed you, sooner. But guess your supernatural powers are on the fritz, huh? Or is it all smoke and mirrors?"

"How did you get mixed up in this?" Beatrix said. "Kidnapping? Then the murder of an innocent man? When I'm found—and I will be found—you will be found guilty of treason. Georgie, do you want that? Do you want to be executed for what you've done? You're only an accomplice right now. You haven't hurt me, and your sister is bullying you, forcing you into this. Any jury would see—"

"Shut up," Willie shouted and slapped Beatrix across the face, knocking her head against the metal siding.

"Sister, you promised," Georgie pleaded, wringing her hands. "You promised to be careful with her, and you never said you'd make the driver kill a man. What is happening? We're going to hang for this if we're caught."

Beatrix knew the truth. Whether she fought back or surrendered, she would not live more than a few days, if that.

She barked, "Georgie's note said something about never seeing my mother again unless I went with her. I'm confused."

"Use your gift, fortune-teller," Willie said. "Oh wait, you can't use it for yourself, can you. If you have one." She chortled.

"We wouldn't really hurt your mother," Georgie said, "but it could be that we might have to kidnap her, too. Unless you help us." She patted Beatrix's shackled hand.

"That's what I don't understand. I told you, my parents are dead."

Willie pressed out the wrinkles from her skirt and straightened the holster, then smoothed her hair and replaced the military-style cap that had fallen to the floor when Beatrix fought to avoid getting in the van.

"Well then, I have some good news for you, amazing soothsayer and clairvoyant. You should sit down. Oh wait, you are my prisoner and you can't stand up. Your mother is alive and well. She just chooses not to know you, or even see you."

Beatrix scoffed. "My mother, according to my dying aunt, probably died birthing another child after she gave me up. You're wrong. So wrong. My aunt told me the truth."

"Well, your aunt was a liar, just like your precious, rich adopted parents. Your Mama is nutty as a fruit cake, that's for sure. She's living in exile as if she were some Catholic Mother Superior or Lady of the Manor. She knows all about you, I'm told, but chooses to reject you. How does that feel? Some mother. But still, we think, if necessary, that we can use her as leverage."

"My mother would never be that way. If she knew I was here in New Orleans ... why, she would ..." Beatrix couldn't get the words out, as if the thoughts were strangling her heart. "No, never. You are wrong." She sobbed. *My mother would want me.*

She could not get her head around why anyone wouldn't long to be with their own child. *When I meet her, will she tell me the truth?*

"This is a trick to break me down for whatever is next on your cruel agenda. It's not going to work."

"It's the truth," Willie said. "Maybe you know her already, because we've watched you and that Asian man go in and out of where she's living. The woman calls herself Mother Adelina. My sources say you've talked to people she works with. She's hiding out, for some wacko reason, at that safe asylum for women, called Poydras House."

While the military van bounced along the city streets, Beatrix closed her eyes. She'd never had interaction with that little French lady who seemed to believe she was some type of angel. Or so the staff said. It didn't take a fake psychic to know the lady had been concealing her identity. But after all, that wasn't uncommon for someone who lives in a safe house.

Willie said, "We found her easily. Just had to ask around. Besides, Flynn Howard's wife is hiding out there, too. Hey, you know that. We just threatened to tell him where she was hiding if she refused to go through the locked files to see if you were born in this city. I scored with that hunch, and your Mama— that weird little woman—had her name right on the birth certificate. It's creepy, these family connections, isn't it, Georgie, and how smells make us think of things. Just like how you are nuts for Evening in Paris perfume, and you've got me hooked on the stuff. But that lady always smells like—"

"Carnations." Beatrix sighed and wanted to slam her head against the steel siding of the van. *The truth was right in front of me. I am so stupid. I've heard about Mother Adelina many times but never thought she'd been avoiding me. Why couldn't I make the connection?*

Before Beatrix could beat herself up, even more, Willie bellowed, with a wide grin across her thin, pale face, "Now that you know your mama— who you might just end up being imprisoned with if we don't get the results we want—I want to break bigger news." She snickered. "Yep, here's the *coup de grâce*," Willie shouted over the rumble of the engine. "1 am delighted to tell you that your father is none other than the most wanted enemy of the Third Reich. None other than Charles de Gaulle."

"No. That's crazy, Willie." She shook her head at this bizarre notion. "He was a close friend of my father's. 1 would have known if he was anything but that. 1 would have. My parents would not have kept this from me, and they wouldn't have prevented me from knowing the truth. Besides, Uncle Charlie is a respected gentleman. He wouldn't have lied to me. He is the kindest man I've ever met." Beatrix's forehead wrinkled at the ludicrous idea.

"1 wish you'd stolen the fancy and expensive tape recorder from Higgins Boatyard, like 1 asked you to, Georgie. 1 could have recorded all that howling when precious and pure Missy Beatrix Patterson learned that her entire life was a big, fat lie. Why, 1 could have included it with our demands."

"Willie, how can you be so callous?" Georgie whined. "Can't you see how you're hurting Miss Patterson? Don't you care at all?"

Beatrix looked at each woman, so weirdly different, yet sisters.

"Why have you abducted me? Does it have to do with my supposed connection to him?"

She couldn't accept that the man she'd thought was a kindly friend of her parents was her biological father. The man had pushed the garden swing when she was a child. He had listened to her tell stories by the hour and had even joined her as they drew imaginary castles a million feet tall, where Beatrix was always the princess.

He was the leader of the French Resistance Fighters, and she had shared confidential information gleaned from high-ranking military officials and the First Lady. He was Charles de Gaulle, who would—in later years, she hoped—become the greatest leader of post-war France and throughout Europe, pulling his country through the reconstruction times and through struggles with Russia.

Beatrix said, "Tell me why I've been kidnapped. I demand to know that, and what your plan has to do with Charles de Gaulle?"

"You can demand anything your heart wants, girly," Willie sneered. "Since I doubt you'll ever be in a position to tell anyone anything, here's what's going to happen."

Georgie, who was sitting next to Beatrix on the van's steel bench, pushed tears off her face with the back of her hand.

"Sister, please. You promised no one would be hurt. You promised. That's the only reason I agreed to help."

"Things have changed. You are dense, Georgianna, but whether you like it or not, you're now in for murder, if I'm wrong about that Brockman guy, as well as treason. That makes you just as guilty as me, so stop your lame-ass whimpering and listen so you know what's going to happen, too."

"Let me out, Willie. Stop the car," Georgie pleaded. "I'll never tell anyone. I bet if Miss Beatrix promises not to tell the police, you can let her go, too."

"Did you not hear anything I just said? Of course not. You could never listen, never understand. Our father always said you were the stupid daughter, and I always agreed with him."

Georgie put her arm over Beatrix's shoulder. "I am so sorry, Miss Patterson. I just thought we'd get some information for Willie and her friends, who want to stop the war and get paid. I just did it for some extra spending money since Mr. Higgins and the boatyard don't pay much."

"I know, Georgie. But like your sister said, things are different now." Beatrix turned to the older sister. "What is your plan for me and the woman you insist is my biological mother?"

"Here's the deal." Willie's malicious grin displayed bright and straight teeth like she could pose for a toothpaste advertisement. "Once we're at the camp, I'll inform my superior that you're in our hands. He will send a telegram to be given to de Gaulle. Don't be stupid, woman. His supposed secret whereabouts have been known by the Nazis for a long time. The kicker? We'll have a photo taken of you holding today's newspaper so that the date is visible. Once the photo has been developed, someone—no, not you, Georgie—someone who can follow orders, and that I can trust, will drop it off at the Old Absinthe and in the hands of the cook, Gillette."

Beatrix's eyes grew wide.

"Don't look so surprised, Miss Patterson. Unquestionably, the pro-Nazi forces I'm proud to serve, right here in New Orleans, know that the bar staff are working with the French Resistance. Haven't you, with all your psychic powers, seen people hanging out on the street, watching you and your lover boy come and go?"

Beatrix tried to dig into her memories, and it didn't take long before she recalled the conversation. *Thomas said that there were odd folks in that part of the French Quarter. But there always are. It's the French Quarter. Could he have felt someone following him? He tried to mention it, but I ignored him. He said something about the patrons at the Old Absinthe and the thug and prostitute he'd seen. I discounted him. How often have I done that to others?*

Beatrix was frozen after that realization. *My play-acting made me so egotistical, I no longer listened. I have ignored the warnings of others. And because I didn't listen, I'm chained in a van with Nazi sympathizers on my way to imprisonment. This is all my fault.*

Her rude dismissal of Thomas's concerns ricocheted like bullets bouncing off cement. Sweat dotted her face as the closeness of the van, and the heat of an early spring day made her clothing, especially the hat, feel constricted.

"I have to get my hat off," she said. "I need to get it off right now."

"Then do it. You think you can try to subdue me with it?" Willie laughed, but her eyes were hard.

Beatrix removed the old-fashion six-inch hatpin that had once belonged to her aunt, then her cloche, and put both behind her back. The point of the pin jabbed her finger. Was it sharp enough to distract the crazy Willie Jones? *Hardly. When I get out, I'll fall again, heave the pin into Willie, then toss my hat as I tried to drop my purse?*

The van screeched to a stop. She heard the driver talking to another man and then the squealing of a metal gate as the van jogged to life again.

"We're almost there," Willie said. "Sorry you won't have any company in solitary confinement, after we take your picture with today's *Times-Picayune*. But just use your supernatural psychic powers and transport yourself out of the camp's jail, to some happy place filled with rainbows, kittens, and chocolate cake."

She grabbed Beatrix's hand and unlocked the handcuff connected to the steel rod, then opened the door and climbed down.

"Welcome home," Willie grunted, forcing Beatrix from the van.

With Willie's mighty yank on her arm as she was about to jump from the back of the van, Beatrix tumbled to the pavement. An accident this time.

"You silly oaf. See what you've done. When we take a photograph to send to your illustrious father, your head will have a big gash on it." Willie looked again at Beatrix's forehead. "Holy cow, you couldn't have gotten that purple lump on the other side from this fall. Have you been in a street brawl, Psychic Princess?" She sniggered.

"Let go of me, and help me get up," Beatrix said.

The hatpin tumbled to the street, and she watched as it fell through a grating. It felt as if she'd gotten been kicked in the stomach. Even if the pin hadn't been much of an effective weapon, it might have given her a chance to run.

She screamed, "I demand that you let go of me."

Willie didn't notice that she'd tossed the hat under the van's tire.

"You're such a comedian," said the deputy warden. "Let you go for even a second? Think I'm nuts? Scream all you want. Lots of the inmates—um, detainees—do. You'll be ignored." She gabbed Beatrix's upper arm and yanked her off the pavement. "You think I'm insane?"

Yes, I do. Beatrix wanted to scream but said, "Actually, I don't think you realize how dangerous this situation is, Deputy Warden Jones. What will you do if Uncle Charlie agrees and gives into the Nazis? They won't have any more use for you. What happens when spies are useless?"

Beatrix twisted back to look at the younger sister, who was dutifully following them into the dark, sooty building that had been repurposed from a warehouse to cells for hostile prisoners.

"Do you know, Georgie?" Beatrix said.

The hallway had cells on each side, and the doors were all open. At the end of the drafty corridor was a cell with a long wooden bench, a bucket in the corner for a toilet, and a tiny slit of a window near the ceiling—nothing else.

Willie grabbed Beatrix and stopped her. Georgie bumped into her back.

"Do you, Georgie?" Beatrix said.

"Willie." The bookkeeper dashed in front of her sister, but Willie pushed her aside. "Either way, we're going to die. The Americans will hang us if the Germans don't kill us first. I'm petrified, Willie, and it's not helping that you're hurting the lady."

Willie shoved her sister once more, and the younger one bent over and wheezed, then tumbled to the stone floor. Beatrix looked back, assuming that Georgie would huddle there and cry, but instead, she jumped up, pulled down her jacket, and hiked up her skirt, which had slipped toward her hips in the scuffle.

"No, Willie, you will not hurt Miss Patterson. I cannot make you release her, but bruising and pushing, as you do with me, is wrong," she growled, which stopped the older sister. "We are not animals. Mama brought us up to care for each other. Or have you forgotten when Mama died and we all huddled together at her funeral, promising that we would be there for each other.

Yes, to help each other, no matter what. What would Mama say right now?"

"Mama's gone," Willie said. "Don't you dare bring her up to me. Look at your life for a second, baby sister. You're eighteen. You're divorced. And the only reason you have a few pretty things is because you're trading sex for them. You're no better than a prostitute. Oh yeah, and now you're in this kidnapping with me." She slowed her steps and barely loosened the iron grip on Beatrix's arm, though her fingers crushed into the skin.

Georgie bellowed, "Remember what you said? You said, 'I will always be here for you both. I'll take care of you. Don't be afraid, little sisters. I'll find a way to make money, and you won't have to worry about never having enough to eat again, just like I promised Mama.'"

Beatrix blinked. So much sorrow surrounded the sisters. Where was the third sister now?

The deputy warden loosened her claw-like fingers and let her captive go. It would do no good to run, but for the first time, she saw a crack in Willie's ugly armor.

"Get in here," Willie barked at Beatrix, but her eyes looked softer and held doubt.

Then she turned and stared at her sister. Beatrix sensed that Willie was fighting a moral battle over the pledge she'd taken.

"Miss Patterson, sit there," she said. "It's clean enough."

"Willie, you cannot expect her to stay in this tiny, damp cell until we know if de Gaulle has yielded to our leader's demands. You don't even use these quarters when detainees act up. It's not humane in here. I saw a rat when we walked in, and there could be snakes, too. She could get bit and die of a snake bite, and then what would you tell those German leaders? It's horrible, like a nightmare in here. And it stinks."

"Stop pleading her case," Willie said. "I am not as evil as either of you seem to think. Georgie, you keep an eye on her while I get water and see if there are pillows and a blanket to be had."

When she looked at Beatrix, her eyes were those of a young girl who was about to bury her mother, not someone who was working for the Nazi war machine.

Beatrix now knew that these women were not brainwashed by the German cause but were just trying to survive. *They've made terrible decisions, but fear can do that.*

Still, neither the women nor their leaders would tolerate anything but cooperation. They expected one result only.

Beatrix knew she'd be dead before the end of the week.

CHAPTER 14

Before Willie could swing the massive door shut, Georgie dashed into the cell.

"I'm staying with the prisoner. It is not right that we leave her unguarded." She plunked down on the wooden bench. "Get her some food, too, Willie. And some for me. We're going to be here until the photographer shows up, and I didn't have any breakfast today, and no dinner last night either, because you said we didn't have money or time."

"Yeah, okay, then. Just let me find a pad and pencil so I can take your order. What would the madam like? Perhaps a medium rare sirloin steak and those fancy soufflé potatoes they serve at Antoine's in the Quarter?" She laughed and started to turn away, then looked back but made no attempt to lock the cell's door. "Don't even imagine you can get away, Miss Patterson. I will secure the building from the outside door. I'll get a guard to stand there, too."

With military precision, she flipped around, and her footsteps echoed down the hall.

Neither spoke until the clank of the outside doors clicked into place.

"Miss Patterson, please know I really want to let you go. But I can't. The Nazi leaders that Willie is working for would kill us at once. I overheard them threatening Willie, and I know they would do it, and probably for sport. After de Gaulle surrenders, we'll be free."

"Georgie, that's a lie." Beatrix looked around the solitary cell meant to punish prisoners; that would be her own final place in life. "I doubt they'll want any witnesses of what has happened here."

"Oh no, they will certainly see that killing you will not help their war efforts or the expansion of the Third Reich."

"What if my uncle refuses, Georgie? My uncle—or if you believe he's my father—is a man of great morals and honor. And my life, one life against many in the cause to stop Hitler's madness throughout Europe and perhaps the entire world, is insignificant."

"You mean, Mr. de Gaulle won't do it, even for you?" Georgie clasped her hands and slapped them to her mouth. "My father was bad. I've never really trusted men. They all seem to be out for themselves. Even Major Davies, who thought I was foolish. You really think your father is that honorable?"

"I know you were abused, Georgie, but there are good men in the world, like Charles de Gaulle and Thomas. Lots of good men."

Georgie looked at her hands as she rubbed them.

"He bullied Mother," she said, "and in a drunken rage, threw her against the fireplace. We buried her three days later, and Willie took me and my other sister, Bertie, and we ran into the night. We never returned, and the horrid man never came looking for us, thank God. We lived in an alley off Saint Louis Street until a kindly lady took us to Poydras House. Bertie got consumption—at least that's what we were told—when we were living on the street. Poor Bertie. She could not stop coughing, and the coughing got bloody. I got scared. Everybody tried to help, even the local doctor. Now she's in Shreveport, being treated like a prisoner, in a sanitarium for paupers. It's filthy, and it'll take lots of money to get her to a better place." She whispered, "After they took Bertie away, Willie and I stayed at the home until she was eighteen. That's when they turn you out. She took me with her. We both worked hard, but we could never save enough money. We just had to find a way to get

Bertie out of that ghastly hospital. We heard that people with an awful cough, like Bertie, do better out in Arizona. That's what we're going to do when Willie gets paid and they let you go. We're going to take Bertie and get on a train and start a new life. I'll never forget the women who were gentle with us. And someday, when I'm rich, I'm going to give Poydras House lots of money to thank them. I made that promise to Bertie, and I always keep my promises."

"The women at Poydras House are good to orphans, honey." Beatrix placed an arm around the young woman and pulled her close. "Is that where you met the woman you think is my biological mother?"

Georgie clung to Beatrix as if starving for a measure of comfort.

"Mother Adelina?" said the young woman. "Yes, she talked about having a baby girl. A girl who would one day tell where things were and help people. When I met you at Higgins Boatyard, I knew you had to be that person, and I went back to Poydras and asked the lady. She just yammered on and on about rockets with passengers circling the world, and get this, men walking on the moon. Don't know what she was drinking, but it had to be good. Is that outrageous talk or what? I think she said that'd happen in 1968." Georgie took a deep breath and laughed. "You've got to hear this. Then she told me that someday, people would carry around tiny telephones, smaller than a sandwich, and some would even use a telephone in a wristwatch, just like in the comic strip character Dick Tracy. Everyone will have them, she tried to tell me. Sure, telephones that will fit in pockets. I laughed in her face. She tried to tell me how people will someday be walking down busy sidewalks and will be able to see the person they're talking to on a telephone—the actual person. Then she tried to convince me that there'll be medicine to stop and cure cancer. Yeah, cancer. Can you believe that?"

Beatrix shook her head.

"Nope, me either," Georgie said. "She was kind and kept patting my hand, but looney as all get out, for sure. Once I got home that night, I told Willie about the coincidence and how this lady also told me about her love affair with Mr. de Gaulle. I remembered that because he's so handsome, with his photo in the newspapers and all."

"Willie then took the information where?" Beatrix said.

"To one of the women here in the camp. She wouldn't tell me who."

"This person is a Nazi sympathizer or a spy?"

"Both, probably, don't you think? A few days later, she got a letter in the mail saying they wanted to meet her and hire us. Her, to be truthful. They gave her lots of money. More money than she or I could make in two years." Georgie's voice cracked, and a wheeze erupted from her throat. "Sorry. It gets worse when I'm afraid. Daddy hated that. Mama tried to protect me."

Even a fake psychic could hear the fear leftover from the abuse.

"That is exactly what I mean about Charles de Gaulle," Beatrix said. "He would want to protect me, but he would know that he needs to protect the millions of people in France even more. I have known him my whole life. He will not trade the future of France for me."

"Or for your mother?" Georgie said. "We can kidnap her, too."

"Again, it won't work. If she really is my mother. He's not like that. It's time to think about what could happen next month and next year, Georgie."

The young woman seemed unable to speak. Then she gulped back a sob.

"I'm not saying or promising anything, mind you. But if I helped you to escape, do you think the American government agents would hang me?"

Thomas had waited exactly thirty-five minutes. He'd had a cup of tea, read the entire *Times-Picayune* newspaper, including the social pages of who was to marry whom. He had paced for ten more minutes and then erupted from the office, slamming the door behind him. He barged into the café, half-expecting to see Beatrix and Georgie whispering and giggling behind their hands, just as his sisters always did, making himself feel even more foolish for worrying.

But that's not what he found.

He stood just inside the door and blinked. Patrons sipped tea and nibbled on delicate pastries. Two young women sweeping the floor in high-necked French maid's dresses with ruffled white aprons stopped and stared at him.

"Where is Miss Patterson?" he bellowed. "I demand to know."

A formidable woman in a flour-splattered apron charged from the kitchen.

"Get out. Get out now. This is my establishment. You must leave. You are upsetting my customers. If you do not get out, I will call the constable." Madam Flambeau started waving her hands and throwing flatware and delicate cups and saucers, along with insults at Thomas.

In three strides, he was in front of the small Parisian and grabbed her hand.

He growled the whisper, "Beatrix Patterson came in here thirty-five minutes ago. She did not leave by the front door, and she is not here. Where is she?" He clamped his strong fingers on her shoulders.

For a second, she looked angry and then let out a wail that rattled the windows. The intensity of her scream jarred customers into action, especially since an Asian was accosting the café's owner.

As if they were fighting the entire Japanese Imperial Army, the women got up and started to pelt sugary petit fours, dainty cream puffs, cucumber sandwiches, and chocolate-covered Napoleons at Thomas. An elderly lady took a hatpin the size of a knitting needle from her cloche, and with words that matched her anger for what happened at Pearl Harbor, waved it in front of his eyes. A fine-boned younger woman, outfitted in white silk draped with an ermine stole, beaned him on the head with a teapot once, then again as he tumbled to the floor, only to have a child kick him while screaming why she hated all the Japanese in the world, and especially him.

How long it would have continued, or if Thomas might have been murdered by the tea-drinking ladies of a certain social level, was never realized. Shouts from a baritone voice stopped the melee.

"Leave him alone. Back off. Stand back. Leave him alone, or deal with me. Lady, put down the plate of croissants. You, there, don't do it. Just leave that teapot on the table. He's not an enemy. He's Chinese."

Thomas started to struggle into a sitting position as a little girl in a frilly pink dress kicked him in the stomach and added some comments her mother probably would have denied ever hearing before.

Henry, Mr. Brockman's driver, stood in the bakery's open door, his arms akimbo, and boomed, "The cops are on their way. You're all going to be arrested. That's enough, ladies."

A second later, tiny John Brockman stepped out from behind the imposing man.

"Come, Dr. Ling. Let's get out of here and clean those French pastries off you."

Brockman's guard lifted him under the arms like a baby and set him down on his feet.

"Beatrix has disappeared," Thomas said. "You don't understand. I know she's been kidnapped. I know who. It's the people who are trying to get money from her parents' estate. She was afraid this might happen."

Brockman flipped flaky crumbs and some custard off Thomas's lapel.

"You're right about being kidnapped," he said. "I saw it all. I saw her being snatched from the back of the bakery. But you're wrong about who did it. These two certainly didn't look like thugs one could hire here in the city. You see, they were women."

It was then that Thomas noticed the bits of dried blood on the man's face and how his right arm fell lank at his side.

"You are hurt, sir," Thomas said. "Whoever took Beatrix, did they attempt to take you as well?"

He couldn't imagine a small man like John Brockman fighting off Beatrix's captors.

Madam Flambeau seemed to get more frantic as her voice grew shriller with each vulgar threat. Her face turned to the color of an overly ripe tomato.

John yelled, "Quickly now. Leave the bakery. She's hysterical."

"No," Thomas said. "She must know what happened. She was here when Beatrix disappeared. We cannot leave without any idea of where they've taken her." He rushed toward the owner. "What have you done with Miss Patterson?"

"You will ruin everything, everything I have worked for," she said. "We must succeed. We must help the Fatherland."

Thomas froze. "Wait? The what? Fatherland? You support Hitler?"

Henry grabbed him by the collar and reined him back just as Madam Flambeau raised her hand and yelled, "Heil Hitler!" She repeated it a dozen more times and mumbled other threats that Thomas couldn't understand. The women who had assaulted him all gasped and moved back toward the walls of the café as if they had been contaminated with plague spores.

Henry held tight to Thomas as Brockman shouted, "She won't help us. She's behind all the sabotage here in New Orleans. I've just learned that this morning. Didn't you hear her? She's said she's waiting for a Nazi submarine to sail up the Mississippi and capture the city, for the Fuhrer will give her a medal. We've no time for this rubbish, as dangerous as she is. Back to my office."

At the door of the bakery, Thomas turned, and the rabid crowd who would have killed him because of his Asian heritage now started to close in on the enemy sympathizer as the screaming and shouting intensified.

"Mr. Brockman, stop," said Thomas. "Tell me where Beatrix has been taken."

Two police cars with sirens blasting swerved through traffic and pulled up on the sidewalk in front of the Le Petite Patisseries.

"Leave this chaos to the cops to sort out," Brockman said. "I don't need to be mixed up in that. Get into your office, now."

Once the three were inside, he slammed the door.

"I fear for her," the bookie said, "especially after she inquired if there was a contract out on her life. She asked me this just two days ago. I inquired and my sources are many, yet the rumors on the street were that a few of the voodoo practitioners are angry because she'd taken business away from them. And one was especially vocal about what she'd do to Beatrix. It was all about money."

"I do not know what to do. I have never been involved in anything like this," Thomas swayed slightly and grabbed the back of a chair.

"I've got to sit." Brockman seemed to crumble in the chair. "Once you stop talking and let me tell you what I know, I'll have an employee take me to the hospital. The getaway van hit me, and my arm was pushed against the wall."

"Oh, sir, please sit on the settee," Thomas said. "Bourbon? Tea?"

"You're a kind gentleman, Dr. Ling. More importantly, I heard the driver of the van say something about Debbie Warner. Could this Miss Warner be the other person involved?"

Brockman accepted a glass of heady liquid and put it to his lips with shaky hands.

"Debbie Warner?" said Thomas. "No, I do not recognize that name. But why would I?" He dashed to Beatrix's desk and flipped through her appointment book. "Maybe the name is here. Maybe she was an old client."

"Pay attention, Dr. Ling. I have had a growing concern for a few weeks that Le Petite Patisseries was a possible headquarters for local Nazi sympathizers. I just never realized that crazy baker was the key to this, until that unfortunate outburst when her true sympathies were made starkly clear. This is about the Germans and something that Beatrix said to me about her uncle and a French connection."

"Wait, that is possible," Thomas replied. "Yes, she is close to that French resistance officer de Gaulle."

"Then you have the reason she's been abducted. They want to use her as collateral as a means to affect the war and de Gaulle's influence."

"Warner. Debbie Warner?" Thomas repeated the name, pacing and wringing his hands.

"I think that was the name," Brockman said. "But everything happened so fast. I could not believe the driver wanted to mow me down. And then ... well, the truck drove at me. If not for the small indention at the back entrance to this building, which I squeezed into at the last second, I would not be here now." He kicked back the Bourbon and held the glass out to Thomas. "I will take a double, although my ulcer will disagree."

"If that copper Flynn Howard is in on this," Thomas said, "his estranged wife might know. She is hiding out at Poydras House. She might know where her husband would take a prisoner, or who this Debbie Warren is. I remember she mentioned he also worked as a night guard at the docks, but that place runs for miles. We will never find Beatrix there. It's a maze. One thing I do know is that Howard has to be a part of it, especially since he clobbered Beatrix the other evening to steal her ruby ring, which the dunce thought held her magic powers."

"At least it's something," Brockman said. "Take Henry and go. Now."

Thomas tore out the door, and Henry lumbered behind him.

"Taxi's never stop for me," Thomas growled. "I look like the enemy."

"Wait there on the curb." Henry stepped right onto Royal Street, and a line of traffic stopped dead.

He walked to the third car, a cab, and opened the door. He said something to the driver and then motioned to Thomas.

"Okay, Doc, no need to wait any longer, because this gentleman wants to take us there."

The cab coasted through the midday traffic, and Thomas drummed his fingers.

"Can't you drive this thing faster, man?" he said. "A woman's life is in danger."

Henry patted the driver's shoulder. "Get going, pal, if you know what's good for you. We don't have time to discuss it. Just drive."

"Drive, drive." Thomas yelled.

"Hold your horses, mister. I don't take no order from a Japanese enemy. But for you, I'll speed up."

The driver took the next turn quick enough to knock both passengers against the doors of the cab.

"I am Chinese. If you will not drive faster, pull to the curb." Thomas shouted, and the driver obeyed.

The second it stopped, Thomas flipped out of the backseat and yanked open the driver's door to drag the cabbie to the curb.

"Get in, Henry, if you still want to help me find Beatrix. Or get out of my way."

Henry hurried to get into the passenger side by the time Thomas put the car in gear. The cabbie sat in the street, flailing his arms as the taxi sped off, belching exhaust as Thomas slammed down on the accelerator.

"Time for us to take a powder, Doc, or that guy will be setting the cops on us."

Thomas had never driven on the *wrong*, or American side, of the road and nearly collided with a streetcar, a bus, and an Army transport vehicle before they reached Poydras House ten minutes later.

"Holy smokes," Henry said as the two rushed up the steps.

"Veronica Howard?" Thomas bellowed. "Where are you? I need to speak to Mrs. Howard at once." He dashed down the hall toward the dining room he had seen on an earlier visit. "Veronica Howard? I need your help, please. Come out. Come out now."

He stopped at the entrance to the dining hall, seeing table after table of women and children. It wasn't the mass of humanity, but the horror in each of their faces, fear of a strange man, an Asian, screaming for one of the staff. Did he look that threatening? Little ones started to cry, and women pulled toddlers to their breasts.

He tried to make his quivering voice sound calm. "Please, please, do not be alarmed. I am only here to talk with Mrs. Howard. Do any of you know where she is?"

Behind him, a voice said, "I'm right here, Dr. Ling. What is it?"

In messy overalls, Veronica Howard was wiping her hands on a greasy rag.

"I believe your husband has kidnapped Beatrix Patterson," said Thomas, "and I know he will try to use her to get you back."

"When did this happen?" she said.

"Earlier this morning, at a café on Royal Street, right near where our office is, just a block from the Gallier House. I am sure you know the neighborhood."

"You're wrong," Veronica said. "Can't be him, Dr. Ling. He couldn't have done it. Although, I wouldn't put it past him, the scumbag. You see, Flynn got his one phone call last night and found me here, wanting me to bail him out. He's known where I've been all along. Mother Adelina predicted it, and she was right. She told me he's never going to hurt anyone again. She knows these things. He's crazy, that man. He thought I'd come up with the money to bail him out of jail. And even if I did have the scratch, there was no way that'd happen. Flynn's lost his mind. This time, he broke a bottle over a man's head, and now he's going to lose his badge. Might be murder if the poor soul he sent to the hospital doesn't make it. He's in the city jail and has been since midnight last night. It couldn't have been Flynn."

Thomas felt the adrenaline rush freeze in his body. *There is no hope now.*

He held Veronica by the shoulders and looked into her eyes.

"Could he have been part of the plan to kidnap Beatrix?"

"Don't shake her." Henry pushed him back. "You'd better not do that, boss. These ladies seen some bad stuff, and they won't stand for you touching one of their own."

"Oh, Mrs. Howard, I am beside myself. Forgive me. But could he, and perhaps some brutes he is associated with, have accepted funds to apprehend Beatrix?"

Veronica squinted and turned to Henry. "What's this guy saying? Can't he speak English?"

Henry snorted. "Think your man wanted to grab the psychic?"

She groaned. "He's always looking for an edge, legal or not. Wouldn't put it past him, especially if he could figure out a way to get the woman to predict the outcome of dog races or ponies."

That's all Thomas needed, and he once more he tore through the dining room, down the great hall of Poydras House, and jumped into the stolen taxicab. Surprisingly, Henry was right behind him.

"Where is the constabulary, man?" said Thomas. "The, um, city jail, where that despicable thug is being held?"

"The Orleans City Jail?" Henry said. "Make a left at the next street. Just some friendly advice? This time, sir, don't pull the dang taxi up on the front steps of the police station like you did at the safe house. By now, that cabbie has probably reported it pinched."

When they arrived at the jail, Thomas realized he had no plans on how to force his way, as an Asian, into the holding area of a jail and demand to speak to one of the prisoners, Flynn Howard. He sat behind the wheel, banging his fingers, unable to move, more lost than at any time in his life.

"Don't know what you thought you'd do once we got here, Doc. But how's about I go into the station, use their phone to call my boss and tell him what we're doing, and then have Mr. Brockman talk to the duty sergeant?"

"Henry, you are brilliant." Thomas sat still, knowing he wanted to reach over and hug the behemoth of a man.

"You stay put. This Flynn character probably would do more talking to me about where they took your lady, than if you go in there and make trouble. Excuse me for saying this, but it wouldn't do no good for some crazy cop to arrest you, all the while you're screaming, like a little girl, *I'm Chinese*." Henry got out of the taxi and lumbered up the steps to Orleans City Jail.

Thomas was tempted to follow him at a distance, but it was impossible to blend into a crowd as an Asian, even if he pulled down the brim of his hat. Then, from the parking place in the alley, he saw two police cars pull to the front, and he slid down so he couldn't be seen as the owner of the cab he'd appropriated, jumped out of the squad car, waving his hands.

It seemed forever, and when Thomas looked at his watch, an hour had passed before Henry calmly opened the door and climbed into the stolen taxi.

"That was a bust, sir," he said. "Yeah, he admits that he took money from some gent to follow the lady. He told me, after a bit of encouragement, that he'd bashed Beatrix on the head and took that big old ring, thinking it would give him magic powers. No powers and no pawnbroker in the city wanted to touch it after Mr. Brockman let it be known that to have the ruby in their possession wouldn't be good for 'em."

"What did he say about Beatrix?" Thomas felt his body quaking.

I am not meant to be a spy. I need to be closed in a laboratory. I cannot handle the tension of being a bodyguard, and most definitely, I am not emotionally suited to have a relationship with a psychic who is constantly in danger.

"I am already emotionally connected to Beatrix." He slammed a fist into his palm and cried out, "Now what?"

He rested his head on the steering wheel and felt Henry waiting and possibly wondering if Thomas was about to have a breakdown.

"What did Veronica say as we left dining hall?" Thomas said.

"Don't know, sir. She yammered on and on about that jailbird husband of hers. I heard something about a mama, as far as I remember. What's her Mama got to do with all this?"

CHAPTER 15

"HENRY, THAT'S IT. How could I be so thick? We must return to Poydras House."

Thomas drove the taxi through alleys and less-traveled streets as they returned to the safe house. He parked in a lot near the home, then dashed between cars to race up the steps.

The receptionist looked up, and fright clouded her face.

"You cannot come back here. The ladies and the children are still terrified from when you were yelling and grabbing Missy Veronica."

"I apologize. Please, please, I must speak to Mother Adelina. It is a matter of life and death." A phrase from one of the many gangster films he'd watched. "You must help me."

The woman picked up the phone and dialed a number. "Principal. Yes, I'm in the front, and that Asian lunatic is here once more, and now he's demanding to see Mother Adelina." There was silence, and then she nodded. "Yes, ma'am."

"I have permission?" Thomas stopped pacing. "Where is the lady?"

"In the chapel. But you cannot go in there, and the principal says if you raise your voice again, she'll have you arrested. She wants you to wait right here for her. You are not allowed anywhere without a guard. Our ladies and children are terrified of you. They're scared enough as it is, without a lunatic screaming at the top of his Asian lungs."

"Yes, yes." He took some deep breaths, but the next sentence came out so loud the receptionist jumped. "Which way to the chapel? Tell me, or I cannot guarantee what might happen next. I am a desperate man."

"Hey, Doc." Henry grabbed Thomas's arm and turned him around. "The room across the hall says *Chapel*, so we don't need her permission."

In the far back of the church, a small, white-clothed figure was kneeling, and initially, Thomas thought she was praying. All too aware that Beatrix's life might depend on every second, his upbringing halted his steps, hesitant to intrude on Mother Adelina in prayer. Then he recognized that she was whistling an off-key version of "La Marseillaise," the French national anthem.

"Madam, if you please? A moment?" He approached her.

"Yes, young man. It is Thomas, is that correct?" She stood, brushing down her white habit, but not before he noticed that she had a cowboy boot on one foot and a ballet shoe on the other.

"That is my name, and I have come to ask you for help. A person I care about greatly is lost. No, that is not true. Someone, or a group of people, have taken her, and I am afraid they will harm her. Can you assist me?"

Mother Adelina took a seat in one of the adjacent pews.

"Please, Thomas, sit with me. Yes, right here. And now, will you hold my right hand? That will help me get a picture in my mind of your dear one."

Thomas grudgingly complied. "What do you need to know? Can you see where she is?"

"You are talking about the girl that is called Beatrix Patterson. What a foolish name. If she would have been mine to name, she would be Margaux, and together we would have been a tiny family, only three to begin with. Just my adored Charlie, little Margaux, and me. It was not to be, and because of my curse to see and know and tell, we never could become the de Gaulle family. However, our baby, I knew from the start, took after my lover's side of the family. They all rely on intelligence, observation, and cleverness, not having any skills with intuition at all."

Thomas had stopped listening when the odd little woman confessed to birthing Beatrix.

"You? Beatrix is your daughter? You and Charles de Gaulle?" His face mirrored the incredulous news he had just heard. "But I thought that Uncle Charlie, as Beatrix always called him, was … well, a symbolic uncle."

Beatrix's mother patted Thomas's hand. "Your beloved will come to no harm."

"Madam, I want to believe you, but she has been kidnapped—snatched from a bakery in the French Quarter. I do not know why, or by who. I do not know where to look for her. I am sick with worry. Do you understand that? She could be hurt or dead this moment. You must concentrate and tell me everything you see."

"I am, Thomas. You apparently are not listening. My daughter is sitting with two ladies, sisters, and they are drinking tea. One has a serious face. Oh, she's bossy, but she has a soft heart for the other woman. She's pretty when she smiles. Wait, I see the other lady joking, and my sweet Margaux, the woman you call Beatrix, is laughing as well. They have all become friends, and they will remain that way throughout this lifetime."

"You are mistaken," Thomas said. "I do not understand why you would tell me something like this. It's madness. Everyone said you were a crazy old lady who does not know what she is talking about."

"Thomas, I only can share what I see. It is this gift that has cursed me throughout my life, and it is why I agreed when Charlie gave our toddler—who I had temporarily relinquished at Poydras House while I was hospitalized—to his best friend, William Randolph Patterson, and his charming wife, to raise as his own. Unbeknownst to either of them, I managed to be hired as the baby's nursemaid. After Mrs. Patterson discovered who I was when I left a photograph of your Beatrix and me on my dresser in my private quarters, she dismissed me. Mr. Patterson had me placed in an asylum. I escaped and returned here to New Orleans, knowing that someday, my baby would look for me. I have hidden from my child, Beatrix, because she couldn't see me like this, a recluse. But I knew the time was coming soon when she could accept that I, her biological mother, had tried to give her a brighter future than I could have ever done." She wiped a tear away. "I swear to you, she will come to no more harm."

"Another man saw her being abducted, Mother Adelina. He thought he heard the name Debbie Warner. Does that mean anything to you?"

"No, he was mistaken. Yet that happens. What he truly heard was *deputy warden*."

"That makes no more sense than the other things you have predicted. This is a total waste of time."

"Wait, Thomas. Let me help you."

"I do not think you can, madam. But if you truly can see what is happening with Beatrix, might you be able to see a vision, or whatever you do, so you can tell me where the ladies are right now. She's in grave peril. Can't you understand that?" Thomas bellowed, and then the fight seemed to drain from him.

Beatrix is lost to me. Beatrix, who I've known just days but want so much to become part of her world. The thoughts were drowning him while not another soul knew of his torment.

"My dear boy," the woman said. "I am telling you what is happening right now. You seem too overwrought because of the intense emotional attachment to my daughter, so you're not listening. Stop that right now," she snapped and slammed a hand on the seat of the wooden pew.

"Now?" Thomas said. "Beatrix is not injured, or worse?"

"They are in a comfortable room, not too large, and my little darling is sitting at a desk. There is a stack of money in front of her. A large pile, actually. Do you know a room where there is a gold settee, and yes, a Monet painting on the wall, a most authentic one? I see soft green leather chairs, like one might find in a grand library, but it seems to be an office."

"No, now that is inconceivable. Is this a vindictive trick? Has someone paid you to tell me this foolishness? I do not believe you, madam. You have just described, in detail, the office that Beatrix rents on Royal Street." Thomas was on his feet, glowering at the lady. "I do not know what game you are playing, but you have wasted my time, and possibly caused harm to the woman you say is your daughter."

He stormed out of the chapel, but Henry grabbed by the arm.

"You know, I heard it all, and the lady may be cracker jacks, but we got nothing else. I say we go to your office and know for sure."

Fool. I am a fool to have wasted my time listening to this charlatan. Thomas stomped to the stolen taxi.

"This time, I'm driving, Doc." Henry snatched the keys from his hand. "If you drive like a maniac again, through midday traffic, the cops are going to pull us over and throw us in the hoosegow."

"Hoosegow?"

"Jail. And you'll be stuck there. Mr. Brockman'll bail me out, cuz he always does. But you? I believe he's got enough pull with most of the politicians in the Big Easy in his pocket. But man, I wouldn't tempt fate again. Remember, we're driving a hot car."

"Then you'd better drive, Henry. To the office."

Henry used all the appropriate arm signals for right and left turns. He obeyed every stop sign and maneuvered through the pedestrian-crowded sections of South Peters and Canal Streets. It felt like hours had passed before they slid into a spot down from Brockman's antique bookstore and Beatrix's storefront office.

"I'll grab some men and Mr. Brockman," Henry yelled, each man heading in a different direction.

Thomas patted his pocket. The pistol was there. Could he use it? *Do I have the nerve?*

He swung back the door of the entrance marked FINDER OF LOST THINGS, then froze.

"Thomas. Thank goodness you've come." Beatrix stood and closed the distance between them and threw her arms around him, only to feel his body stiffen, muscles tensed like a tiger ready to pounce on its prey. "Wait. Thomas, listen to me. Now, don't jump to conclusions. This is not what it seems."

He looked at the deputy warden from the internment camp and the floozy bookkeeper, who was swayed by the mysterious charms of an Army officer to the money in the middle of Beatrix's desk.

"You are paying your own ransom?" he said. "That is what's happening here. It's extortion, and I am here to stop it." He put an arm out and shielded Beatrix with his body as he reached into his pocket for the gun. "Whatever you're thinking, I will let no more harm come to Beatrix."

He surveyed her. The dove-gray suit was muddy, and strands of her hair tumbled in twenty directions. But it was the scrape on her chin that made him gasp.

"They did this to you?" He tilted her chin up. "Tell me."

Georgie and Willie stared at Thomas, one strong and militant in a green uniform and the other with red shoes and a dowdy dress. Georgie stood slightly behind the militant one as if she would safeguard her from the crazy Asian who seemed unable to stop waving a gun.

"Thomas, give me the gun," Beatrix said in a quiet voice.

"After we call authorities. This might be America, but kidnapping is against the law."

"No, Thomas. That's not necessary. Come sit with me, here on the settee. Just hear me out, and then after we talk, if you still want to call the police, the telephone is yours."

"You are certain that you are not in danger?"

"Yes, and I'll tell you all the details, if you will just sit down."

More than an hour passed before Beatrix finished telling Thomas how she'd been abducted from the bakery and how she thought that the deputy warden, Willie, who was Georgie's sister, had ordered the van driver to rundown John. But the driver, instead, had driven over some laundry, and this was verified when they returned to the Royal Street office and John

Brockman, arm in a sling, met them as they walked inside.

"Willie and Georgie made terrible mistakes, Thomas," said Beatrix. "But desperate people do desperate things. They needed the money. Their sister Bertie suffers from tuberculous, which is called consumption here in the states. Willie knew there was a Nazi spy cell at the internment camp, and when she found it, she approached the woman who seemed to be in charge. The inmate denied it, of course. Then the bakery owner, Madam Flambeau, approached Willie with a letter first, and then directly when the Parisian had been delivering bread to the camp. The baker asked if Willie wanted to make some real money."

"l saw it as a way to get out of New Orleans," Willie said. "To get Bertie from the squalor of a sanitarium, then move to Arizona so she can breathe better. The three of us would start new. A good, honest life together," She never looked up from her work shoes.

"We never hurt Miss Patterson," Georgie said. "I've never hurt anyone."

"They're telling the truth," Beatrix said. "We talked about why they agreed to kidnap me. Which was so the pro-Nazi forces here in New Orleans could manipulate my, um ... my father, Charles de Gaulle, and have him surrender to the Germans. That plan would destroy the hopes for France's resistance in the war, and perhaps even change the total outcome of the war. l could not let that happen. And when l explained it to these sensible women that l had a way of exonerating them, and that l would give them money to help them go out West, they agreed."

"We are gravely sorry." Willie pushed back a tear.

"Exonerate?" Thomas said. "How can they ever be vindicated from kidnapping you, hurting you, and nearly killing John?"

"Because it's time to forgive," Beatrix said. "To do the right thing. Have you ever done things you're not proud of, Thomas?"

"Do you mean like just hours ago, yanking a cabbie out of a taxi so l could steal it?" He blinked. "But they have broken a lot of laws, including collaborating with the enemy and accepting bribes from saboteurs. Will those deeds go unpunished?"

Georgie gasped and wheezed, clinging to her big sister's arm as she had when their mother was murdered by their father.

"Will we have to go to jail?" Willie said. "What will happen to Bertie? We have to get her to a better hospital. We have to."

Major Davies flipped back the door to the office with an entourage of military police on his heels.

"Miss Patterson. Good day, ladies," he said, seemingly unaware of the emotional tableau before him.

"Good of you to come, major." Beatrix stood. "If you will walk to the end of the block with me, I would like to speak with you about that matter we first discussed—the Nazi spy cells in New Orleans."

He stood taller, realizing he would soon have news he hoped would help his career, and released the breath he'd been holding when he realized Georgie wasn't going to pounce on him again.

"Men, step aside," he said. "Better yet, wait outside and stand guard. You there," he pointed to a private, "go around back and secure that entrance. Miss Patterson and I will be right back."

As they strolled, Beatrix disclosed what was happening at Camp Algiers, from hanging the swastika to bullying the Jewish detainees. She explained the complicity of the warden and how the deputy warden, Willamina Jones, came forward, and with her sister's help, exposed the pro-Nazi bakery owner, as well as the spy ring that the Parisian woman controlled right from Royal Street bakery shop next door.

"Now, let's talk about the welfare and the future of the ladies in my office, Major. The deputy warden, a brave young patriotic civil servant, had to pose as a Nazi sympathizer to gather this information. She put her life at stake to amass vital intelligence. I cannot imagine doing all she did, knowing I could be killed by the warden, or one of the saboteurs, at any second. As you can imagine, she was just getting that information in order to turn it over to you. There may be a few others, civilians, like her sister, who, if this got out of hand and into the newspapers, would jump to the wrong conclusions. Now, for someone as shrewd as you, you can see that often, there are unique circumstances, especially in wartime, when a few might falsely assume the sisters have broken laws. If these women have done anything wrong, it is that they should have come to me, or perhaps you, much sooner. Everything just happened so quickly, as you can understand."

"Nonsense," said Major Davies. "We must follow protocol. After a hearing, everything will be rectified. It will be a military hearing, so the community doesn't need to be involved in this little matter of the Nazi enclaves."

"A little matter, Major?" Beatrix shook her head and attempted to contain her outrage. "No, that won't do. Here." She shoved a list in his hand. "Now you have the names of connections for the spy cells here in the city, plus the connection with the Nazi bakery owner and others in her enemy ring, thanks to those brave young women. Which of your men could have done that?"

"I don't know—"

"You can, and you must. You must absolve them of any wrongdoing. Then you must take the credit. Which is where the credit should go since this was your original plan. You can blame me for any misdeeds."

He seemed to be calculating how his career would prosper.

Beatrix continued, "When we first negotiated, I told you I would not take money, but I needed one favor."

"Yes? You want me to give them immunity?"

"New identities. The women and their convalescing sister, who is in an infirmary for the destitute, need to be transported to Arizona. I know you'll agree. After all they've done, they deserve a fresh start in life. They saved New Orleans from German spies, and worse, such as allowing submarines up the mouth of Mississippi, which could easily have happened. You'll need to interrogate Madam Flambeau, who is already in custody with the local police. Although, they probably don't know she's a Nazi, unless she's still screaming it at the top of her lungs." Beatrix looked at the major. "You are the hero in all this for orchestrating the plan, and not only your commanding officers will know this, but as soon as we part this afternoon, I must tell my good friend Eleanor Roosevelt about your role in the covert operation."

The major's chest puffed out even more, dangerously taxing the brass buttons on his tan uniform.

"Miss Patterson, thank you. Yes, patriotic citizens like these ladies should be given help. Why, they've risked their lives for the good old USA."

Beatrix smiled. He'd probably get a medal for the operation to capture spies, terrorists, infiltrators, and secret agents. By the time they got back to Beatrix's office, the major had singlehandedly driven submarines out of the Mississippi River. Or so he thought.

"I'll arrange transport at once, probably late this afternoon," he said. "Would it be acceptable if the women stayed with you until then? Well, I know the answer since you've already helped bring them to me and our government. Thank you, madam. Now, I must be off. Your government is grateful for the introductions to these heroines. They deserve the best treatment, and I will see to it that's what they get."

Later that evening, Beatrix and Thomas said goodbye to Georgie and Willie, who were being escorted to the hospital in Shreveport, and then flown by Army transport to Phoenix in order to start a new life.

The two agreed to a lavish celebration dinner at Antoine's on St. Louis, thanks to John Brockman, who could always pull strings to get a table at the finest of all New Orleans' restaurants.

Beatrix smoothed the white tablecloth. "You met my mother? This is going to sound silly, but what did she smell like?"

"A bit of perfume, flowery. Maybe carnations? Yes, carnations. Now, considering the close and limited association I have had with you, I see a resemblance. It's not physical—but then again, she's shrouded in a nun's habit—but in kindness and determination.

"She's avoided me all the time I've been here in New Orleans.

She had to know her sister-in-law, my aunt, was dying. Why didn't she come? I'm afraid, Thomas. I'm afraid she'll reject me if I go to see her."

"I am sure she had reasons. What would you tell me to do in a situation like this, noting that I am not psychic?"

Beatrix smiled back at him as he poured champagne.

"First off, I am not a psychic. It's an act, a way to get information about where my mother could have gone, and yes, to make money."

He shook his head. "I knew you weren't really a *wu* or psychic."

"Yeah? When exactly did that come about?"

"As of yesterday, to be precise. So what would you tell me to do if the tables were turned?"

"I would tell you to try and give her a second chance," Beatrix said. "That's the only way to know the truth. And as for truth, no more lies. I promise."

A weight seemed to tumble from her shoulders.

"Will you go with me to Poydras House tomorrow?" she said.

"Shall we drink to that?" Thomas held up his glass full of champagne. "Now we have a celebration here. And honestly, more times than I want to consider, I doubted if I would still be alive by the end of this week."

"I had those exact thoughts earlier today," she said.

Merrymaking filled the restaurant, and it felt as if the war was a million miles away—at least for the next hour.

"This is an extravagance I never thought possible in these treacherous times," Thomas said. "It has only been four days since I became entangled into your clutches. It is a time I shall never forget." He again raised his champagne glass. "To good health and friendships that will last forever."

Beatrix sipped the bubbling drink and looked a bit shyer than Thomas had come to know of her.

"A few days ago, I asked if you wanted to know about the future," she said. "It would have been fairytales with a fairytale ending."

"I said no. At least, that's what I think. Being with you, Beatrix, I have lost touch, at times, on what is real and what could be magic or my outrageous imagination, which I had not discovered before being with you. It now runs wild."

"I appreciate that," she said. "Maybe it was the head clobbering Flynn Howard gave me before snatching my ring, or perhaps it was time for me to personally come to a greater understanding of myself. You don't think I'm growing up, do you?"

Beatrix laughed at herself with a lightness Thomas had longed to hear again.

After a few moments, she said, "By the way, I will no longer need a bodyguard. You see, my long, unresolved financial issues are going to be settled, and I will be safe. Tomorrow, after we visit Poydras House, I have an appointment with a new attorney, thanks to John's recommendation, who is going to take the matter to court in Santa Barbara, where it belongs. I confirmed Mother and Dad officially adopted me. The paperwork was in the courthouse record room mistakenly filed under de Gaulle and not Patterson. Yes, there all along and only required a telephone call, which was all Mr. Brockman's doing. He has connections even in California. As for the estate, I will let a judge and a jury rule on the case and put this to rest. I cannot pretend to predict the future, but I'm trusting in the judicial system to do what is right. It also means I have half siblings. I have a family but not in Santa Barbara, of course."

"Yes, Santa Barbara," Thomas said. "That's far away. Especially from London. I left work undone. Although, now it seems superfluous compared to the technology here in America. Perhaps someday I will visit you in California?" He leaned forward and smiled.

"I won't need these scarves in Santa Barbara, since it's like springtime most of the year." She pulled the silvery-white scarf from her throat and flipped it onto the back of an empty chair.

"I will always be your friend, Beatrix." Thomas reached out to touch her fingers.

She took his hand and kissed the palm. "Now, back to your future. That's what I want to tell you, you stoic, stalwart, scientific Chinese Brit. Your future includes me."

"Excuse me, Miss Patterson. You told me you do not have a psychic gift, and it is all do to a hyper-ability for remembering and observing? Then you tell me you know my future? I'm lost."

She giggled, a sound that was surprising to her ears, as it had been so long since happiness had been part of her life.

"I'm changing your future right now," she said. "It's going to be with me. You are stuck with me, and I don't know what that means to your traditional family, because not only will you marry a fake *wu*, but she'll bear your children. We'll just have to buck up and figure it out as we go along. Your grandmother, the one who tortured you with stories of witches, I believe she'll be pleased."

"Grandmother?" Thomas said.

"Don't play coy," Beatrix said. "Those stories you heard, and the secrets she shared. She wanted you to think she was a *wu*. That's why you seemed to accept it in me, because I am not a good actress."

"Absolutely. It was acting, and I never truly believed. Wait, you said *marry*? You hardly know me." He leaned forward to nuzzle her neck.

"Will you, or won't you? And if you say no, then my dearest Dr. Thomas Ling, you are in eminent danger of being put under a lifelong spell. And if you say yes, the same thing will happen."

"Yes. My life will never be dull again, will it, my darling Beatrix?"

"Do you want dull?"

"Absolutely not."

However, that is the beginning of another story.

For book club and group discussion questions:
www.torchflamebooks.com/seer-questions

ABOUT THE AUTHOR

Eva Shaw is one of the country's premier ghostwriters and the author of more than 100 award-winning books including *Doubts of the Heart, Games of the Heart, Ghostwriting: The Complete Guide, Writeriffic 2: Creativity Training for Writers, Write Your Book in 20 Minutes, Garden Therapy: Nature's Health Plan,* and *What to Do When a Loved One Dies.* She teaches university-level writing courses available online at 4000 colleges and universities.

A breast cancer survivor, Eva is an active volunteer with causes affecting women and children and with her church. She loves to travel, read, shop, garden, play the banjolele and paint, focusing on folk art and California landscapes.

When not at her desk, you can find Eva walking around the village of Carlsbad, California with Coco Rose, a rambunctious Welsh terrier.

Connect with Eva at:
evashaw.com
facebook.com/eva.shaw.96
instagram.com/shaw.eva

YOU MIGHT ALSO ENJOY

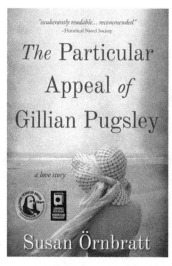

The Particular Appeal of Gillian Pugsley
Susan Örnbratt

Nicole Graves Mystery Novels
Nancy Boyarsky